Hard Time

Maureen Carter

First published in 2007
by Crème de la Crime
P O Box 523, Chesterfield, S40 9AT

Typesetting by Yvette Warren
Cover design by Yvette Warren
Front cover image by Peter Roman

Printed and bound in Great Britain by
Cox & Wyman Ltd, Reading, Berkshire

ISBN 978-0-9551589-6-4
A CIP catalogue reference for this book is available from the British
Library

www.cremedelacrime.com

About the author:
Maureen Carter has worked extensively in the media. She lives in Birmingham with her husband and daughter. Visit her website:

www.maureencarter.co.uk

Huge thanks as ever go to Douglas Hill, whose editorial advice and acuity are beyond measure. *Hard Time* would not be the book it is without his expertise, enthusiasm and support.

I am again enormously indebted to Lynne Patrick for her faith and focus, and her inspirational team at Crème de la Crime.

For his valuable insight from both police and press points of view, I thank Richard Lakin.

And for helping me see through Bev's eyes, massive thanks to my favourite detective sergeant in the Midlands.

Writing would be a lonelier place without the support of some special people. For 'being there' even when they're miles away, my love and affection go to: Peter Shannon, Veronique Shannon, Corby and Stephen Young, Anne Hamilton, Frances Lally, Jane Howell, Henrietta Lockhart, Suzanne Lee, Paula and Charles Morris and Helen and Alan Mackay.

Finally, my thanks to readers everywhere – as always, this is for you.

For Sophie

December 1984

It was snowing when she dumped the baby. She laid the newborn on the ice-cold floor, winced as the pitted concrete dug into her knees. The blanket had loosened slightly during the short walk. She pulled it tighter, then drew the hood of the shawl over the baby's head. Delicate mauve eyelids fluttered in protest, though the child didn't wake.

The young mother studied the tiny face, perfect in every detail. It was an image that would stay with her forever, returning unbidden over the years to torture her with feelings of guilt and shame and sorrow. Little more than a child herself, she believed the baby would be better off without her. It didn't make the decision easy.

Outside the cubicle, she paused, leaned against the door for support. What harm was there in one last look? She shook her head, nails drawing blood as they dug into her freezing palms.

Seconds later, she emerged from the breezeblock building, raised the fur-edged hood of a grubby parka and glanced round. She'd never been to Stafford before, probably never would again. It was just a name on a map, a town with a railway station where she could break the journey south. No planning, no great design, no inkling of what the future held for herself – or the baby.

She made her way across the Square. It was scattered now in icing-sugar snow and lay in darkness save for festive lights slung like gaudy necklaces between lampposts. Others nestled in the branches of a huge Christmas tree. Santa Claus and snowmen, reindeer and robins: the scene seemed to mock the young mother's black despair.

1

She found a place to watch from the shadows. Her pale face glistened with tears as she waited and watched. Waited for a stranger to take her baby.

Stafford Weekly Observer, 22 December 1984

'Miracle' baby cheats death

A newborn baby abandoned in public toilets in Stafford town centre is lucky to be alive, according to Staffordshire police.

Sergeant Neil Jackson told the *Chronicle*: "It was the coldest December night in a generation. It's a miracle the baby didn't freeze to death."

Sergeant Jackson said a passer-by who found the little girl undoubtedly saved her life. Bridget Mackay, from Lark Rise in Stafford, was walking through Market Square when she heard cries from the ladies' toilet.

Mrs Mackay alerted the emergency services, then kept the baby warm until medical help arrived. "I only did what anyone would do," she said.

PRESENT

The baby was rushed by ambulance to the Princess Margaret hospital where she is now recovering from her ordeal. Miss Susan Green, a nurse in the children's ward, said: "She's a poppet. We've been calling her Holly because it's so close to Christmas. Being reunited with her mum would be the best present ever."

Police want to talk to anyone who was in or near Market Square last night and who may have noticed anything suspicious. They particularly want to trace a young woman who was seen leaving the toilets at about 11 pm. A special hot-line number has been set up and all calls will be treated in strictest confidence.

The police have also issued an appeal to the baby's mother to come forward. "The woman has nothing to fear from us," Sergeant Jackson said. "She's the mother of a beautiful little girl. We just want the story to have a happy ending."

3

Present Day

A man in a trench coat walked his dog down a wide pavement still slick with rain. It was past midnight, the street dark and otherwise deserted. Tall with stooped shoulders, the man carried a heavy torch. The young black labrador pranced at his side, pausing to investigate the damp bark of a dying oak tree. Through the fretwork of gnarled branches, indigo clouds skittered across a sallow moon.

Robbie Crawford observed his dog with affection; a lazy smile softened the hard angles of his lined face. The former police officer was in no hurry. He knew sleep would be a long time coming; had no idea his life was almost over.

He walked at night to combat insomnia worsened by early retirement. He'd held detective chief superintendent rank before quitting the West Midlands force two months earlier, at the age of fifty-three. Since then he'd learned more about his home patch, wandering around it, than in his previous twelve years' residence.

Wake Green was solid, respectable, not plagued by street crime. Thieves were more likely to target its large semi-detached houses, half-timbered properties full of rich pickings. Crawford knew the location of every burglar alarm, which systems were linked to the police, which buildings were soft targets. He gave a wry smile. Luckily, he was one of the good guys.

As a few spots of rain began to fall he lifted his collar, tugged gently at Jasper's lead. If the heavens opened again, the walk would have to be cut short. He hoped it wouldn't come to that. The nightly routine, the regular exercise, helped him sleep – eventually. Like most officers, serving or not, Crawford suffered flashbacks, unsettling images he thought he'd learned to live with. Nowadays, he found it more difficult to stave off ugly memories. Hopefully the new job would help. Security chief at the National Indoor Arena was a prestige post. He hadn't expected to land it.

Suddenly the dog yanked its lead. Crawford swore under his breath, almost lost his footing. Jasper strained forward, tail bristling; the deep growl in his throat was normally a prelude to prolonged barking. Crawford spoke gently while he scanned the street, wondering what had spooked the animal. Rustling leaves? A cat lurking in the bushes? No matter. The dog was already distracted, sniffing a gatepost as if his life depended on it.

Crawford relaxed, thought again about the future. The NIA contract would start when he and Josie returned from New York next month. She wanted to renew their wedding vows during the trip. It wasn't a lot to ask. At times over the years it seemed he'd been married to the job more than his wife. There was ground to make up; he looked forward to it.

Panting, Jasper halted obediently at the kerb, waited for Crawford's go-ahead. The ex-cop patted the dog's head, whispered soothing words as they began to cross.

Just as the black four-by-four burst out from shadows on the right. No lights. No warning. Engine gunned, aimed at Crawford.

Wide-eyed, panic-stricken, he tried to leap away, but the vehicle was moving too fast. There was nowhere to run, no place to hide. His last coherent thought was that the driver had been lying in wait: it was no accident.

The impact flung both Crawford and the dog into the air. Crushing blinding pain lasted only seconds. The final sound he heard was the sickening crunch of his skull smashing into concrete. Motionless, he lay on his side; torchlight flickered on the planes of his face as he stared sightlessly down the street.

Jasper whimpered pitifully as he crawled closer, nuzzled his master's hand. Only the dog saw the dark shape among the bushes. Only the dog saw the glint in the camera lens. The dog was dead, too, before help arrived.

FRIDAY

1

Daniel Page was the cleverest little boy in Year One, probably the smartest five-year-old in the entire universe. His mummy said so. And she was always right.

He was at the classroom window now, looking out for her. It was wet playtime and the air reeked of Marmite fingers and Monster Munchies. Daniel was dying for the bell to ring. Mummy would be here any minute to take him to the dentist. It meant missing two whole lessons: Daniel didn't mind. He'd rather have five fillings than be in school any day. Not that his teeth had the tiniest hole. They were perfect. Mummy said so.

He bared them now, tilting his head from side to side as he admired his reflection in the window. He hadn't mastered winking yet so he practised that for a while as well. Daddy always said Daniel had his mummy's eyes. It made the little boy laugh. How could he have someone else's eyes? Of course he knew what Daddy meant: their eyes were exactly the same shade of green.

He frowned. Where *was* she? He pressed his nose against the glass. It was pouring down. Everything was fuzzy because the window was steamed up inside and rain streamed down outside. He rubbed a porthole with the elbow of his jumper. Then his face lit up.

"Miss!" he shouted. "Mummy's here! Can I go?"

Daniel's teacher, Mrs Wilson, gave a tetchy sigh. She hated wet playtime; it meant she had no real break and she was trying to finish a letter to her son in Australia. "You'll have to wait, young man." The classroom assistant had popped to the staff room and there was no way Shirley

Wilson was leaving thirty hyperactive infants to their own devices while she escorted the Page boy out.

Daniel stamped a petulant foot. "I want to go now! Mummy's getting wet. She'll be very cross."

Tough, thought Mrs Wilson. Like a lot of beautiful women, Jenny Page imagined she only had to snap her elegant fingers and the world would come running. Shirley Wilson was two years off retirement: she only ran baths.

"I'll be late for the dentist," Daniel wailed.

It was a cue to the other kids. "Cry-baby, cissy-boy."

"That's quite enough!" She had to shout to drown out the chorus. Daniel's lower lip trembled as he pleaded with her to let him go. Mrs Wilson pushed her glasses up into her candyfloss perm and dragged weary legs to the window. Sure enough, Jenny Page was at the electric gates, tapping an equally petulant foot. Must be genetic. The teacher sighed. Presumably there was no one in the office or they'd have buzzed her in. Security was tight these days, even at The Manor prep school.

Mrs Wilson squinted through the glass. The boy's mother was tapping her other foot now. The teacher masked a spiteful smile. It could be worse. At least that ridiculous golf umbrella was keeping the poor dear dry.

The classroom door opened and a young woman with a purple bob and parrot earrings backed in, carrying two mugs.

"Tanya, before you settle, take Daniel out to his mother, will you?"

"Sure." The classroom assistant grinned, reached out a hand. "Come on, Tiger."

Ordinarily he'd have pointed out that his name was Daniel but he let it go this time. Miss was new and like most grown-ups was nice to him. Tanya led the little boy to the cloakroom and helped him on with his coat. "I'll get Mr Gallagher to open the gates, then we'll make a dash for it." She tousled his blond thatch of hair. "If we were ducks, we could swim across."

He laughed. He liked Tanya. Though he doubted the puddles were that deep. While he waited for her to come back, Daniel wondered if Mummy would remember about the Disney Store. She'd promised they could go after the dentist.

"OK, Tiger." Tanya held the main door, pulled a face. If anything, the rain was worse. "Got your swimming trunks?"

"And my goggles." Daniel giggled, then looked concerned. Tanya hadn't even got a coat. "Stay in the dry, miss. I'll be OK."

"No way, mate. I have to escort you to the gates." She gave a mock frown. "Don't want me to get into deep water, do you?"

They burst out laughing.

"Come on, Daniel, we'll be late."

Daniel shot a glance at his mother, then back at Tanya. "Mummy," he called. "Miss doesn't have to come out, does she?"

The woman struggled as a sudden gust of wind caught the umbrella. "Only if she wants to be blown away." There was laughter in her voice.

"See?" The little boy's eyes shone. "I told you it'd be OK."

Of course it would. Even so, Tanya waited in the doorway until Daniel reached his mother, and lingered there watching as they walked away hand in hand.

2

Short of a terrorist alert or a royal visit, Detective Sergeant Bev Morriss had rarely seen so many uniforms. But then she hadn't been to many police funerals. And never in rain masquerading as a monsoon.

Cruising past, she glanced in the rear-view mirror. Tired blue eyes and matching bags told a tale she didn't want to hear. Instead, she clocked the picture outside the church. Cops in black macs shuffling about like a bunch of crows. Murder of crows, wasn't it? She grimaced. Ought to be a collective noun for coppers as well. Line-up, perhaps? Conviction?

Or killing.

Bev gripped the wheel, wished she could do the same with her thoughts. A hit-and-run might not be cold-blooded murder, but the end result was the same: Detective Chief Superintendent Robbie Crawford was no less dead.

She nudged the MG into a tight spot. Not that its body-work was at risk. She knew its contours better than some of her old boyfriends'. And loved them more, despite the dodgy spray job. The original mustard yellow showed through the black in places, which meant when the boot was open the Midget looked like a giant wasp.

The motor's soft-top was currently being pelted with sharp stinging rain. Wet stuff bounced off the bonnet and paddling-pool potholes scarred the road surface. It was more April than early July. Momentarily cocooned against a storm both meteorological and mental, Bev sat head in hands, taking deep calming breaths. Her inner tempest had been going on pretty much all year.

She straightened, let out a deep sigh that lifted a short fringe the shade of Guinness. A final check in the mirror confirmed her mascara wasn't waterproof. She wiped licked fingers under panda eyes then, using an old *Evening News* as a rain-hat, reluctantly left the haven of the car. Three o'clock. Time to strengthen a few sinews. Assuming she could find any.

The church, silhouetted against a pewter sky in the distance, was like something out of a Hammer horror: Vampire Towers, hot and cold running bats. It glowered and towered over rows of tired terraces. The Victorian two-up-two-downs were relatively new kids on the block. Bev reckoned St Luke's was *faux* late Gothic – the sort of place you'd *only* want to be seen dead in.

Button it. It was a funeral, not the Comedy Store.

She paused halfway up the steep incline, slightly out of breath and not impressed with her fitness level. This close, the church looked more workhouse than God's house. Not that it mattered. Minarets outnumbered missals in Balsall Heath.

Soggy now, the newspaper was doing a crap job. She dumped it in a bin, glimpsed a local dial-a-quote, the ubiquitous Grant Young, on the front page. She wondered idly what he was banging on about this time. *For Christ's sake, woman, get a move on.* She hiked the collar of a black trench coat (borrowed) and broke into a trot.

Her tardy arrival was due to a panic attack. Usually she recognised the signs, but this one had caught her off guard crossing the car park back at Highgate. They'd been happening off and on for six months or so. An unwanted legacy from the bastard who'd raped her. One of several unwanted legacies. Mind, she hid them well.

"You look shit." Sergeant Oz Khan. His outstretched hand

didn't quite touch her. Bev still thought of him as detective constable. Still thought of him as her lover. Copulating cops – they'd made a fucking good team. *Bitter? Moi?*

"Nice one, Khanie."

Oz's sculpted jaw tightened a fraction, though she doubted anyone else would've noticed. She'd forgotten how beautiful he was, how she used to lie awake just watching him sleep: the tip of his tongue peeking between soft lips, the curve of his cheek, the… *Fuck's sake, woman.*

He shrugged, did his best to match her casual delivery. "Coming tonight?"

His leaving do? Genuinely wouldn't miss it for the world. She gave an indifferent sniff. "Dunno yet."

Oz had walked the sergeant's exams a few months back, piss-easy given his Oxford law degree. The new posting with the Met had only just come through. He started Monday. Not that his departure featured in their split. There was a chasm between them anyway: her reluctance to let anyone close, Oz's problem with her increasing aggression. Oh, and a dead serial rapist called Will Browne.

"Suit yourself," he said. "You generally do." She watched as he rejoined Darren New and Mike Powell, huddled under the only tree in the street. If they didn't stop staring, she'd give them a bow. Did she really look shit?

Carol Pemberton didn't. The DC was waiting for Bev on the steps of the church. Tall and willowy in classy black velvet, Carol's curtains of dark glossy hair were drawn back for once, showcasing a seriously attractive woman. At thirty-four, she was five years older than Bev, looked ten younger. How did that work?

"Cutting it fine, aren't you, sarge? Thought you were catching a ride." The Highgate contingent had hired a minibus.

"So did I." Only she hadn't fancied an audience: hyperventilating into a brown paper bag was not cool.

Carol tilted her head at the church. "They're running late anyway."

Late? "You're joking."

"Hardly. There's another funeral going on."

Christ Almighty. It'd be the last place Bev'd choose to make a final exit. She glanced round. How bad would it look to light a ciggie? She fingered a crumpled pack of Silk Cut in her pocket. Yeah, right. The cardboard was almost as damp as her best mate Frankie's trench coat. And Carol's brolly was a waste of space. Other mourners were sheltering under a choppy sea of the things but piercing rain still homed in on the gaps.

"Good turn-out," Carol said. "More police than family."

No more than you'd expect. For a popular cop who should be on early retirement, not permanent leave.

"And vultures." Bev nodded at a sheepish-looking bunch keeping a discreet distance across the road. The press was out in force. A police officer's death in suspicious circumstances was still rare enough to make the news.

The car that killed Crawford hadn't been traced, nor the scumbag driver. It was most likely an accident, but like any cop Robbie Crawford had made enemies. A possible revenge attack was among the lines of inquiry. Which explained the media interest. It wasn't Bev's case, but she knew a number of suspects had been questioned and eliminated. No one was in the frame. Yet.

Crawford's widow looked shell-shocked. Bev's heart went out to her. At least with illness there was a chance to say goodbye to the people you love. But when it comes out of the blue... She swallowed hard, closed her eyes, until a sudden tap on her elbow brought her spinning round in fury.

"What the f…" *Whoops.*

"Sergeant?" Detective Superintendent Bill Byford lifted a curious eyebrow. "You were saying?"

"Guv. How you doing?" She aimed for an engaging smile. "Better late than never, eh?"

3

Why was Daniel always the last to emerge? Jenny Page smiled indulgently as she kept an eager eye on the infants' exit. It was already 3.20. Apart from a select band of yummy-mummies exchanging juicy gossip outside the school gates, she was the only parent there. At least it wasn't raining now, bar the odd spot. Under her breath she muttered, "Come on, Dan-Dan."

Not that she really minded. Daniel was a sunny, sociable little creature. He'd be bending Mrs Wilson's ear, describing the Pages' plans for the weekend, giving away all the family secrets. She shook her head, picturing the little boy who'd stolen her heart the second he was born. Any minute now he'd come hurtling through the double doors, huge grin lighting his lovely face. On the way home she'd be lucky to get a word in as he chatterboxed her through his day in excruciating detail. Jenny's smile turned wistful as she thought about the teenage years ahead when she'd be lucky if he threw a surly grunt in her direction.

"Mrs Page? How may I help you?"

The voice was distinctive; Jenny concealed a wince. Gruesome Gallagher, the head with halitosis and a yen for Hawaiian shirts. The old lech talked through a mouth full of rotting plums. Taking a step back, Jenny swiftly masked her distaste. "Mr Gallagher. How nice to see you. You couldn't chivvy Daniel along, could you?" And while you're at it, get out of my face.

"*Doctor* Gallagher." His pointed index finger, a touch too close, reinforced the reprimand. His rubbery lips were spread in a smarmy smile that displayed tiny pointed teeth not quite taking root in anaemic gums. "Come with me, my dear."

For the umpteenth time since Daniel started at The Manor, Jenny Page neatly sidestepped a wandering hand as the head tried to shepherd her along. Short of a burqa or a bin liner, she couldn't avoid his roving eye. The left one was currently traversing the contours of her body, even though they were all but swamped in a green leather swing coat.

Gallagher's small talk during the short walk majored on the weather; Jenny was more interested in the children's gaudy daubings that brightened the dark panelled walls on which they were displayed. The sights and smells evoked memories of her school days. Though God knows why: The Manor was more beeswax and potpourri than sweaty trainers and over-boiled brassica. She concentrated on the present: Corporation Street wasn't a place to revisit, even in her thoughts.

"Ah, Mrs Wilson. Where are you hiding Daniel?"

The teacher was rummaging in the bottom of a cupboard, inadvertently offering a rear view. Jenny looked expectantly at the teacher, pointedly ignored the head's laboured wink. His jocularity was forced, too, unlike the genuine confusion that flashed across Shirley Wilson's moon face. Her troubled glance flitted between Gallagher and Jenny; she opened her mouth a couple of times but didn't get as far as actually speaking.

"Well?" Gallagher boomed, hoisting a straining waistband over a flabby gut.

The teacher's uncertainty increased. "But Daniel's not here." She gave a tentative smile as if the head and Mrs Page were sharing a private joke. "He had a dental appointment. He left at playtime." Her no less troubled glance settled on Jenny. "With you."

The blonde woman shook her head, more cross than concerned. "We changed the arrangement. I couldn't get away. Daniel's father…" Jenny's jade eyes narrowed as she worked it out. Richard was always moaning about not seeing enough of Daniel. He'd have taken him to the dentist, then rather than dash back to the office they'd have indulged in some father-and-son bonding. Naughty but nice – Rich really should have phoned to let her know. Knowing her boys, they'd be catching a movie, then demolishing a pizza.

"But, Mrs Page, I saw you at the gates."

Lost in thought, Jenny only half heard. "Sorry…?"

"I *saw* you." She tilted her head towards the window. "At the gates."

The teacher's absolute conviction was slightly unsettling, but Jenny was equally adamant. "I was nowhere near the school." Unless it had an annexe at Chez Jules where she'd lunched *avec* Justin. "You're mistaken, Mrs Wilson."

"I don't think so."

"Come now, ladies." Gallagher simpered. "I'm sure there's a simple explanation. Why not call your husband, Mrs Page?"

"This is ridiculous." Jenny snatched her mobile from her bag. Rich's was switched off. Great.

Mrs Wilson was having more joy. After a short hushed conversation, she handed her own phone to Jenny. "Tanya Woodall, my classroom assistant."

Tanya described how she'd watched Daniel walk away from the school hand in hand with a woman she'd swear was his mother. As Jenny listened, she felt the first faint chill in her veins. She passed the phone back without a word. Maybe Richard had been unable to make it. He must've arranged for Daniel to be collected by someone

17

from the office.

But she knew everyone who worked for Richard; none looked remotely like her. And why the hell hadn't he called?

Angry now, she speed-dialled his number at the agency, Full Page Ads. No answer. The machine kicked in at home.

"Would you like to sit down, Mrs Page?" Gallagher offered a seat. "While we gather our thoughts."

Her thoughts were beyond gathering and of the countless questions crowding in her head two were uppermost. Who had taken her son? And where the hell was he?

Byford was in the pulpit. Bev reckoned he was a natural, could just imagine him in a dog collar taking confessions. Great voice too; touch of Anthony Hopkins. *Space control to Beverley: come in, please.* She tried concentrating but he was reading that Auden piece about stopped clocks and dogs not barking. *Four Weddings and a Funeral* had a lot to answer for.

Tapping fingers on knee, she glanced round, shuddered. The church was crammed: cops and chrysanthemums. And a coffin.

As Byford reached the line about traffic police and black cotton gloves, her mobile vibrated against her hipbone. The message was short but sent another tremor – this time down her spine.

Dear God. Not again. The most traumatic case of her career had involved an abducted baby. Now it looked as if another child was missing.

When the guv resumed his pew, she tapped him on the shoulder, showed him the text.

Five minutes later, Bev and DC Darren New were dodging

and weaving through rush-hour traffic on the Bristol Road, heading for Edgbaston.

She double-checked the school's address, then stuffed the phone back in her pocket. These days, female cops didn't always get the kiddie cases: she'd just been the only dummy not to switch off her mobile.

"Could've been worse," she said.

"What?" Daz eyed the Mars bar she was unwrapping. "Getting a call in church?"

She nodded. "My mate Frankie?" Like any man with a heartbeat, Daz had hit on Frankie Perlagio once or twice. "Coupla weeks back, she's at some big wheeley-dealy do at the Buddhist temple in Moseley. They're all sitting round cross-legged, dead intense, doing that om thing." She gave him a bite of the Mars. "Her mobile goes off. Full blast. *Doctor Who* theme tune."

"Exterminate her. Exterminate her."

Dazza's Dalek didn't raise a smile but Frankie's brass neck did. "It's across the room in her bag," Bev wrapped up the story. "No one knows it's hers, so she just throws dirty looks like everyone else and bangs on about people showing a bit of respect." Bev shook her head: typical.

Daz skirted a skinny pigeon making a meal of the tarmac. "Frankie still at your place?"

She stiffened. He wasn't savvy like Oz. There was a touch of the Andrex puppy about Daz: eager, enthusiastic, boundless bounce but not much sense of direction. Otherwise he'd know he'd crossed a line. "Next left."

Quick learner, though. He didn't go any further. Lucky, given the taut messages her body was sending. She suppressed a sigh: her life had more no-go areas than Baghdad. If she'd kept personal cards close to her chest before the rape, they were buried there now. Even Frankie

19

couldn't prise them all out. "Right at the crossroads."

Frankie had taken up temporary residence in Baldwin Street after the attack, theoretically until Bev was back on track. Seven months down the line, she was still in the spare room. As for Bev, she resented her best friend being there and dreaded the day she'd go.

Daz was tapping the wheel in time with one of his tuneless whistles; it could've been Frank Sinatra or Frankie Goes To Hollywood. She sneaked a glance. Open, friendly face, dark, strong features. He wasn't pissed at her – he was just being Daz: one of the lads, bright enough, amiable, bit of a bird-fancier. The guv hadn't assigned her a new partner yet but Daz'd probably fit the bill. If she took him under her wing.

"What's tickled you, sarge?"

The prospect of Daz nestling on her breast was not one to share. "Trust me, you don't want to know."

Hampton Place was next right: a wide tree-lined road, all very blue-plaque-listed-building posh. Except for the brace of squad cars parked two-thirds along.

"That'll do a lot for property prices," she muttered. Daz was on the radio to control. She stretched her legs, had a look round.

Like its not-near neighbours, The Manor prep school boasted substantial grounds, screened by mature hedges. Closer inspection revealed the school's grounds were mostly concrete, marked out with hopscotch grids and a kids' footie area. The herringbone façade sported all the green stuff: lush ivy all but concealed the brick. Barley-sugar chimneys and diamond-leaded windows completed the look. All very National Trust – apart from the security gates and the odd CCTV lens twinkling in the foliage.

"Wotcha." Bev raised a hand as a uniform approached

school-side. PC Simon Wells was a fit twenty-something, despite the twenty-a-day habit that occasionally subsidised Bev's.

Simon's forehead was uncharacteristically rumpled. "I don't like it, sarge. Something's not right." A five-year-old gone walkabout? You could say that. "We're playing it by the book, but…"

"Just a tick." Daz was approaching: no sense going over it twice. They listened carefully as Simon related the conflicting accounts he'd gleaned from Daniel Page's mother and teacher. Shirley Wilson's having been confirmed by a classroom assistant on the phone.

"Check the dentist?" Stupid question but she had to ask.

"Natch."

Daz nodded at the all-but-hidden lenses. "Anything on camera?"

Simon shrugged. "System pre-dates the wheel. There's a few grainy images on one of the tapes. It's being biked to the lab."

"Mother's seen it?" Again, Bev knew the answer.

He nodded. "Reckons it could be anyone."

"OK." She rubbed her hands, eager to get on. "What's happening?"

"Patrols are out, door-to-door underway, dog handlers en route. Obviously we're taking it seriously but – mystery woman aside – the mother's still desperately hoping he's on a jolly with his dad."

"And if he's not?" Bev checked her watch: 4.15. It was nearly four hours since Daniel Page had been taken from the school.

4

Five minutes later Bev was in the head teacher's plush wood-panelled office with one of the most striking women she'd ever seen. If Bev had balls, she'd probably be making a pass. Jenny Page, the missing boy's mother, had that glacial Nordic look: long blonde hair, flawless skin; it was difficult to believe she was pushing forty. The eyes were like tiny circles of new grass. Daz couldn't keep his gaze off.

In the same vein, no one would give Shirley Wilson a second glance. The boy's teacher was all fuzzy perm and faded polyester. Bev'd had a few words, then asked Wilson and the fatso in the loud shirt to wait next door.

So far she'd listened to Mrs Page without interruption, allowing her to say what she wanted, in the way she wanted. And decide what to omit. The recital had been unemotional, robotic, as if relating events that didn't touch her. Could be shock or denial, but the story had holes. If Jenny Page was involved in any way in Daniel's disappearance, her attitude could also be indifference. Morriss golden rule number two: don't believe a word anyone tells you, even if you're talking to your gran.

"So let me get this straight." She mimed note-taking at Daz, then leaned forward to narrow the gap with the mother. This close, Bev discerned holes of a different nature: defunct piercings at the side of the nose and below the bottom lip. Youthful rebellion now regretted? Also apparent, despite the perfectly applied make-up, was a lattice of fine lines round the eyes. Not crow's feet, perhaps, but getting there. "You couldn't collect Daniel yourself…"

"Something came up at the last minute. I couldn't make it." She crossed a well-toned leg.

"Work?" Bev asked.

"No." The smile was a tad smug.

"Right." Bev cleared her throat. "So you rang your husband from home this morning and asked him to go to the school?"

"Rich was fine. He loves spending time with Daniel."

"But he didn't arrive." It wasn't a question. She let it sink in but nothing surfaced. "Where were you?"

Jenny glanced in Daz's direction. "Sorry?"

"You couldn't get here? To pick Daniel up?" *Hello, come in, please.* "Where were you?"

The hesitation could've been genuine. "A medical appointment. It slipped my mind." She gave a faltering smile.

Bev didn't return it, felt strongly the woman was lying. "I'll need details."

Jenny Page nodded, impatient. "Look, officer, I still think it's a misunderstanding. I'm sure Richard must have asked one of the girls to collect Dan-Dan."

The quick change of subject was not subtle. "Girls?"

She shrugged. "Secretary, PA, someone from the agency."

Bev sat back, arms crossed. "Got a double then, Mrs Page?"

"Sorry?" She patently wasn't. Bev was clearly ascending Jenny Page's perfect nostrils.

"A double? At the agency?" The cues weren't picked up. Bev threw another. "The woman at the gates looked so much like you, Shirley Wilson and Tanya Woodall let Daniel go with her."

"The old biddy wasn't wearing her glasses. I asked."

"And Miss Woodall?"

"How should I know? She's only been here five minutes.

Trust me: they're mistaken."

"And Daniel?" Bev snapped. "Was he wrong too?" A tad harsh. But Jenny Page was a big girl. The little boy was Bev's prime concern. And she had to admit there was still distance between her and the woman. She'd come across similar bimbos before: leg-flashing eyelash-flutterers who – if they noticed other women at all – looked straight through them. The Jenny Pages of this world felt easier with men because men were a soft touch. Bev didn't do little woman.

"Where's your husband now, Mrs Page?"

The eyes closed briefly. "I don't know. I can't raise him."

"Is that unusual?" She kept her voice neutral.

"Extremely."

"Are you happily married, Mrs Page?" She returned the woman's glare, letting the silence linger, aware Daz was shifting in his seat.

"I see now." Page rose, shrugged on a leather coat that matched her eyes. "You don't believe me. You think I'm wasting your time."

Or your husband is. "Right now I don't know what to think, Mrs Page."

True. At this stage, they were starting from scratch, knew naff-all about the Pages. Depending how things panned out, they'd soon know the lot. Cops were like the media: digging into private lives, uncovering intimate details. Big difference: the police didn't splash the goods all over the front page.

As for the Pages' possible involvement in Daniel's disappearance... Like it or not, parents harmed their children. Bev wasn't pussyfooting around so as not to hurt a few feelings.

Jenny Page looked down, hands on hips over a still seated

Bev. "Know what? I don't care what you think. Your attitude stinks. I'm going home. I'll wait for my husband there."

Before she reached the door, the phone in her bag trilled. The tension in her face eased as she checked caller ID. Turning her back, Jenny Page listened more than she talked.

Bev didn't need to hear. The ice maiden was losing her cool. "That was Richard." The woman was shaking. "He hasn't seen Daniel since breakfast." A single tear ran down the almost perfect face. "He says I called. Told him he didn't have to collect Daniel. That I'd do it after all."

Mummy always said never to go with strangers. But the nice lady wasn't really a stranger, was she? Even so, Daniel had hesitated just for a second when he saw who was at the gates. He wasn't scared or anything but he'd been so looking forward to seeing mummy. He'd met the nice lady before. It would be OK. And the bag from the Disney store must be for him, mustn't it?

5

"What you reckon, guv?"

Byford was on the phone, listening to Bev's take on the interview with Jenny Page. The superintendent reckoned that his wayward sergeant shouldn't need to ask for his input. That she needed guidance too often these days. That she was in danger of losing her direction. And failing to give it. In part the big man was flattered she sought his advice; in greater part he was afraid where it might lead. Professionally and personally.

He'd detected changes in Bev over recent months, not just in her appearance. The shorter spikier hair did nothing to soften her face; the tongue, always sharp, could now be lacerating.

Byford hoped Will Browne was rotting in hell for what he'd done to her. And for what he'd taken from her.

The big man suppressed a weary sigh. "You tell me, Bev."

Long black mac flapping in the wind, he cut a lone figure in the huge bleak cemetery. Other mourners gone now, the grounds were deserted and silent apart from a chorus of rooks cawing in the wings. Byford had been paying his last respects to ex-DCS Robbie Crawford. The two men went back a long way. As young cops, they'd patrolled the same patch in Aston, moved to CID within a few months of each other, worked a handful of big cases together and socialised off-duty occasionally. Bev's call was disturbing more than his private sorrow at a friend's senseless and untimely death.

If that's what it was. The superintendent had been unable to shake off a faint sense of unease about the hit-and-run.

Difficult to describe, impossible to pin down but there all the same, a niggle at the back of his mind.

"It's a bugger, guv." On the phone he heard the rasp of a match followed by the sharp intake of what would undoubtedly be smoky breath.

Byford glanced at his watch: 4.50. Alarm raised 3.30. Daniel last seen 12.20. Given that the first sixty minutes in any inquiry were the most crucial, the so-called golden hour, by his calculations they were already in extra time. "What's priority, Bev?"

"The boy." Ten out of ten.

"Well, then?" All the fast actions were underway: tracker dogs, chopper, every available body searching, Bev en route to interview the father. Byford couldn't see the problem.

"It's not that simple." More aural smoke signals. He'd already heard her out, read the silences, sensed the nuances. It was clear she had a problem with the boy's mother.

"Jenny Page..."

That was as far as he let her go. "Sergeant, don't let personal..."

"Not."

"You are. I'm aware the woman doesn't fit your image of a distraught parent, but..." He didn't need to spell it out. "A five-year-old boy's missing. That's the bottom line, the top line, every line in between." He paused. "It is that simple."

And Bev didn't need him to tell her that. The operation was textbook so far, couldn't be faulted. It was her attitude that was out of line.

"It doesn't add up, guv. There's..."

He supplied the word. "Discrepancies."

"Exactly."

His sigh went unsuppressed this time. "Is Mike Powell up to speed?"

The DI. He'd been on the phone to Bev, said he'd handle the press. No surprise there: it could be a biggie and Powell was a media tart. "Yeah?" *Why?*

"Where are you now?" Byford stroked an eyebrow. In guv-speak that was not good. She'd picked up the signals in his voice anyway.

"Almost at the house."

Their unmarked police Vauxhall was just behind Jenny's Audi. The woman had insisted on driving herself home. Like Bev, the Pages lived in Moseley, though the couple's house in The Close was more Georgian pile than her Edwardian pad.

"I'll get Mike over there. Make your way back to Highgate." He heard the teeth grit. When she spoke, it was sweetness and light.

"S'OK, guv. Daz is here. Virtually on the doorstep. We can handle it."

"Mike'll want it." There was no way to break it gently. "I'm making him SIO."

Senior investigating officer.

The phone coughed and died. Doubtless they'd been cut off. He'd give her the benefit – this time.

"Double shit with shit on top." Bev rooted in the foot-well to retrieve her mobile, then lowered the window. Hot air; stinking mood.

"New pizza topping?" DC Darren New's grin-cum-smirk was ill-judged.

"Fuck off."

"Please."

His deadpan delivery made her lip twitch. "Daft sod." She twirled a finger in a U-ey, sighing from the soles of her Doc Martens. She conveyed the guv's change of plan: that

Powell was now on parent duty. That she was pissed off didn't need explanation.

"Not *flavour* of the month then?"

"Darren. Let's not do flavour jokes. OK?" His witty repartee, like his whistling, was well flat, both were distracting and she had a load on her plate.

Despite chucking the phone and throwing a wobbly, she privately conceded the guv had probably made the right call. Admitting it hurt – but, like a lot of stuff lately, she'd not done herself any favours with Jenny Page. If he'd let her loose on the boy's father, odds were she'd have cocked up again.

She rubbed a hand over her face. The over-the-top tantrum was for Dazza's benefit: very Bev Morriss. If she acted the same as always, no one would know how shit-scared she was. Scared of responsibility, scared of decision-taking; her judgment was down the pan, searching for her confidence. Maintaining the Morriss façade was like treading a tightrope over the Grand Canyon. In stilettos. On stilts.

Daz broke the silence and her thoughts. "Where to, boss?"

She snorted at the unwitting irony. "Drop me at the school. I'll catch you back at the nick."

Pursed lips ready to launch into another tuneless rendition, Daz took a look at her face and changed his mind. Stomach-rumbling starving, she raided the glove compartment for food, came up with half a packet of beef and onion crisps. She sniffed the contents, curled a lip, stuffed her face anyway.

No pigging out, though, Beverley. The slinky little number she'd bought for Oz's leaving do didn't leave much to the imagination. And didn't have a lot of slack. She pictured her grand entrance, designed to give Oz an eyeful, make sure the man knew what he'd be missing. That didn't include lumpy bits and visible panty line. On the other hand, lunchtime was practically prehistoric. She crammed in another mouthful, casting a covetous glance at Subway Moseley as they drove past.

Moseley Village. She gave an affectionate snort. A scrubby patch of green soaking up exhaust fumes was as rural as Moseley got. Bev had lived there for the better part of a year, loved its ethnic blend and urban buzz. The place was jammed with pubs, wine bars, restaurants, some already gearing up for a Friday night *al fresco*. Pavements were dry now, tables already filling. Rain would not stop play.

"Prob'ly as well, you know, sarge."

Life, the universe, everything? Had she missed something? "What's that, Daz?"

"Not having another go at the Page woman."

"Another go?" she spluttered.

"If you don't mind me saying…" So she would. "I thought you gave her a hard time."

The criticism was brushed off, along with a smattering of crisp crumbs. "She's lying. Kid's missing. No mileage pissing round."

"Maybe she is." He shrugged. "Doesn't mean she's lying about the kid, though."

"She's a fake. Christ, I bet even the emerald eyes are plastic."

"They're not, actually," Daz corrected her. "I took a close look."

"Yeah. I noticed."

Ostentatiously she rummaged in the depths of a bottomless shoulder bag, withdrew a jotter and started making notes. Did Daz have a point? She'd always prized herself on getting along with anyone: empathy, rapport, whatever, she was *simpatico* on legs. Was she losing that as well? Best watch it, make an effort.

"Hard time?" She sneered. "Not me, mate. It was you creaming your jeans."

6

Hampton Place was chocka with cops and squad cars; uniform had thrown a police cordon round the school and the force helicopter was circling in a slate sky. If this were a shoot for *The Bill* or an incident in Small Heath, gawpers would be lining the road. But this was real and Hampton Place didn't do nosy buggers. Posh with a capital P, Big Brother round here meant George Orwell, not Jade Goody.

That was a point. No telly cameras. Bev frowned, scanning both sides of the street as she headed for The Manor. Where were the journos? The pack? Not so much as a cub reporter. DI Powell obviously hadn't got the media circus together yet, and the newshounds clearly hadn't picked up the incident or Hampton Place'd be crawling with sniffer hacks.

A stony-faced Daz had dropped her as far from the school as he dared, saying the exercise would do her good. She sniffed: another mate's nose she'd put out of joint.

"Beverley Morriss. Light of my life. How you doing, babe?"

My God, that voice took her back. She turned and grinned. "Jack Pope, as I live and – got a baccy, old son?"

"For you, precious…" He proffered a pack of Marlboro. "Looking tasty as ever, kid."

She rolled her eyes, took a light as well. She and Jack had done basic training together. Eighteen weeks at Ryton. They'd hit it off from the word go, even gone as far as the odd grope behind the motorbike sheds. But she had no illusions: he'd always been full of shit, no matter how sweet it smelt. Jack was the original lad: twinkling grey eyes, ink-black curls, more boyish charm than anyone she'd met, though the tight black cords left no doubt that he was a big boy now.

"When did you make CID?" Last she heard, Jack was a beat officer in Oxford. "Thought you were slumming it under the dreaming spires."

"Thought wrong, babe. I could fill you in, though." The twinkle turned into a glint. "Fancy a pint later?"

Hiding a smile, she shook her head. "Where you based?" Nowadays it was Christmas cards they exchanged, not bodily fluids.

"Birmingham."

Ta for mentioning it.

"No need to get arsy, Ms Morriss. I'd've given you a bell. I don't start till next week." He jabbed his thumb at the action. "Heard this kicking off. Thought I'd take a look."

"You gonna be working out of Highgate?" Jack was a good mate, but as partner? Pain in the butt.

"Why?" He overdid the eyebrow waggling. "Would you like that, little lady?" Seeing the audience reaction, he cut the drama. "Sorry, mate. Nah. City centre."

She nodded at the school gates, carried on walking towards them. "What you picked up?"

"Only just got here. I was hoping you'd tell me."

"The kid's been missing five hours. Taken by some woman the spit of his mum. And that's it. Earth. Face of. Vanished. No sightings. No calls. Nothing. Big fat nada."

"Door-to-door?"

She flicked the butt in the gutter. "Place is full of disabled monkeys: deaf, blind, dumb."

"No leads at all?"

"Where do we always look first?" He shrugged. "Come

on, Jack. You know as well as me – nearest isn't necessarily dearest."

Sage nod. Murder, rape, abuse, the stats showed it every time. Victims – especially women and children – suffer at the hands of the people they love.

"Close to home," she went on. "Not so far to lash out."

"Who's your money on?"

"Early days, mate."

"Gut instinct?" He offered another baccy. "You used to swear by it."

"If the mother's not in it up to her neck –" she grabbed two for later – "I'm Naomi Campbell."

He pulled an ear lobe. "Listen, Bev…"

Through the gates the woman Bev wanted a word with was about to get in a Ford Ka. Bev cut him off. "Gotta go, Jack." She ducked under the tape, flashed him a smile. "Catch you later."

"Prince 'bout nine?" he called. "Got something to tell you."

Shirley Wilson had probably seen better days. That was the best Bev could say. Seated in the Ka's passenger seat, Bev saw on the teacher's face what was probably going through her troubled mind, sensed the guilt she felt.

Bev had just established that – as Jenny Page claimed – the older woman wasn't wearing her glasses when she'd looked through the classroom window. What Page hadn't pointed out was that the teacher didn't need them for distance.

But that was no comfort to Mrs Wilson. "I should have taken him down myself." She picked compulsively with paint-stained fingers at her frumpy skirt.

Bev wasn't there to make her feel worse. "You had no reason to doubt the woman was his mother."

The teacher shook her head. "That's not really the point, sergeant. I expected to see Mrs Page. I saw a blonde-haired woman with an umbrella and made an assumption."

Shee-it. If the woman had been concealing her face, Shirley Wilson could've had a telescope – it would've made no difference. "So you never actually saw the woman's face?" She tried to keep the accusation out of her voice.

"The window was misted, it was pouring with rain, Daniel was eager to get away. I was in the middle of…"

Bev waited as long as she could. "What?"

"Writing a letter." The teacher made eye contact for the first time. "To my son."

That was the big stick, then. Keeping in touch with her own son, Shirley Wilson had failed to look out for someone else's. It wasn't the only reason she was giving herself a hard time.

"Tanya had never even seen Daniel's mother before. How was she to know who was waiting outside?"

The ID thing had been bugging Bev too. "You're right, Mrs Wilson. Tanya wouldn't know." She reached to touch the older woman's hand. "But *Daniel* would."

According to the classroom assistant, he'd gone without a second's hesitation. Which meant Jenny Page had been there and was lying. Or Daniel had been taken by someone he knew.

Jack Pope sat in his Boxster tapping a biro on the steering wheel and wrestling with an alien concept: his conscience. Even if he hadn't bumped into Bev Morriss, he'd have looked her up. She'd been a good mate way back and whatever *it* was, young Beverley had it in spades. And, boy, did she still have a mouth on her.

He needed contacts like that in the police.

Jack glanced at the notes and quotes he'd jotted from memory: *disabled monkeys…big fat nada…lying mother…* OK, Bev hadn't actually called her a liar, but *If the mother's not in it up to her neck, I'm Naomi Campbell* wasn't the biggest vote of confidence.

Pope could see the headline now. Not that he'd write it; the subs did that. But the story was his baby; the smile suggested this was one he'd love. Technically he didn't start until Monday. But he could file early, get a piece in this week's *Sunday Chronicle*. Every new boy needed brownie points.

Naomi Campbell. Pope shook his head. If Bev ever needed a proper job, she could try stand-up. Pope had switched to news reporting because he was sick of a police culture so politically correct that cops were scared of their own farts. It stank because in the main it was still all lip service. Gobby headstrong mavericks like Morriss were the new endangered species.

Mind, for a woman sharper than a syringe factory she'd not cottoned on to his career move. Pope told himself he hadn't lied, hadn't tried to hide the fact that he'd turned in the badge. Bev had made all the assumptions. It had always been a failing: rushing in, jumping to, presuming that, this and the other. If she hadn't dashed off, he'd have put her straight there and then. Probably.

Question was: would he keep her name out of it? Quoting her direct would drop her in shit so deep she'd be struggling for air. He didn't relish doing that to a mate. And he might need her again.

Glancing in the mirror, he eased the motor into early evening city-bound traffic. He could murder a drink and there was no deadline to worry about. He'd give the Morriss thing some thought over a pint or three.

7

"Dead original." DI Mike Powell tilted his blond head at a discreet road sign: The Close. Behind the wheel, DC Carol Pemberton could care less; she was keeping an eye out for the Page place. It was a *tres* des res in what was becoming Moseley's most prestigious development. The Close's classic Georgian dimensions were pretty convincing, considering a screw factory had occupied the site three years back.

Powell checked his teeth in the mirror for green bits, and after a quick adjustment to his dove-grey necktie reckoned he was ready for anything. The guv's order had come as a bit of a shock. Bev Morriss should've been a natural to interview the boy's father but she'd got another bloody beehive in her bonnet. And Powell had to pick up the pieces. Talk about making allowances. It was the police service, not the social. Powell had worked his arse off arranging a six-thirty news conference. It was five-fifteen now; if they didn't get a move on he'd miss the action. Suppose he could leave Carol mopping up the dregs; girl needed the experience.

"There." He thrust a finger across her line of sight, indicating a pristine property on the right, aptly named The White House.

Already pulling over, Carol shot him a pointed *gee thanks* look.

The man waiting anxiously in the doorway had to be Daniel's father. His arms were tight across his chest, the left leg jerked like it was wired. Even Powell could feel the tension. The DI extended a hand that went either unnoticed or ignored. Richard Page wasn't into polite preamble.

"Have you found him?"

"Not yet, Mr Page." Powell reckoned any other time Page would be Mr Smoothie. Chestnut hair, caramel eyes, expensive tan; he was a top earner, good looker, clearly successful. But at the moment the man was as crumpled as his Hugo Boss suit.

"You'd better come in."

The hall was bigger than Powell's flat. He had a quick butcher's, but it was all a bit ostentatious for his taste: yellow stripes, massive gilt mirror, showy white flowers everywhere. Place smelt like a florist's. Or a funeral parlour.

Page was about to disappear through high double doors at the end. Powell caught up, cocked a disapproving eyebrow. He so didn't like ponytails on men. Made them look well gay.

The DI wasn't up on interior-design trends, but presumably green was the new black. The huge sitting room was wall-to-wall pea with a dash of avocado. Even the shag-pile looked as if it could do with a mow. As for the woman…

Powell hadn't registered Jenny Page initially, now couldn't take his eyes off her. Like a sculpture in ice, she perched on the edge of an upright chair gazing through a casement window. He had a hard spot for cool classy blondes, and they didn't come much chillier or more classic. As she turned her head at his approach, he clocked the eyes. They made the other greens looked insipid.

"No news, darling," Page answered his wife's unspoken question as he took her hand in both his. Touching tableau though it was, Powell had a stack of questions he wanted off his chest. And he was damned if he'd conduct the interview on his hind legs. Carol interpreted the rapid hand-and-eye movements, dragged over a couple of straight-backs, pulled out a tattered notebook.

The DI kicked off with the easy ones: full names, ages, occupations, then significant movements and timings during the day. Throughout, Page hovered at his wife's side, gently massaging her elegant neck and shoulders. *Jammy sod.* Powell took off the kid gloves.

"The phone call bothers me," he said to Page. "When the arrangement was changed, you had no doubt you were speaking to your wife?"

"None."

"What was said exactly?"

"That she could get to the school, so not to worry about Daniel. I was a bit disappointed. I'd been quite looking forward to seeing him. I don't spend enough time with the boy as it is." He pinched the bridge of his nose. "Sorry. I…"

"Take your time," Carol said. Powell glared at his colleague.

"That was it, really. It was a bad line. Lot of background noise."

"Yet you were convinced it was your wife?" Powell asked.

"It was her voice!" His was raised. "Sorry. It sounded like Jenny. That's all I know."

"Mrs Page?" Powell asked.

"It wasn't me."

Powell tended to believe her; they'd find out either way when the techie boys traced the call. *If* they traced the call.

"Can either of you think why anyone would take Daniel?"

A glance passed between husband and wife. Powell couldn't read it. Page shook his head.

"He's just a little boy." Jenny circled a white gold ring on her wedding finger. "Why would anyone take Dan-Dan?"

"These are difficult questions, I know, but what about enemies? Have you rowed with anyone recently? Anyone out there who might bear a grudge?"

"Jenny and I have discussed this already. We can't come up with anything."

"Has anyone followed you? Any strangers hanging round? Either of you seen anything suspicious?"

Page sighed. "Don't you think we might have called the police if we had?"

"You're a successful businessman, Mr Page…"

"So?"

Powell paused, prepared the ground. "Is it possible Daniel's being held for ransom?"

"Kidnapped?" The guffaw was a shock but appeared genuine. "Don't be ridiculous. We're comfortable, not rolling in it."

The answers were predictable, automatic. "You both need to think about these things. We can't rule anything out." Seed planted, Powell changed tack. "You had a medical appointment, Mrs Page?" Did she start slightly? Page's fingers definitely stilled momentarily.

"I…" An ornate ormolu clock on an Adam fireplace ticked the seconds: ten before Jenny Page spread her hands. "I'm sorry. It was the first thing that came into my head." She bowed it now. "It was a stupid thing to say."

"You lied." Carol stated a fact, not asked a question. She locked her gaze on Jenny. The blonde failed to meet it, sent distress flares to Powell, leaning towards him, jade eyes welling.

"The officer at the school… I felt harassed. I wasn't thinking straight."

Powell frowned. What had Morriss been playing at? The Highgate rumour mill reckoned she was losing it, crumbly as a chocolate flake. He'd not go that far, but she could be her own worst enemy.

"I'll have a word with her, Mrs Page."

"So will I." Carol paused. "It'll be interesting to see if that's how she sees it."

Powell flapped a hand at the DC. "So where were you, Mrs Page?"

Lowering her head, she did the Diana thing through thick eyelashes. "In town. Having lunch. It just seemed so… so *frivolous*, with Dan-Dan…"

Powell nearly reached to comfort her. Carol didn't. "Which restaurant?"

"Chez Jules." Not so much as a glance at Carol.

"With?" she persisted.

Jenny appealed to the DI. "Is it important?"

"Yes," Carol said.

"Is that the door?" Powell asked.

Page squeezed his wife's shoulder. "I'll check. Back in a minute, darling."

Jenny touched the DI's knee, softened her voice. "Quick thinking. Thank you, inspector." He was nonplussed; he'd only mentioned a noise outside. "I was with an old friend," Jenny revealed. "A man called Justin Weaver. He lives in Northfield, Tudor Rise. Number's in the book. Please don't tell my husband. He'll kill me." She slapped an overdramatic hand to her mouth. "Sorry. That was a slip of the tongue. Richard's not a violent man. I've known Justin for years. It's entirely platonic, but my husband hates it when I see other men."

Powell had no idea how long Page had been standing in the doorway, but the man clearly had more important things on his mind than his wife's lunch partners. Staring at a sheet of paper fluttering in his hand, his skin tone blended with the décor. He tried to control his voice, but it broke as he read out the message.

"*Involve the police and the boy dies. Instructions for payment will follow.*" The note floated to the ground.

Carol ran into The Close as Powell rang control. Given the level of police activity over the last two hours, Daniel Page was as good as dead.

8

The ransom note changed everything. Taking a child was sick, maybe sad; kidnapping was calculated evil. Within minutes of its arrival, established procedures were activated, an immediate news blackout requested. Less than an hour down the line from Powell's call to control and Operation Sapphire was in almost-full swing.

The force's top family liaison officer was on his way to The White House. No cushy berth this. Colin Henfield wouldn't just be there to brew tea and burn toast. As well as getting close to the Pages, he'd be the eyes and ears of the police. Throughout the inquiry, skilled operators would monitor home and business calls; surveillance teams and gear would be installed at a neighbouring property. If a suspected perp so much as sneezed, cops would be there with a tissue. And cuffs.

Back at Highgate, a kidnap room had been set up and was now crammed with forty-plus officers raring to get out there. Early arrivals had seats, others lined the walls or took floor space. Canteen smells clung to the clothes of guys who'd been called in off their break. Not that there'd be any complaints. Not while there was a chance Daniel was alive. The atmosphere was electric and then some. Bev, next to Daz in the front row, could feel the sparks.

The DI had just brought everyone up to speed with events at The Close and was now perched on a table at one side, ankles crossed. Current focus was centre stage where Byford wielded a pointer across a line of whiteboards covered with street maps, aerial shots and blow-up photographs. Key locations were highlighted: the school, the Page home, possible routes taken by the kidnapper. "It seems likely a vehicle was involved," Byford speculated. "It's yet another thing we don't know."

The superintendent had relieved Powell of SIO status, opted to take the reins of the inquiry himself. The hands-on role suited. Six-five and well covered, his fifty-plus years had started to show just recently but Bev reckoned right now he was as wired as anyone in the room. She detected flashes of the younger Byford, especially the sparkle in his slate-grey eyes. Not for the first time, she wished she'd known the big man before he was old enough to be her dad.

Byford told the squad he'd run twice-daily briefings for the duration. Made it clear he wanted as many bodies there as possible and it was up to those who couldn't make it to familiarise themselves with updates. Johnnie Blake would be their first port of call. The tough-talking Lancastrian was Operation Sapphire's newly assigned information officer.

There'd be regular news conferences as well but not a word printed or broadcast until the outcome was known. No cop or reporter wanted a repeat of the Black Panther fuck-up back in the seventies. Donald Nielson had kidnapped the Midlands teenager Lesley Whittle; the press got wind of it, details appeared, the girl died. Reporting restrictions had been tight ever since. The media would have its day when the police had a result: Daniel Page's release or the discovery of his body. Right now the press pack was milling downstairs, keen to be put in the picture.

"Fucking miracle they didn't get a sniff." The nasal drawl was pure Bernie Flowers, head of the police news bureau. Bev reckoned the grey-civil-servant image was carefully cultivated and deliberately misleading. In a former life

Bernie had edited a national redtop and was sharp as a blade. He'd be holding her hand shortly when she faced the hacks. That was another role the guv has assigned: Bev Morriss, media liaison. On top of DS duties.

Not that she needed a fancy title to know Bernie's assessment was sound. All conspicuous police activity had been called off the instant they knew what they were dealing with, but for two hours the full works had been up and running: helicopter, tracker dogs, uniforms on the knock. The kidnapper must've known the all-singing all-dancing police show would kick off the minute Daniel was reported missing; must've realised there was every chance it would hit the news.

"Something on your mind, Bev?" Byford was loosening his tie. Maybe he was feeling the heat too.

She dropped the frown. "Can't get my head round the delay," she said. "The kid's snatched at lunchtime. The note's not delivered for five hours."

It had bothered the superintendent as well, but at this early stage the kidnapper held every card. All the police could do was try to force a hand. "And?"

She tried to ignore the line of sweat trickling down her spine. "Everyone knows when a kid goes missing, the cops are on the case like a rash."

"As we were."

"Exactly. Kidnappers aren't stupid. These characters knew exactly what they were playing at. They wanted us out there. Now they want us to stop. They want to call the shots. Show who's boss."

"You keep saying 'they'?" Byford asked.

"A kid needs guarding 24/7. Can't do that and run errands; needs teamwork." A few heads nodded. "Daniel wasn't just snatched off the street; the pickup took meticulous planning, precision timing. And insider gen."

"Kidnappers always learn everything they can about their victims," Byford said. They'd often shadow a target for days, weeks, months even.

"Or pick it up from an expert." It sounded like a sneer. She didn't mean it to. "The woman who took Daniel knew about the dental appointment, knew to be at the school and when; knew to call off the father. She looked like Jenny Page, sounded like Jenny Page. What if...?"

"For Christ's sake," Powell exploded. "The poor bloody woman's catatonic."

"That's one way of putting it," Bev muttered. She spread her hands. "Maybe she's sick, maybe she needs help..."

"Sarge," Carol Pemberton intervened. "She didn't pick the boy up. I've checked. She was in town lunching with a mate. I've spoken to the guy."

Wind. Sails. Out of. Then a puff of breeze. "But if she lied about the medical appointment...?" The implication was clear: for Jenny Page, truth was a moveable feast.

"You're lucky she's not putting in a complaint," Powell said. "Bullying, intimidation." He tucked hands under armpits. "Touch of the green eyes, sergeant?"

Jealous? Never. Then a sudden thought; she narrowed blue ones. "Did Jenny Page leave the room while you were there?"

Powell sighed impatience. "Let it go."

"Was she out of your sight any time?" *Long enough to drop a ransom note?*

"For Christ's sake," Powell said.

She ignored him. "What's your take, Carol? Anything iffy?"

DC Pemberton shrugged. "She's a cold fish, I'll give you that. And she didn't just lie to us; her old man didn't know she had a lunch date. As for this guy she was with – I don't think he's the only one she sees."

Powell crossed his arms. "How's that work, Rosie Lee?"

Carol riffled the pages in her notebook. "She said, *Richard hates it when I see other men.*" She looked pointedly at Powell. "Plural."

"No crime, is it?" He sniffed. "She's not a bad-looking woman. No reason why she shouldn't meet up with an old mate."

Secrets and lies. Bev made a mental note.

"One other point," Carol added. "It may be nothing but… the place wasn't exactly child-friendly. No toys scattered round, no sticky finger marks. They had to root round to find a photo."

"Big deal," Powell said.

Byford picked up on the visuals. "What about the pic, Mike?" Richard Page had sorted out the most recent image of Daniel. It was being copied.

"Ready any time, boss."

Everyone in the team needed a copy; needed to know Daniel's face better than their own. "Thoughts on the note, anybody?" Byford asked.

All eyes turned to one of the kidnap boards where the kidnappers' message, now copied and enlarged, was displayed. Just eleven words. Not a lot to go on: certainly nothing forensics could sink their scientific teeth into. The original had been clean as a bleached sheet. Byford waited a few seconds, but what was there to say?

"OK. This is the current situation." He paused, wanted everyone's full attention. "We're looking at virtually a blank page. It's up to all of us to fill it. Obviously we look at the parents but we talk to everyone. And I mean everyone the Pages have ever had contact with: family, friends, neighbours, colleagues, butcher, baker… Check every word. Don't take anything for granted." Another pause. "And keep an open mind."

Bums shifted, throats were cleared; a few questions were thrown, then the guv dished out the fast actions and the donkeywork, the key interviews and the slightly less urgent. No one needed reminding that kidnap was a big crime like no other. It carried the highest risk and the lowest profile. While the victim was still being held there'd be not be a whisper in the media and all police activity would be covert.

One slip could cost a little boy his life.

Bernie was hanging round outside the room where the press conference was to be held, skimming what looked like the local rag. "Wotcha, Bev."

She'd just had time for a coke and a pee before entering the lions' den. Below-the-belt noises suggested indigestion or nerves. Either way she was windy.

"Word in your shell-like." Bernie pushed up from the corridor wall. "Clear how we play this?"

"You bet." She zipped her lips.

"Good girl." Bernie's crooked smile displayed a chipped front tooth. Story went that some Right Hon took a swing after starring in a kiss-and-tell on a Bernie front page. *A tooth for the truth* was Bernie's favourite tag-line. "Watch every syllable. Keep it short. Don't offer a thing. If in doubt, no comment."

Her hand was on the door. "Nothing new there, then."

He didn't return the smile. "These embargos are voluntary, Bev. None of them'll break it; that don't worry me. But they'll beaver away so they can make a splash soon as we know the score. They'll track down anyone with a pulse as long as they add to the story. Specially if they've got any dirt. And the more people in the know, the greater the danger it'll leak."

She nodded, laid a hand on his arm. "Trust me, Bernie."

Almost as many hacks were gathered as there'd been cops upstairs. Pecking order was same old same old: TV, radio then print. She nodded at a few familiar faces: Matt Snow, a Tintin look-alike from the *Evening News*; Nick Lockwood, the Beeb's Mr Midlands; even Celia Bissell, who looked after features for the *Chronicle*. She'd be working on colour pieces to run when the story broke; flimflam to pad out a few inside pages.

Vague mutterings faded as Bev ran through the intros for those not already in the know. She threw out the barest of bones, then outlined what would happen over the next few days: regular off-the-record updates and more formal sessions where they could record material with the SIO and other main players for later use.

Just about everyone in the room jumped on that. "What about the parents?"

Bev broke the bad news that the family's identity was being withheld for the moment. Then she handed over to Bernie, who reinforced the imperative of keeping the news blackout in place. It was a no-brainer; protests were token. Ten minutes in and Bev was beginning to relax; this liaison lark was a piece of piss. She glanced at her watch: getting on for half-seven. When this little lot was over, she'd be heading for home and a scrub-up. Bases were covered, she'd cleared it with the guv, and she'd be on the end of a phone if anything broke. The glimpse she'd caught earlier of Oz clearing his locker wasn't going to be her final memory.

"Can I run a name past you, Sergeant Morriss?" The clipped tone was familiar. Bev looked up to find Celia

Bissell flicking though her notebook, red talons clutching what looked like a Mont Blanc.

"Say again?"

"Can I run the victim's name past you?" The tight smile didn't reach the caked mascara. "Our crime correspondent says it's from a reliable source."

Bev stiffened. How the fuck did it get out so quick? "Who's that, then?"

"I never reveal sources." Smug bint.

"She meant who's your crime guy these days?" The query was Bernie's. It wasn't as nonchalant as it sounded, going by the clenched fist under the table.

"New operator, just joined us," Bissell said. "His name's Pope. Jack Pope."

9

Jack Pope was propping up the bar at The Prince of Wales when Bev rolled up an hour later, itching for a fight, still staggering from a bollocking. It had been damage limitation all round, back at Highgate, after Bissell dropped the name-bomb. Then came the inquest. Without a body. The normally laconic Bernie lost it big-time; the guv was incandescent. But it was nothing compared with her self-imposed mauling. *Fucking idiot.* She'd trusted Pope and he'd stitched her up like a baby kipper. The fact that the victim's identity was almost certain to come out eventually was no comfort.

"Beverley. I was beginning to give up on you." Waving a ciggie in welcome, Pope aimed a peck at her cheek. She flinched, not just from the beery breath and fag mouth. "What's up, doll?"

"Bastard." Her lips barely parted.

His laugh, though nervous, was a mistake. "What?"

"Arsehole," she hissed.

Pope glanced round, hating scenes. Not a big crowd. The Prince was a police pub; tonight most cops were occupied elsewhere. "Come on, Bev." The playful tap was a major error. "Knock it off."

"My pleasure." She moved in. "Where do I start?" She needed to know how far he'd betrayed her.

"I was gonna tell you." He scratched his nose. First sign of veracity deficit.

"Lying toe-rag." Another step backed him flush against the bar, her index finger lodged in his chest hair kept him there. "I don't care about looking a complete moron." She did. "Don't give a shit that you dropped me in it." Untrue. "Fact you looked me in the eye and lied through your teeth – *that* pisses me off, Pope."

Apart from cops, the pub's nicotine-and-sawdust interior was a geriatrics' haven: real-ale drinkers and serious domino players. Several pairs of rheumy eyes were agog at the sight of a woman at the bar about to knock spots off some bloke. Livid, Bev was oblivious, but maybe the audience was getting to Pope.

He swatted her arm away. "Back off, lady." At five-ten, he had four inches on Bev. She edged back, palms damp, heart racing. Scared what she'd do to him.

"Go back through what I said," he sneered. "Every word was true. You jumped to your own conclusions, kid."

Momentarily flustered, she ran a mental check. OK, he'd never actually said he was with CID. On the other hand, he hadn't exactly put her straight. "You let me think…"

"No one *lets* you think." He swigged from a full pint. "Supposed to be some shit-hot detective, aren't you?"

She felt the flush hit her cheeks, spat the next words. "You should have fucking *told* me!"

"You should've listened, lady. Instead of mouthing off."

Tears pricked; she had to look away. The uncharacteristic vulnerability had a softening effect. Pope put an arm around her shoulders, drew her close. "Come on, Bevy. You rushed off before I had chance to say a word."

She nestled her head against his chest, all nods and muffled sobs. "I could lose my job over this, Jack."

"No way." He wanted her to face him but she clung tighter when he tried to pull her away. "Listen, Bev, I only gave Celia the name. That disabled-monkey business and the stuff about the mother? It'll go no further." He smoothed her hair, hated seeing her like this. "You have my word."

"Promise?"

"I'd never do that to you, Bev."

"Sure?"

"Absolutely."

"Hundred per cent?"

"Hundred and ten."

"Your maths is shite as well."

He was too late to protect his balls. She was there first.

"OK, Bev. Let go."

"Cross me again, Pope…" She squeezed hard. "Your chances of fatherhood are fucked. Clear? *Kid*?"

He croaked what had to be a yes.

She smiled as she tightened her fingers. "Mother's-life clear?"

Beyond words, Pope nodded.

"One slip…" She turned the screw. "And you'll look back on tonight as one of life's pleasures."

Grip released, she picked up his glass, a glint in her eye. "Hot in here, innit?"

Pope raised his palms as she took aim. "Bev. No."

His top half was the last place she had in mind. Especially when below the belt was an open goal.

Two minutes later, Bev's sobs in the MG were the real deal. Hugging herself, head bowed, she drew deep breaths, heart still on double time. The crocodile tears and weasel words in The Prince had done the trick but the cost was high. Truth hurt. And she'd enjoyed inflicting the pain. Pope had seen that in her eyes and it had scared the pants off him. He'd not go back on his word: she'd got what she wanted. *Bully for Bev.* The thought choked her up again. But what if he was right? Did she have the listening skills of a dead slug? And as for foot in mouth, was there a sodding shoe shop in there? The snipes would have been water off a duck's back before the attack. But now? Her confidence and judgment were shot to shit.

She wound the window, lit a Silk Cut. *Bullying?* Jenny Page had slung the same accusation at her. Had she gone in heavy-handed? *Christ, Bev. Who do you think you are? Robocop?* She snorted, not sure who she was any more.

That was one of the problems.

After the rape, the police welfare people had leaned on her to see one of their therapists. No real choice. A sceptical Bev had gone along with it, was still hearing the same psycho-crap every week: her aggression was a direct result of the rape; every time she lashed out, verbally or otherwise, she was hitting back at Will Browne.

Bullshit. Hard-ass had always been her middle name. She'd always given better than she got. But what if it was out of hand? What if the trick cyclist was right? Sigmund, as she called him, said she must learn to pull her punches, count to ten, stay calm, trust people again. Like yeah. And find a cure for bird flu.

She smacked the wheel with her palms. Why couldn't she let go? She had to move on; couldn't see the way forward. And the road behind was littered with burnt bridges.

Nice one, Bev. *Clichés 'r' us.* She flicked the butt through the window. Last time she looked, she still had a job to do. Just. She picked up an envelope from the passenger seat, took out a photograph. She'd not had chance to study it yet. And little Daniel Page was what it was all about.

"Drink your milk, Dan-Dan." The nice lady smiled as she ruffled Daniel's corn-thatch hair, gave him his beaker.

It was the Harry Potter one from home, his favourite.

Not enough sugar; still, he always drank warm milk last thing at night. She took the mug back and tucked the Doctor Who duvet under his chin. It was good to have his own things around him.

"Sleep tight, little man."

The nice lady blew him a kiss. She knew he was afraid of the dark so she left the nightlight. He yawned even though he wasn't a tiny bit sleepy. He wasn't frightened or anything, either, just very, very worried. He hadn't known Mummy was ill. The nice lady had told him Mummy was in hospital, and he had to stay here for a while. He'd forgotten the lady's name but she said Daddy would come to take him home soon so it didn't really matter.

Daniel thought he might call her Aunty, even though he didn't have any aunties. Picturing the lady's face, he recalled her eyes: green eyes like Mummy's. Daniel's eyelids fluttered, and fell. The little boy yawned and snuggled into the pillow. Sleepy after all.

10

The slinky little number didn't get an outing. It was late and Bev couldn't be arsed to go home and change. Nor was she in the mood after her pop at Pope. It meant that when she slipped into the prefab annexe at the back of Highgate for Oz's leaving do, she was still in the funeral weeds she'd worn all day.

Fitting, then. Given it felt like a bereavement.

Except for the music floating into the lobby. Not so much *Abide With Me* as *Get Off of My Cloud*. She gave a slow smile. Oz was an old tart for the Stones. She ran her fingers through her hair, licked her lips and made an entrance of sorts.

"How's it going, Bev?" A familiar face at the bar, tombstone teeth and flapping jowls; Vince Hanlon had a permanently avuncular grin. Deceptive. The sergeant had nearly thirty years' service and had felt more collars than Sketchley's.

"Tickety, Vincie." She tapped a salute.

"Drinkin'?"

"Diet coke. Not." Wide grin. She could murder a large pinot. "Cheers, Vince."

She spied out the land as she sipped the wine. Oz was at a table with the usual suspects: Pembers, Daz, Del Chambers, Ken Rose, Brian Latham. DCs tended to stick together. Not that Oz was DC any more. To the right, Powell was chatting up Gorgeous Goshie at the far end of the bar. Like that would work. Sumitra Gosh had a functioning brain.

Vince nodded at the DI. "Has he come up with a new one yet?"

She gave a rueful smile. "Nah." The whole nick knew

Powell had a problem knowing what to call Bev. For years, she'd just been Morriss, occasionally sergeant. He'd used her first name only once: when he comforted her immediately after the rape. That subject was taboo, never mentioned let alone discussed. Given the intimacy – however unwilling – they'd shared, Morriss was now too impersonal, but he balked at calling her Bev because she still got up his nose. She and Vince monitored the DI's dilemma daily, notched up the ways he got round it. "Hey, you" was current favourite.

Vince tilted his grizzly-bear head. "Will you miss young Khanie, Bev?"

Like an arm. "Who?"

"Daft sod."

"Guv around?" Easier territory.

"Popped his head in earlier."

Good. Bev nodded, took a few more sips. It was a piss-poor turnout, really. Maybe no surprise, given the kidnap, but even so the Highgate hard men had kept away. Oz had never been admitted into the crusty club: too cute, too clever, wrong colour.

"'Nother drink, Vincie?"

"Why not?"

She did the honours and chinked her glass against his pint. "Bottoms up, old girl."

"Less of the girl," Vince tutted.

Girl? That reminded her. Jenny Page had been convinced initially that one of the 'girls', the women at Page's ad agency, had collected Daniel from school. She'd bear that in mind when she and Daz did the staff interviews first thing.

Daz was on sparkling form. Looked as if he was stringing out one of his jokes. Shame the guv had bowed out early;

she could've asked if he was teaming her up with Daz for the foreseeable rather than the current job-by-job footing.

Jagger had moved on to *You Can't Always Get What You Want*. You can say that again, she thought. Oz was strolling over. Black linen pants, sexy black shirt, dark floppy hair.

"Bev." He nodded. "Glad you made it. What you drinking?"

Two large vinos were making their presence felt in an otherwise empty stomach. Her head wasn't exactly spinning but… "Pinot. Cool."

"I'm off." Vince drained his glass. "Best of luck, Khanie. Don't do anything I wouldn't."

"Cheers, mate."

A handshake, Vince left, then silence. It wasn't that they had nothing to say – they had too much. But for months now they'd been talking on eggshells. Scratching round for safe ground, both pounced simultaneously on Vince's departing bulk.

"Nice guy…" she started.

"Good bloke…" Oz began. Their laughter was too loud. The eye contact between them was rare these days. It said more than either was willing to put into words. She watched as he positioned his glass dead centre on a beer mat, then ran both hands through his fringe. The gesture was habitual and she interpreted it accurately. He was about to spout.

"Sod it, Bev. I'm sick of messing about."

So was she, despite the so-what shrug.

"I'm going tomorrow. I don't want to leave it like this."

The eyebrow was raised and arch. "*It?*"

"You. Me. Us. Unfinished business."

Neither did Bev, but hell would host winter sports before she'd admit it. Oz could read her body, too: knew she had a

PhD in pig-headedness. He reached to touch her; for once she didn't pull back. "I won't be around any more, Bev, but I'll always be there for you." He paused, brown eyes shining. "If that's what you want."

Does fire burn? She had to look away.

"If you won't say it, Bev…I will." He left another gap she didn't fill. "What we had was precious." Gently he turned her head to face his. "It was to me, anyway."

Another Stones track: *It's All Over Now.* "Listen to the words, mate." She removed Oz's hand, gulped the wine. "Catch you later."

Oz was still at the bar when she reached the door and looked back. Her heart did that flip-thing like when she first met him. She'd never wanted him more. And he'd never appeared so hurt. Maybe it was his pain or her pinot but she drew a deep breath and sauntered back. If he told her to fuck off, so be it; she couldn't leave it like this. She whispered in his ear. *Let's Spend the Night Together* usually had the desired effect.

It was late. The multi-storey car park in Northfield was badly lit and virtually deserted. Emerging from a foul-smelling lift, the man staggered, almost fell. His flushed face had the broken veins and spreading purple nose of a boozer. Doug Edensor was over the limit and, as a former police officer, knew he'd be stupid to get behind the wheel.

His Jaguar was in the far corner, the only car on this level. He fumbled with the key, caught movement out of the corner of his eye. Two hooded figures. Edensor presumed they'd been hiding behind one of the concrete pillars: muggers or druggies. He put a protective hand on his wallet but the swaggering bastards weren't interested.

He lashed out but they were younger, quicker, stronger. His muscles screamed in mute agony as one of them twisted his arms behind him. The pain was so intense he barely felt the needle enter his chest.

Supporting his body between theirs, his assailants mounted the stairs. Edensor was barely conscious when they emerged at roof level.

He was dead before he hit the ground.

Where to locate the camera had been a difficult decision. A top-shot would have captured the body's flight. But the long lens would show the crash landing. The shadowy figure at the end of the street gave a satisfied smile, whispered, "Cut." The choice had been a good call.

Dark thoughts about Daniel Page's kidnap were keeping Byford awake. When the phone rang in the early hours, his heart sank. He expected the worst when he reached for the receiver. It was Highgate control and it took a while for the news to sink in. Two traffic officers had found Doug Edensor's body smashed almost beyond recognition in a street in Northfield.

"It looks like suicide," the duty inspector said. "We thought you'd want to know."

Dougie had been a good friend before he left the police. "Of course," Byford said. "Thanks for telling me." Deep in thought, he ended the call, swung his legs out of bed, headed for the kitchen.

Two minutes later, he lay back in a recliner, a crystal glass of single malt in his hand as he gazed through the window at the city skyline. The view usually helped put his troubled thoughts into some sort of perspective but tonight all he could see was Dougie. Byford found it difficult to imagine his ex-colleague dead, impossible to picture him taking his own life.

He sipped the Laphroaig, saw another figure jostling for attention in his mind's eye. The unease he'd felt since Robbie Crawford's hit-and-run accident was no longer faint. If there was the merest sniff of suspicion about Doug's death… He shook his head. SOCOs were still out there; he'd study the reports first thing before jumping to conclusions. He laid his head back, closed his eyes. The view's customary magic wasn't working; neither was the malt's.

In less than a week, two senior police officers – both old friends – had died. And Byford didn't do coincidence.

January 1994

Holly wasn't scared the first night the bedroom door was inched open – she was excited. The little girl shivered under the duvet, hardly daring to look. From an early age she'd fantasised about it: Mummy finding her, telling her it had all been a terrible mistake and now it was time to come home. Not for one second had she doubted her mother would return.

So that first night, she wasn't scared. Not really. Hardly at all. In her child's head, she'd worked it all out. Obviously Mummy would have to steal her back. The people who'd adopted Holly wouldn't let Mummy anywhere near her, would they? They hated it when Holly asked questions; she wasn't even allowed to talk about her.

Her mummy could be a princess or a movie star. It didn't matter. She was Holly's Mummy and she loved her. And Mummy loved Holly. The little girl knew something awful must've forced her mother to let her go. But none of that mattered. One day she'd return. The little girl just knew her mother followed her every move, would have watched over Holly from afar – until the moment was right.

So the first time a shadowy figure crept into Holly's room in the middle of the night, the little girl was excited as could be. Even when that figure slipped into bed beside her, Holly wasn't frightened. Mummy would want to catch up on all those cuddles she'd missed. Mummy would want to hold her darling girl as tightly as could be.

Wouldn't she?

SATURDAY

11

Oz's smell lingered on the pillow, and other places, but he was gone when Bev woke. Better that way. She lay still, eyes closed, savouring the moment – a morning when she felt good, fighting fit. Will Browne was not the last man inside her. She and Oz had made gentle tender love and she'd clung and cried and confided and confessed. Ironic or what? She'd let him close at last and now he'd buggered off. She laughed, not really concerned. He was going to the Met, not the dark side of the moon. What was it her dad used to say? *Que sera sera*. What'll pan out'll pan out.

She flung off the duvet, headed for the loo and a shower. Frankie was clearly on galley duties. Bacon odours and Bizet wafted up from below. Frankie was bellowing out a number from *Carmen*. Girl must be in a good mood.

When Bev entered the kitchen ten minutes later, her friend whirled round, raven curls flying, mouth a perfect O. Bev frowned. "Wind changes, you could catch flies for a living, mate."

Frankie Perlagio missed nothing. "Did we have a little company last night, my friend?"

Trying to keep a straight face wasn't going to happen. "This the Italian inquisition?"

"Drawer there." Frankie pointed. "Pass the thumbscrews."

Bev flapped a hand, took a seat at the table. Frankie tilted her head. "Are you going in today?"

"Doh." Flexi-hours Frankie didn't know what full time meant. If she wasn't giving her dad a hand in the family restaurant, she busked it as a session singer. A kind of Katie-Melua-Nigella-Lawson hybrid. Her current incredulity wasn't down to the fact it was a Saturday.

"But you're…" She pointed to Bev's legs. "And you're…" Wearing make-up.

"Yeah, yeah." So she hadn't forgotten how to put on slap and a skirt. Bev's main concern was the angle of the plates in her friend's hands. "Shall we eat or are you just gonna drop them?" For a half-Italian, Frankie cooked a mean full English. And she had the nous not to talk with her mouth full.

Early brief. Highgate. Nineteen hours since Daniel Page was seen being led away from The Manor prep school by an unknown woman. Any of the thirty-plus officers present who doubted what was at stake only had to look at the posters pinned on every wall in the kidnap room. Little people didn't figure large in Bev's life but she'd never seen a more angelic-looking child. Only the halo was missing. Halo. Wings. Afterlife. That train of thought made her shudder.

The guv gave her a glance but didn't break verbal stride. There'd been nothing earth-shattering overnight, not even a minuscule flicker on the Richter scale. Hardly surprising, given a news blackout was operating. How could the public call if it didn't know about the kidnap? Cops depended to a large extent on witness information. The case wasn't so much hamstrung as straitjacketed.

"On the plus side." The guv was key-jangling, a sign he was keen to get on. "Obs are in place near the Page house. And comms are on the case." Observation officers had set up in a property over the road. And telecommunications officers were ready to monitor, record and trace every conversation. "Covert surveillance teams are cruising the immediate area plus the key locations we're aware of so far." The school and the ad agency. "And Colin reckons he's establishing pretty good rapport with the couple." Colin Henfield, family liaison, pivotal role in a kidnap. Pembers lobbed in a question about FLOs and the boy's grandparents but Bev was distracted, another issue playing on her mind.

Culpable or not, the Pages were crucial to the case. The fact she'd made herself *persona non grata* with the mother was giving Bev grief. On reflection, her behaviour hadn't just been insensitive; it was unprofessional. She was paid to help women like Jenny Page; they didn't have to be best buddies. She waited for a lull, then lifted a hand. "Can I have another shot at the Pages, guv?"

"Revolver or Kalashnikov?" Powell muttered.

Bev glared, then turned in mute appeal to the guv. Getting people to open up had always been one of her strengths. The guv knew that, probably why he gave it some thought. "No."

Shoulders slumped. "Aw, go on, guv."

"We need to keep the Pages sweet, sergeant."

"I can do sweet." The smile was a kind of sickly-simper. It didn't work. She sat up straight, cut the crap. "Seriously, sir, my manner with the mother was entirely inappropriate. I'd welcome the opportunity to rectify the situation and develop a more constructive future relationship with Mr and Mrs Page."

"At ease, sergeant."

She fixed him with blue bayonets. "Another chance, guv? I'd really appreciate it."

The plea was real, the voice told him that. He told her to leave it with him, then turned to the troops. He tasked a couple of DCs to check if the Pages were known to social services, child protection. Not looking the type meant zilch. Child abusers don't have it tattooed on their forehead.

Other interviews had already been assigned; officers in pairs would continue questioning intimates and acquaintances of the family. Byford ran through the strategies: what they were after, what they should listen and look for. Discrepancies, especially: conflicting statements, information that didn't tally. Until they'd gathered the facts there was little to go on. And as most officers in the room knew, even if few acknowledged, it was piss in the wind.

Byford voiced everyone's thoughts. "We need whoever's holding the boy to make contact again." His gaze was fixed on one of the posters. It showed a bright beautiful child with his mother's jade eyes. "Till then, like Daniel, we're in the hands of the kidnappers."

Daniel didn't know what time it was. He could tell the time, of course, but he seemed to have lost his watch. Aunty – as he was calling the nice lady – said they could get another one if he liked. He asked if they could go and buy one today but he didn't think Aunty had heard. He supposed it didn't matter. Not if Daddy was coming soon.

Mummy was still in hospital. Aunty hadn't said anything but Daniel could tell by the way her face sort of crumpled that Mummy was very sick. Aunty had told him not to worry, in that voice grown-ups use when they don't want to talk about something.

Daniel had been watching a Harry Potter DVD but could barely keep his eyes open. Maybe it was later than he thought. He turned his head when the door opened.

"Here you go, Dan-Dan."

"Thank you, Aunty." The little boy smiled politely, then drank his milk.

12

Post-brief, Byford perched on the corner of his desk staring at a sepia news cutting. He'd retrieved it from the back of a drawer where it had been gathering dust and Hobnob crumbs. Photographs, even press pictures, were something he rarely junked. The attic at home was crammed with shoeboxes spilling out happy snaps. The Byfords at play: Margaret and the boys at every age and virtually every angle. He never looked through them; the potent memories of a shared history would make his present solitary life seem even lonelier. His wife had died seven years earlier. And though Chris and Rich were on the end of a phone, he missed that daily contact with someone who cared.

"Guv! Can you get the door?" Bev calling. Byford frowned. Why couldn't she let herself in? He laid the cutting on the desk and wandered across. He could just about see her face.

"Got my hands full, guv." With the biggest cactus he'd ever clapped eyes on. It could star in a western movie; John Wayne could live in it. She'd had to drive in with the sunroof down.

It was his sergeant's first horticultural peace offering for months. She'd said sorry with cacti so many times his windowsill used to resemble a succulents' superstore. It had dried up since the attack.

"What's brought this on?" he asked.

"Gift horse? Mouth?" she admonished. The bloody thing wouldn't fit on the ledge. "It's a simple token of my appreciation."

He laughed, recalled her words at the briefing a few

moments ago. The cactus was in the way of a bribe, as well as an apology. "You won't get round me with that."

"Won't get round anything with this," she groaned.

He watched as she struggled to position the monster growth on the floor in the corner, waited until he had her full attention. "I'll give it some thought, but no promises."

Her eyes shone. "Ta, guv."

It was a look he'd not seen in a while. He nodded at the cactus. "Where did you lay your hands on that at this time in the morning?"

"Had it ages, saving it for a rainy day."

It was early July. The sun had already turned the guv's office into a greenhouse. He made no comment. Her glance fell on the news cutting as she passed his desk. The picture showed a group of people on the steps of the city's old law courts in the mid-eighties. The briefs stood out in wigs and gowns but there were plain-clothes lawmen as well.

Byford resumed his preferred perch on the windowsill. "Are you off to the ad agency now?" She'd not heard or wasn't listening. "Bev?" She'd obviously spotted a face in the crowd and was now taking a closer look.

"Hey, guv, you never said…" There was mischief in her eyes.

Despite himself he asked. "What?"

"You and George Clooney." Crossed fingers added sign language. "Peas in a pod, back then." She grinned.

"I'm taller than him," Byford mumbled.

"This just after you joined the force?"

He opened his mouth to say *not long*, but her focus was back on the picture, another face. She frowned. "Is that…?"

Her index finger hovered over a smiling man on the guv's right. "Robbie Crawford," Byford supplied. "DC then. I was sergeant."

She nodded, still studying the line-up. "Big case, guv?"

"Operation Rainbow."

Her blank look was no surprise. She'd have been in pig-tails when Reg Maxwell was sent down. He gave her the top lines: Maxwell had been a Birmingham crime boss behind a huge porn and prostitution racket. Until he'd raped and murdered a ten-year-old boy.

"This guy Reg?" Bev frowned. "He any relation to Harry Maxwell?" Every cop knew that name. Harry Maxwell's crime empire extended far beyond the Midlands.

"Was," Byford said. "They were brothers. Past tense." Reg Maxwell had served five years before a vicious beating by another prisoner put him on life support. "And when the plug was pulled –" Byford stared into the distance – "only Harry shed any tears."

A ringing phone brought him back to the present. His features sharpened as he grabbed a pen. She read the urgency in his voice – as well as the name and address he wrote. "Looks like we've got a witness," Byford said. "A man says he saw a child being forced into a car."

She was on her feet before he replaced the receiver. "It's on the way."

"Call in…" Her heels echoed in the corridor. He shook his head, then studied the cutting again. Maybe she'd never come across Doug Edensor, or she'd have picked his face out too.

He reread the note that crime scenes had dropped off first thing. It was in way of a favour from one of the officers who'd attended Doug's broken body. This was early stuff; a detailed report would follow, but the note appeared to confirm that ex-DCS Edensor had committed suicide. No evidence pointed to an accident, nothing suggested the fall was forced.

Byford pinched the bridge of his nose. Two cops' sudden deaths. Maybe it *was* coincidence. Maybe there was no link. Even so, pending the follow-up report on Doug's death, he'd have another look at Crawford's hit-and-run, go through the police reports, re-read the statements and interviews.

He'd already had a word with the DI in charge at Wake Green. The accident was still being treated as suspicious even though no one was in the frame. Byford knew everyone who'd been questioned. Harry Maxwell had been among the first.

And Harry Maxwell had more reason than most to hate cops – not primarily because of Reg's death in prison. Twelve years earlier, Harry's only son had died instantly when the driver of a stolen BMW lost control and ploughed into Maxwell junior's Mini. A police car had been chasing the stolen motor. Robbie Crawford had been one of the officers in the pursuit vehicle.

It was the norm for witnesses to be nervy round police officers. Even Bev felt stressed if a traffic cop was on her tail. But Stephen Cross was totally unfazed: cucumber on ice. And not just cool, but aloof and condescending. He lived in a swanky show-off pad in Priory Rise, Edgbaston, the road parallel to Hampton Place where Daniel's school was situated. Popular location this morning; hacks were already in the area, knocking on doors.

Cross led Bev and Daz through to the kitchen as if they were there to clean the place. Like it needed cleaning. It resembled a theatre, operating not playhouse. Every latest gadget and bit of kit gleamed, probably all for show. Bev doubted if Cross had ever shelled an egg, let alone boiled one.

"Can't offer you anything, I'm afraid." Most people would have concocted a polite excuse. "Can we get on with it?"

Taking her time, Bev strolled to a bum-numbing chair round a glass-topped table. Daz took the other. Cross decided to pose against the stainless steel sink, maybe because it faced the mirrored wall. Tall and graceful, he moved like a dancer: ballroom, not ballet. Receding bland blond hair accentuated a high shiny dome. Hazel eyes bulged slightly; the nose was a real stonker. If it was Bev's she'd have it taken in.

She unbuttoned her blue linen jacket. "Tell us exactly what you saw, please, sir."

"I've alread…"

"From the beginning."

He folded his arms, ankles already crossed. "I was on my run." Four-mile circuit, three times a week. "I was waiting at the top of Hampton Place, checking for traffic, and saw a woman bundling a small child into a car. She had her hand on his head, and was forcing him into the back seat. The kid was kicking and screaming."

So why didn't you do something? "Did you consider taking a closer look, sir?" Her smile was forced. He was admiring his in the mirror.

"Have-a-go hero? You're joking. Wouldn't stick my nose in if you paid me."

She tried to keep her voice non-judgmental. "But a woman… and a little boy?"

He shrugged. "Why get involved? She could've been armed, stoned off her face. You never know these days." He studied his nails. "Anyway, little Johnnie was probably just throwing a tantrum and mummy lost it."

"So what did she look like, sir?" This mad axe-murdering mummy.

"Didn't see much. I wasn't that close and she was leaning into the car. Blonde hair, though, and I'd guess above average height."

"And the boy?" Daz asked.

"Again, the only thing I can recall was the hair, blond and lots of it."

Bev glanced at Daz, who was clearly sharing the same thought. Clock on the wall chimed the hour: nine am. Time to turn up the heat. But after closer questioning not much more emerged except the timing fit: Cross had left his place at twelve-twenty. Apart from that, he wasn't sure but thought the car could have been a Merc, maybe a BMW, definitely silver. Or grey. Or light blue. He seemed to recall a P or D in the number but wouldn't swear to it. He hadn't registered other vehicles in the road but he'd not been looking. He couldn't remember what the boy or the woman was wearing but wouldn't rule out green.

Suppressing a sigh, she handed him a card. "You've been very helpful, sir. Anything else comes to mind, give me a bell. Any time."

None of it was conclusive. But it was a start.

Daz checked the mirror, eased the Vauxhall into a stream of city-bound traffic. Richard Page's firm, Full Page Ads, occupied pole position in Saint Paul's Square, Hockley. "Tosser or what?" Daz was muttering about Cross. "Talk about hooray bleedin'…"

"Henrietta." Bev's saucy tone was accompanied by a leer and a wink.

"Never!" Daz said. "How's that work?"

"Bloke couldn't keep his beadies off you."

"You're jok…" He caught the glint in hers, shifted uneasily in his seat. Poor Daz. He protected his macho image like the crown jewels. She gave him a break, put a call through to the guv, brought him up to speed.

Byford wasn't surprised reporters were doorstepping properties round the school. The media were as desperate for a lead as the cops. He'd already deployed plain-clothes teams down the same path, all canvassing potential witnesses. Christ, they'd be falling over each other in the rush. Her query as to whether they were chasing CCTV footage was met with a *what do you think?*

She ended the call, ripped the wrapping off a Lion bar and swatted Daz's open palm; guy could buy his own this time. He gave an easy-come-easy-go shrug and pulled out to pass a 2CV with go-faster stripes. "I thought you showed amazing restraint back there," Daz said.

Dog. Bone. God, he was still on that. Mind, she had bitten her tongue a few times. The concept that Cross could've thwarted the kidnap if he'd intervened was a tough one. Part of her empathised: the papers were full of horror stories about attacks on innocent passers-by, a man or woman in the wrong place at the wrong time making inadvertent eye contact with the wrong yob. But Cross was well fit and he'd not so much walked by as run past a young woman struggling with a little boy. Still, easy to be wise after the event and nobody liked a smart-arse.

"Sir this, sir that," Daz mocked. "Talk about three bags full."

"It's the new me."

He shot her an old-fashioned look. "Turning over a new tree?"

She ignored the quip. "I need the practice for when I interview Jenny Page."

"How long've you got?"

13

The only genuine Georgian real estate left in Birmingham, Saint Paul's Square was an attractive mish-mash of red brick and white stucco, garnished with pinks and purples spilling from window boxes and hanging baskets. Neat properties of three or four storeys surrounded a well-kept green. Brass-topped railings, a grade-one listed church and the occasional Doric column completed the eighteenth-century ambience. Close your eyes and smell the horseshit. Gleaming horsepower lined the kerbs now. Daz spotted a gap between a Jag and a Porsche.

Bev scanned the square, taking in the trendy restaurants and chic wine bars dotted among classy commercial premises. Discreet brass plaques were the only clue to what went on behind highly polished doors. Mostly it was media-connected. Like Page's ad agency.

The reception area was all bamboo, water features and koi carp. Those glassy eyes gave Bev the creeps; she shuddered as she crossed the expensive carpet. She and Daz had already decided to split the interviews: saved time, made sense. Bev would take Page's second-in-command.

Laura Foster didn't need a badge to indicate she was in charge during the boss's absence. Not with her presence and posture. Bev almost searched for the wires. A couple of inches taller than Bev and a couple of dress sizes thinner, Ms Foster's combination of glossy elfin-cut black hair and pale blue eyes was knockout. Even the glasses were sexy. The scarlet silk shift dress would look tarty on most women. Not on Bev; she'd look like a post box.

There were three other staff members, all female.

Frighteningly well-groomed, if not actually starched, Maggie Searle and Imogen Boateng were clearly older than the twenty-something Foster. Auburn-haired teenage Chelsea, face mapped in freckles, made up the numbers. She was the office junior, had worked there less than a month. Laura asked her to look after the coffee.

Leaving Daz to make a start with the others, Bev trailed Ms Foster's subtle sashay through a glass-panelled door. One side of the huge space was kitted out like a control deck from *Star Trek*: banks of monitors, levers, knobs, dials. The name of the agency said more about the size of Page's ego than the area in which it operated: this was visual media, not newsprint. Bev hoped to God she didn't press anything irrevocable.

"Do sit down, sergeant." Laura waved Bev into a huge black-leather swivel chair. The castors were well oiled; she tested. A few times. Glancing round, it was obvious whose space they'd invaded. Most men kept a family photograph on their desk at work; Richard Page had covered almost an entire wall. Pictures of the little boy dominated: Daniel from birthday-suit days to fancy-dress parties; Daniel building sandcastles and snowmen; Daniel scoffing Easter eggs and Christmas cake.

"As you can see," Laura said, "Richard's wife and son mean the world to him. I so hope nothing awful's happened." It was a platitude but didn't sound it.

Bev focused on Laura, who now sat poker-straight on the other side of the desk, hands neatly folded in her lap. "Have you met the little boy?"

"Once or twice when Richard brought him in. He's such a happy child, always smiling."

"Friendly? Outgoing?"

"Oh, absolutely." Laura hesitated, catching the implication.

"You mean would he go with someone?"

"Would he?"

The response wasn't pat; she gave it some thought. "I don't know is the honest answer. Who knows how perverts entice children?"

Puppies, promises, pretence. But not this time. "I don't know what you've been told, Ms Foster…"

"Laura. Please."

"I don't know what you've been told, but it appears Daniel went quite happily with a woman a couple of people at the school mistook for his mother."

Laura frowned. Bev explained the initial confusion, some of which still lingered. Because originally Mrs Page was under the impression someone from the agency had collected Daniel.

Laura's frown deepened. "That doesn't make sense. Richard would never dream of asking anyone here to do that sort of thing. And how could anyone mistake Imogen or Maggie for Daniel's mother?" Imogen and Maggie were black. As for Laura, her hair colour was the polar opposite to Jenny Page's.

Bev said nothing; waited for the other woman to come up with an idea.

"So Jenny must have got the wrong impression somehow," Laura went on, then paused. "Or she's lying…" She shook her head. "No. That's ridiculous."

She made it sound so simple. "Do you know Mrs Page well?"

Laura took off her glasses, polished them with a tissue. "Not terribly," she finally conceded. "But enough to be certain she loves her child." She glanced at the picture gallery, warm smile on her face. "You can see that in her eyes, can't you?"

"How long have you known Mr Page?"

The abrupt change didn't throw Laura. "I've worked for Richard for about eighteen months."

Worked, not known; *for*, not with. "How do you get on?"

"I can't see the relevance…" Curious, not hostile.

Bev reckoned if Page chased skirts, he'd definitely be on Laura's tail. No sense stirring, though. "Just trying to build pictures, Ms Foster."

"Of course." She smoothed the silk dress over a shapely knee. "We have an excellent working relationship. Everyone here does. We're a strong team."

"What is it you do exactly?" Not an easy one to put her at ease; Laura was well cool.

"I build the client list, chase the big campaigns, organise the corporate stuff. I used to do a little modelling, still have contacts, know how to network."

Bev nodded. That would explain the walk and the way Laura held herself. Bev had noted the habitual hair-flicking as well: very Kate Moss.

"And the others?" she prompted.

"Richard and Imogen are the creative brains. Maggie looks after finance and marketing."

"I'll need a copy of your client list." The door opened and Chelsea entered with a tray holding cafetière and white china. The interruption dragged on as Laura poured, then handed Bev a cup. The request hadn't been forgotten or dodged.

"I'll get a list together before you leave." She met Bev's eyes. "I can see why you want it."

"Thanks." Not that Bev had any great hope that the kidnapper was a disgruntled customer. More that she was trying to rattle the impossibly phlegmatic Ms Foster.

And she wasn't even sure why. Except Laura seemed almost too good to be true. Another little shake, then. "Any problems in the Page marriage?"

Laura flushed. Anger? Embarrassment? Something else? "I know you have to ask these questions, sergeant, but that's one I can't help with." Perfectly civil.

"Can't or won't?"

"Both, actually." Firm but polite.

Bev let it go, asked about Richard Page's movements the day before. Laura indicated the desk diary. It and she confirmed Page's three client meetings and a working lunch at the agency. His alibi appeared kosher.

Asking if Laura had seen anything suspicious would be useless. *Like kidnappers advertise?* She posed it anyway.

"I wish I had." The woman had feelings after all. "I can't bear to think of Daniel with a stranger." Eyes welling, she turned her head.

Bev started at an unfamiliar sound. Someone had changed the ring tone on her mobile. Rummaging in her bag, her mouth twitched as she recognised the strains of *Miss You*. Bet Oz had downloaded it.

The smile playing round her mouth didn't last. The guv was on the end of the line. "The kidnap. We've got a lead. I want you back at Highgate."

Wayne Dunston had been arrested less than a minute after delivering a ransom note to The White House. The second Bev heard the name on the police radio, she had her doubts. Far from being a Mister Big, Dunston was a petty thief, short on common sense let alone the intelligence to plan and execute a kidnap. He'd served time in both juvie and Winson Green for burglaries that went pear-shaped. But if he didn't have the nous, could he point the finger at someone who did?

After an hour in Interview One with the guy, Bev was convinced Dunston's only lead was clipped to a dog's collar. She passed the verbal baton to Byford again, then took a metaphorical back seat, observing. Dunston was mid-twenties with thin beige hair and an inane grin. Bev always thought of him as Nearly Man: nearly tall, nearly fit, nearly all there. But not quite. He teetered on the fine line between slow and special needs.

She listened again as he repeated his story almost word for word. Maybe he'd been well coached; maybe he'd learned his lines. Or maybe he was telling the truth. The Postman Pat act had netted him a pony. According to Dunston, it was a favour for a friend of a mate of a pal. No names, no pack-drill, he said, tapping the side of his bent nose. With twenty-five quid cash in hand, he didn't give a toss where it came from. As to what was in the note he'd been carrying, Dunston didn't have a clue. Bev could buy that; the guy was illiterate.

With the interview wrapped and Mastermind in a prison cell, Bev and Byford were grabbing an early lunch in the canteen. Dunston was on a holding charge of demanding money with menaces; Bev doubted he even knew what it meant. The premature hope of a break was now replaced by a pissed-off resignation. If her fish and chips were supposed to be comfort food, they weren't working. "Waste of sodding space." She scowled. "Talk about useless."

Byford shook his head, impatient. "Obviously the note originated from the kidnappers. There's a link somewhere. It's up to us to dig it out." Along with the search team currently taking apart Dunston's grotty bed-sit in Lozells. It was just possible they'd unearth something incriminating. No one was holding their breath.

Bev glanced up as she constructed a chip butty. "What you thinking, guv?" His stare and knotted eyebrows were dead giveaways.

"Why Dunston?"

She shrugged. "Just an errand boy, isn't he?"

"Goes without saying." He flapped a dismissive hand. "But they didn't just pluck him off the street." Byford pushed away the remains of a plain omelette, and now sipped peppermint tea; the irritable bowel must be playing up again. "The kidnappers would have to have been pretty sure Dunston would deliver without too many awkward questions. So they must have known him beforehand. Or someone pointed them in his direction."

Bev shrugged, nodded. "But we don't know who…"

"No, we don't." He scraped back his chair. "Yet."

She stood, grabbed a few chips. "Get the spade, shall I?"

14

The spacious sitting room at The White House was like a West End set, the elegant figures of Jenny and Richard Page draped in theatrical poses on peppermint damask furnishings. Lit by shafts of sunlight, DI Mike Powell paced the carpet, long fingers stroking lantern jaw. "You're sure you've never seen him hanging round?"

A pair of heads shook in unison. The Pages were adamant. They didn't know Wayne Dunston, they'd never met Wayne Dunston. Until he turned up at the house, they'd never laid eyes on Wayne Dunston. They'd made the points, several times.

DC Carol Pemberton observing, taking notes, sensed the couple's growing impatience. As far as the Pages were concerned, Dunston was a minor player in the unfurling drama. Unlike their son.

The couple's edginess confirmed a concern expressed by the family liaison officer. Colin Henfield was away, grabbing a change of clothes, but he'd taken Carol aside for a quick word on the QT. He reckoned the pressure was getting to the Pages, especially the father. Richard had stormed out several times to cruise the streets, searching for Daniel. Colin had tried restraining him, tried talking sense, but Page had been beyond reason and reasoning.

Carol recognised the pattern. Fathers often need to get out, to *do* something; mothers stay home, can't *do* anything. She watched Page wander to the window to gaze across a manicured lawn. Frown lines suggested deep unease. For a successful businessman accustomed to a lead role, playing and needing support clearly didn't come easy.

Mr Ad Man of the day before now looked more Big Issue salesman, unshaven unkempt underdog.

He turned, shoulders sagging, hands stuffed deep in casual cords. "How do we play this?" The ransom demand had been clear: half a million or Daniel would be killed. Details for the drop would follow.

The DI stopped pacing, consciously or otherwise mirrored Page's stance. "By the book."

Carol, face a blank, glanced up. *As if there was one.*

Still, precedents and police procedures existed, even if no case was the same. And there were consistent factors, as Powell explained in a general way. Duty of care to the child was paramount, and a non-confrontational set-up had to be in place for the handover. Of course, that could only be activated when the kidnapper released instructions.

"Meaning?" Jenny Page appeared ghost-like, ethereal. Except she was the haunted one. In her pale arms lay a Dennis the Menace t-shirt. It belonged to the angelic Daniel, the scarlet and black in stark contrast to the trailing ivory dressing gown Jenny still wore at lunchtime. Every few minutes she lifted the soft material to her face, inhaled little boy and lost love.

Powell sank into a deep armchair at right angles to her. "The kidnapper has to believe you'll do what he says."

"We will." No hesitation.

"It's not that simple, Mrs Page."

Gaze fixed on Powell, she made it easy for him. "Someone's holding Daniel. We pay. He comes home. End of story."

But it wasn't. They weren't writing it. A happy ending wasn't a given.

Powell didn't go there. He gave a tight smile, brisk nod. "We'll have a clearer idea, Mrs Page, when we know what's in the kidnapper's head."

"How much longer, inspector?" she groaned. "I can't…"
She buried her face in Daniel's shirt. Carol felt huge
sympathy, even felt sorry for a floundering Powell, who
was clearly out of his emotional depth.

The ormolu clock ticked away long seconds. A black-
bird's song drifted through the open window, thin curtains
rustled in a gentle breeze. Everyone jumped at the sudden
shattering of the near silence. Everyone but Jenny Page: the
agonised scream of an animal in pain was hers.

Daniel was trying very hard not to cry. His bottom lip
quivered and his green eyes welled with bright shiny tears.
Clutching Eeyore in his tiny hands, he pleaded with the
lady he called Aunty. "But *why* isn't Daddy coming? You
said he'd be here today."

The woman tried to put comforting arms round Daniel
but he ducked away, shuffled along the settee as far he
could. She'd tried to hide it, but he'd seen the look on her
face. She was smiling now, but underneath she was very
cross.

"He's sure to be here tomorrow, Dan-Dan."

"Don't call me that!" Daniel shouted, leg kicking out.
"Only Mummy can call me Dan-Dan."

The woman raised an eyebrow. "Mummy isn't calling
you anything at the moment, little boy."

Daniel glared. He didn't quite understand what she
meant but knew it wasn't very kind. He turned his back,
snuggled into the arm of the settee. She tried to stroke his
shoulder but again he pulled away sharply. He heard her
sigh and felt the cushion move as she stood.

"Look, Daniel. I didn't want to tell you this…" He
clamped his hands over his ears.

Only pretend.

"I don't know when Daddy'll get away. He's with your mummy in the hospital. She's very sick, Daniel. Much worse than we thought. I'm so sorry."

She sounded so kind but Daniel didn't know if he could trust her any more. His tears were soaking the soft material but he didn't want her to know he was crying.

"Thing is, Daniel darling, Mummy might not get better. Ever."

His shoulders trembled, then his whole body shook. He was frightened, needed a cuddle. When she stroked his back he flung himself into her arms, sobbing hysterically.

She hugged him tightly, calmed him, smoothed his brow. "Daddy'll come when he can, Daniel. You wouldn't want him to leave Mummy all on her own, would you?"

Chastened, the little boy shook his head, wiped his nose with a sleeve, gave a shuddering sigh. The nice lady settled him into a nest of cushions, and ruffled his hair. "I'll get your milk now. It's nearly bedtime, Dan-Dan."

Bev had spent most of the afternoon chasing some of Wayne Dunston's known associates. Known to the law, that was; associates as in criminal partners. A few feelers were out but Wayne had a lot of mates. She stretched the kink in her spine, reached fingertips towards the ceiling and let out a sigh. It was a shit job but someone had to do it. Wouldn't be so bad if she was sure of a break but it was all a bit iffy.

If the kidnappers had handpicked Dunston to do their dirty work, chances were they'd come across him inside. Prison had its old boys' network too.

She pushed back the chair, crossed Doc Martens on the desk, sucked a biro. First poser had been a piece of piss. Wayne's cellmates and prison peers were on record. Winson Green had dished out the baddies, no prob. She'd thought sheer numbers'd prove a bugger but logic told her asthmatic bigamists from Brazil could probably be crossed off the hit list. No sense pursuing extremes. Even with the discounts, deadbeats and deceaseds, it still left a bunch.

A bunch of habitual criminals, most of who would rather poke a rusty needle in their scrotum than stitch up a mate. On the other hand kidnapping, especially a child, was one of those crimes where even hardened lags had been known to turn a blind eye to the code-of-silence crap.

Absentmindedly she ripped the pull ring from a Red Bull. It was her third can. She could open a Starbucks with the caffeine in her system. She took a slug, scrolled through data on the screen. Once she'd whittled down names she'd spread the honours among the squad. The cons still inside were a captive audience, so to speak. She'd get a team over to Winson Green, see what, if anything, was what. As for the ex-cons, it was a case of tracking down where they lived. She recognised names on the list, could put faces to a few.

She'd seen one the day before, though not in the flesh. Grant Young's photograph had been on the front page of the newspaper cum rain-hat she'd used walking to the church. She tapped a finger against her lip, recalling what she knew about the ex-con who was now a C-list celebrity.

Young had been sentenced to life for child murder and served twenty years before the real killer confessed. He'd been released a couple of years back and awarded two hundred and fifty grand compensation. Since then the media dragged him out every time they needed a quote on miscarriage of justice or anything along the lines of 'the law's an ass'. And the guy knew his stuff: twenty years of inside information plus degrees in law and criminology. He'd carved a career in news and documentaries, even used the guv from time to time when he needed a police quote.

At least she knew where to find Young and that he could string two words together.

She pulled a face, heart not really in it. What was Young or any of the gorillas gonna say? "Yeah, love, kidnapper's a mate. Here you go... name, address, inside leg." As if.

Daniel gazed at Bev from the photo she'd pinned to her corkboard. Talk about an infectious smile. She studied his face, took in every detail. Again. "Where are you, little boy?" She sighed, shook her head. It was the Pages, especially the mother, that quickened the Morriss heartbeat. The parents were closer to the crime than anyone and, even if they didn't know it, they had to be closer to the solution.

15

Saturday, late brief, kidnap room, Highgate. Operation Sapphire was in its thirtieth hour; if anything, the squad was more fired up than on day one. Reasoning went that as the minutes ticked away, a result had to be closer. The kidnappers would make contact again, and each time they made a move they risked making a mistake.

Bev was slumped in a chair near the front, listening to that theory being bandied about. Sounded like wishful thinking to her. The kidnappers hadn't put a foot wrong and they were patently several steps ahead.

The guv's up-sum hadn't exactly inspired confidence. Predictably the ransom notes were a forensic wasteland: untraceable paper, untraceable PC, untraceable printer. Prints, no problem: Richard Page's on Friday's missive, Dunston's all over today's.

As to sightings, covert canvassing carried out round Daniel's school in Edgbaston had revealed diddly. Forty-nine residents had been interviewed. Each statement was virtually identical, invariably negative. Posh-boy Stephen Cross's report of a woman struggling with a small boy was the only incident of any potential significance, but was unconfirmed by anyone. Bev was beginning to think the guy had been on something.

Other lines of inquiry were proving equally barren. Daz hadn't elicited anything useful from his share of the interviews at the ad agency. He and a couple of other DCs were now working their way through Richard Page's client list, faxed through by the super-efficient Laura Foster. Bev had found it on her desk after lunch, Ms Foster's professionalism as impressive as her posture. Like everything else, the list was going nowhere.

Bev waved a few sheets of paper in the air. "I have a little list too." There was a chorus of groans from the troops. Everyone knew it meant more phone bashing, more plod work. She passed copies round, talked through what she'd done, what was still needed.

"Grant Young rings a bell," Carol Pemberton said. "He's on the telly a lot, isn't he?"

"I can do Young," Byford offered. "I'm seeing him later."

The guv didn't elaborate, but Bev reckoned Young was probably after a talking head for yet another programme he was putting together.

"Gonna be a star, guv?" Daz asked.

The big man ignored the quip, moved on to the search results from Wayne Dunston's pad. It was a predictable lot of nicked MP3s, Play Stations, SatNavs. Not that Dunston would need satellite guidance in the back of a prison van. No link with the kidnap had been uncovered.

No surprise there, then. Big fat zeros all round. Bev's exasperated sigh wasn't meant to be so loud.

"And?" Byford queried, tapping a brogue.

She shrugged. "It's all going-through-the-motions stuff."

"Solid routine police work; it has to be done."

"Yeah, yeah." She knew that. "But it's all peripheral. The kid's parents are where it's at. We need to get in there, get them talking."

Mike Powell bristled. The DI had spent the better part of the day with the couple, come back with a blank Page. "Fuck you think I've been doing? Waxing my legs?"

She shrugged. Pembers, who'd pulled out of the house when the FLO returned, had been pretty withering about the DI's interview technique.

"No, come on, Oprah. Tell it like it is." Powell leaned back, hands tucked under his arms.

The grovel was going to be a first; she drew a deep breath. "I fucked up big-time with Jenny Page, OK? Taking pops when I'd only just met her was a no-brainer. Fact she's not saying much is prob'ly down to me." Jenny's withdrawn state was a coping mechanism, according to Powell, not a question of being unco-operative.

"Way I see it," Bev went on, "the parents are still the key. Me mouthing off might've jeopardised our relationship with them. Least I can do is try and sort it."

"How'll you manage that, Mrs Springer?"

Byford saw Bev's clenched fists, the slight quiver in her limbs. The admission was taking it out of her. Contrition took courage. The emotions might be wobbly but the reasoning was sound. And she needed a bit of support, not shooting down. "It's already arranged, Mike. Bev's going over first thing."

It was news to her.

Byford tucked his battered brown fedora under his arm and headed for the back stairs.

He'd expected Bev to drop by after the brief but the coast was clear. Now home was calling, though not as loudly as a pie and a pint at The Prince.

"Hey, guv, what was all that about?" Sheepish, he looked up. Bev framed in the stairwell, glared down. Fair cop, not.

He lifted a hand. "Tomorrow."

She'd see it differently then. Maybe he shouldn't have stuck his oar in but she'd looked decidedly shaky in the face of the DI's snide digs. Byford had donned shining armour, but Bev didn't do distressed damsel. He still thought it'd been the right thing to do. He reckoned he'd spotted the green shoots of a re-emerging confidence. They didn't need trampling by Powell's size tens.

The evening was still warm, an almost Mediterranean azure sky, humid air scented with sunscreen and Indian cuisine. Byford breathed it in, relished a relatively early night. When Operation Sapphire really kicked off he'd be lucky to get away at all. Maybe a balti instead? The tap on his shoulder wasn't a complete surprise.

"Pile of poo. Nothing's arranged for tomorrow, is it?"

Bluff or bullshit? "Absolutely nothing."

"Good job you butted in." A smile twitched her lips.

"Oh?"

"Yeah. I was about to land him one."

He masked a smile as she fell into step. Tough talk? Fake veneer? He read body language like most people read books. Maybe Bev had sent the wrong signals. Or maybe he didn't know her as well as he thought.

"Mind, guv, I'm well ahead in the name stakes." She kicked a pebble across the car park. "Me and Vincie got a tenner on it."

He'd heard a whisper, not the full story. "Go on."

"What the DI calls me." She explained the rules. It was quality and quantity. He couldn't just keep saying "hey you"; it had to be something ingenious and it had to be used six times. When someone else picked up on it, it counted double.

"Ingenious."

"Yeah, I know." She twisted her mouth. They were at the guv's Rover. "Could be a sticking point, that." Definition of an oxymoron – ingenuity and DI Powell. "Oprah wasn't bad," she conceded. "Can't see it getting another airing, though."

"Glad your priorities are sorted." The silence was uneasy.

"Just a bit of fun, guv." She scuffed the concrete. The mock reprimand had been taken to heart.

He softened, knew she generally pulled more than her weight. "What are you up to tonight?"

She hoisted her shoulder bag. "Hot date with Johnny."

"Johnnie Blake?" His eyebrows disappeared. The information officer was gay – never looked at another man besides his partner.

"Depp. As in *Pirates of the Caribbean*. DVD's just out." The grin was endearing. He didn't see enough of it.

"Enjoy." He saluted her with a smile.

"'Less you've got a better offer."

"Sorry, Oprah." The door clicked open. "Got a date."

Not a date. Grant Young was more business than pleasure. Earlier, the media man had floated another programme idea and wanted to tap into Byford's expertise. Young's Kings Heath terrace was on the detective's way home anyway.

The place was pristine compared with its neighbours. No rusting bikes or greasy engines out front, paintwork wasn't peeling and intact windows sparkled. Byford reckoned a man with Young's capital and kudos could afford something more upmarket, but that sort of thing wasn't important to him. Byford admired the guy for turning his life round.

"Bill. Thanks for dropping by." Young stepped back to let the detective in.

"Flying visit, Grant. Can't stop long."

He'd been there before and followed Young through to the office. Floor-to-ceiling shelves crammed with books covered three walls. Dotted among legal tomes and textbooks were bulging files and tapes. Young videoed every show he appeared on. Byford raised a vaguely amused eyebrow. Made a change from showing your etchings.

"Before we get down to your programme idea, I want to pick your brain," Byford said.

"Sure. Take a pew." Young perched on the edge of a desk. He was taller in the flesh than on the box, sinewy, obviously familiar with the inside of a gym. He wore a white round-necked shirt and black linen trousers. The hair was in a curiously dated Beatle cut except for the grey streaks, seeming at odds with the goatee and half-moon glasses that added a vaguely academic air.

"The name Wayne Dunston mean anything to you?"

"A vague ringing," Young said with a frown. "Nothing special. Why?"

"I need to know who his friends are. Whether he's in with any of the major players."

Young shrugged. "I can ask round if you like."

"I'd appreciate it." Byford was disappointed but not surprised. Young moved in more rarefied circles these days. "Tell me more about this show, then."

Young wanted to take a wider look at the implications, when justice went wrong: the impact not just on the person wrongfully convicted but on the parents, wife or husband, children. Further still, what were the effects on the police and the judiciary? The individuals whose collective actions not only led to the wrong person going down but allowed the real perpetrator to escape punishment?

"Working title's *Hard Time* – what do you think?" Young's enthusiasm was laudable but somewhat naïve. Byford didn't want to burst the bubble but he thought Channel Four had more chance of getting the pope on *Celebrity Love Island*. Sure, some people would take the money and run their mouths off – a wronged wife, a bitter father. But as to getting the closed ranks of senior police and judges to open up… No way.

"Great idea…"

"I hear a but," Young prompted.

Byford shrugged. "What cases have you got in mind?"

Young ran through a number of *causes célèbres*: individuals and a couple of groups championed by the media over years of high-profile campaigning, cases that had all invariably ended in jubilation on the steps of the appeal court.

"I'm hoping to get a few big guns on board. Michael, Chris, a couple of the Birmingham Six." His wavering hand said it could go either way. "And you, of course."

Byford masked a wry amusement. He was hardly in the same league as the Mansfields and Mullins of this world. "What about your own story?"

"Not sexy enough. No wife. No kids."

No people to rip into the system, baying for pints of blood and pounds of flesh. "Who else have you approached?"

"Police-wise, you're the first. Actually, no. I dropped Mr Crawford a line. Talk about bad timing. I didn't know till I saw the coverage of the funeral in the paper."

"Paper?" Byford hadn't seen anything.

Young riffled through a pile of newspapers and magazines on the floor. "Yeah. Thought I'd kept it. Here you go."

It wasn't the story that transfixed Byford. It was one of the pictures. Presumably to indicate the level of media interest, one of the photographers had snapped the other snappers. Among the line of lens-men, one figure stood out, video camera on his shoulder, crooked smile on his face. He was known to his friends as Jazz – a benign affectionate name for one of the most ruthless thugs in the city.

He was known to the police as Jaswinder Ghai. And Byford had seen him many times before. Never far from Harry Maxwell's right hand.

December 1995

The second time Holly's bedroom door had inched open in the middle of the night, she had known who it was and what he would do – had known she must endure the pain and shame. Who could she tell? Who could she turn to? Who would believe her? He came when everyone was asleep, the house silent but for his moist breath in her ear, the animal grunting as he took her.

She lost count after the first year. And lost every vestige of faith. The little girl no longer believed her mother would return and take her away, tell her it had all been a terrible mistake, beg her for forgiveness. At eleven years of age, Holly recognised the hopes for what they were: childish fantasies.

After twelve months of rape and vile assaults, Holly lived in hell and harboured only dreams of revenge against her mother.

Vivid dreams. Against a woman she'd never seen.

SUNDAY

16

Highgate, Sunday, 9.12am. Operation Sapphire. Day Three.

Bev had a hangover the size of Wales. She blamed it on curry, carousing and half a bottle of Armagnac. Gingerly, she stroked her temple. It was all coming back to her now. She and Frankie had stayed up half the night playing Desert Island Dicks. Bev's wish list featured the guv for the first time. How did that work?

She seemed to recall, around two am, texting knock-knock jokes to Oz. And finally called it a day just after three, persuaded by a compulsive urge to belt out *I Will Survive*. Right now, that was a moot point.

Groaning, she plopped a couple of Alka-Seltzers into water. When the phone rang she nearly sent the glass flying. The call was sobering. Laura Foster had found a Jiffy bag at the ad agency marked urgent.

"And, sergeant, it's addressed to Jenny Page." The unflappable Ms Foster sounded ruffled.

Bev beckoned to Daz, who was en route to the brief. Muffling the phone, she mouthed, "Something's come up, I'll get there soon as."

"Later, sarge." He tapped the side of his head but her full focus was now on Laura. Apparently she'd popped into the agency to collect a portfolio she needed to work on at home. The package was the first thing she noticed on opening up.

"Obviously there's no post today, so I was a little surprised but not unduly concerned. We do get items delivered by hand."

"But this one worries you?" It was beginning to bug Bev.

"Well, yes. I can't ever remember anything coming here

for Mrs Page." There was a slight pause. "I'm probably wasting your time, but you did say. And in view of…"

Bev's glance fell on Daniel's picture. "Fifteen minutes, max. See you there."

The tingle in her palms could be premature. But at the very least the package was her calling card for Jenny Page.

Byford's desk phone rang just as he was leaving for the brief. Doctor Gillian Overdale was the relatively new police pathologist. She had a penchant for berets and brogues and an attitude that veered between businesslike and brusque. "There was a note attached to the Doug Edensor file? I was asked to keep you informed?"

No greeting, polite or otherwise, and her habitual antipodean inflection got up Byford's nose. To be fair, whatever her verbal idiosyncrasies, she was a skilled operator. She'd succeeded Harry Gough who'd grabbed early retirement and headed for sunnier climes with a laptop, fancying himself as the next Ian Rankin. Byford wished Overdale had inherited Harry's skills with live bodies as well as stiffs. "Thanks, doctor. What…?"

"Edensor had multiple injuries consistent with a fall. Broken bones, internal bleeding? He was a mess. But the fall probably didn't kill him, and anyway he wouldn't have felt a thing."

"Sorry?" What had she said?

"Completely out of it. Enough medication in him to down a rhino."

A faint alarm bell sounded in Byford's head. "What had he taken?"

"Who said anything about *taken*?"

The alarm was so loud Byford could barely hear himself think. According to Overdale, a lethal dose of insulin had been administered. Doug Edensor wasn't diabetic. It appeared that Doug had been murdered and the death made to look like suicide. Which made it increasingly likely that Robbie Crawford's hit-and-run had been no accident.

"How did you move it?" Bev asked, fingers crossed. The package lay on a low table in reception at Full Page Ads. She and Laura were the only people in the building.

"I used a tissue. I hope that's all right."

"Nice one." *Thank you, CSI.* Amazing how much savvy viewers picked up from cop shows; shame villains watched telly too.

Laura sounded her old self now and as far as Bev knew also looked it. The ebony hair and alabaster complexion put her in mind of Snow White. Bev felt like one of the dwarves standing next to her. "Sit for a minute, shall we?"

La Foster's crisp white suit looked classic and cool. Bev was feeling the heat in navy cords. It wasn't a brilliant colour for summer but her entire working wardrobe was blue: saved thinking first thing. Came in handy earlier that morning. "It definitely arrived after you left yesterday?" she asked.

"Absolutely." Straight-backed, knees together, she nudged her glasses up her nose, like she was taking an oral exam.

"How often do you come in on a Sunday?"

"Hardly ever." Her mouth turned down. "Ah... so it's probably nothing to do with Daniel's disappearance, is it? The kidnappers wouldn't want any delay. They'd contact the family direct, not leave something here."

Wasn't the way Bev saw it. Kidnappers generally played a waiting game, convinced they had all the time in the world – because they drew up the timetable. Their main priority wasn't the victim or the family's trauma. It was not to get caught. Given how tight security was round The White

House, the agency could've seemed a safer bet. They'd not give a rat's arse when it was found. Assuming that's who it was from.

"Hold this for us, will you?" she asked.

Laura held open an evidence bag; Bev carefully slipped in the package.

There was only one way to find out.

The MG was like a furnace and it wasn't half ten yet. Thank God she'd eschewed yesterday's skirt, her bum would be melting into the plastic. She lowered the windows, then put a call through to the guv, brought him up to speed before heading out for Moseley and the Page house.

"Might be nothing, guv, but…" Her instinct said otherwise. A temperature nudging thirty wasn't the only cause of damp palms. He didn't respond; come to think of it, he'd not said much at all.

"Anything back there I need to know, guv?" Silence. "Guv?"

"Sorry. What'd you say?"

The big man was distracted. "Something up, boss?" She couldn't unscrew the top on her Highland Spring. Wedging it between her thighs, she tried again.

"Doug Edensor didn't kill himself."

Spring water was apt; she just managed to dodge a squirt. "Say again, guv?"

"Doug Edensor. He didn't commit suicide." She took a swig, frowned. The name rang a bell. Had it been on a recent crime report? She skimmed them every day, didn't retain every detail. "He took a dive…?

"No," Byford corrected. "He didn't. Looks like he had a helping hand." The crime-scene guys hadn't picked up signs of a struggle because Edensor had been dead to the world before he'd gone over. "Insulin overdose." A rasp filled a pause as Byford rubbed a hand across his chin. "Doug wasn't diabetic." Once Overdale had the tox results, she'd re-examined every inch of Edensor's flesh. The puncture mark was in his chest.

"Right." She tapped fingers on the wheel. "Nasty."

Shitty way to go, but she couldn't get worked up about it. Not with an ongoing kidnap. A five-year-old life on the line versus some middle-aged bloke who'd crossed it? No contest. 'Course they'd investigate, but Edensor was beyond help. Whereas Daniel...

"By the way, guv," she said. "Know those feelers I put out on Dunston?"

"Yes." Like he could care less.

"A guy called, wouldn't give his name, reckons Dunston does odd jobs for Harry Maxwell."

"What?"

"Yeah, I know. Maxwell must be scraping the bottom of the barrel." Crime lord and low-life.

"Why wasn't this in a report?" The voice was way too quiet.

"Come on, guv. I only just heard."

"What else did you only just hear?" Sarcastic. Not like Byford.

"That's it. Odd jobs. Bit of driving."

"And delivery boy?" As in ransom demand?

She frowned. "Maxwell involved in the kidnap? You can't be serious."

"Don't tell me what I can or can't be."

"But guv, we know he doesn't touch kid stuff. Porn, prostitution, protection, trafficking but never..."

"You're wrong," he snapped. "The vice squad's been hearing whispers for months." Byford had checked with his counterpart in the squad that morning.

"Whispers?"

"*Child* pornography." It made twisted sick sense. Maxwell already owned the equipment and a list of potential clients. It made Byford's blood run cold, but was kidnapping a way of obtaining young victims?

"I'll get someone to check…"

"Don't bother. I'll do it myself."

Why was he being so arsey? He'd been off since the start of the call. Then a thought occurred. "This guy, Doug Edensor, guv?"

"Ex-detective superintendent. He retired a few years back." Retired was a euphemism for shown the door. The former cop had been offered treatment for alcoholism. Twice undergone re-hab but couldn't give up the bottle.

"Mate of yours, was he?"

"He was in the photograph you saw yesterday." She heard a phone ring. "I've got another call," Byford said. "Let me know the minute anything moves."

She pressed the end button, deep in thought. Doug Edensor and Robbie Crawford. Both friends of the guv. Both dead. No wonder he was distracted. She started the car, circuited the square. What was that Oscar Wilde line? *To lose one police mate's a misfortune – to lose two…* She snorted. The quote was close enough. Except she didn't buy careless. She wasn't sure what she'd put her money on. Yet.

Byford wasn't a betting man, but Harry Maxwell had been front-runner in the detective's uneasy mind even before the link with Wayne Dunston emerged. Not in connection with the kidnap – like Bev, he had severe doubts on that score. But why had the crime boss sent one of his lieutenants to film Robbie Crawford's funeral? That question had kept the big man awake for much of the night.

Then he'd picked up the child-porn rumour. And now Doug...

Byford walked to the window, stared across the car park. He'd hoped it was in the past – the road accident that killed Maxwell's son. He could still recall every detail of that night twelve years ago. Not surprising, given he'd been driving the police pursuit vehicle. The stolen car – a BMW – had careered into the side of James Maxwell's Mini on Fiveways roundabout. The teenage joy rider had been killed outright. Fire crews had to cut James's mangled body from the wreckage.

For several years on the anniversary of the crash, Byford had received thinly veiled death threats: sympathy cards, black armbands, funeral wreaths. It didn't take intelligence to work out who sent them. The detective had two sons; sympathised to an extent with Maxwell's grief. But when the tyres were slashed on his motor six years back, he'd pulled Maxwell in and issued a few threats of his own. The unsolicited mail had dried up since then.

It was one of the reasons why Maxwell had been among the first suspects questioned after the hit-and-run that killed Crawford. Robbie had been Byford's passenger that night. Doug Edensor, if Byford remembered rightly, had been one of the officers who'd broken the news to Maxwell.

The detective returned to his desk, reread a transcript of the interview he'd copied first thing. According to this, Maxwell had been flying back from India when Crawford died. Travel documents and holiday videos corroborated the alibi. Byford sniffed. *So what?* The crime boss never got his hands dirty: he hired heavies for that. Mostly Asian.

It didn't mean he was clean.

Byford picked up a pen, tried to marshal his thoughts. He'd been surprised Maxwell had agreed to see him. It wouldn't be an easy meeting – assuming all hell didn't break loose and he could get away from Highgate. He sighed, rubbed his chin. God, he could do without this. The priority had to be Daniel Page. He couldn't afford to get sidetracked.

Unless Harry Maxwell did know something about the kidnap.

17

Glare on the glass? Trick of the sunlight? For one glorious second, as she neared the Page house, Bev was convinced the little boy was back. The green eyes she'd glimpsed at a downstairs window were the spit of Daniel's. But they were Jenny Page's, now full of loathing before she turned and vanished from sight. Bev took a deep breath and girded mental loins. No one said it'd be easy. At least the hangover was history.

Colin Henfield opened the door before she knocked. She'd never seen the FLO in anything but a neat suit and tie. He dealt with messy lives, people at the lowest ebb; maybe it was his way of showing respect. The job was about connecting, communicating; Bev reckoned he could wear a bin liner and people would open up. Which could explain his pained expression as he blocked her path.

"Can't let you in, Bev." It was Jenny Page's order and clearly difficult for him. Though Highgate's finest liaison officer, Colin held the rank of constable.

"I'm not leaving, Col." She folded her arms.

He smoothed a cap of short black hair. "She's adamant. Doesn't want you here."

"Tough."

She felt sorry for Col, a tad sorry for Jenny Page, but the real compassion lay with a little boy she'd never met who was being held by strangers God knew where. Unpalatable though it was, she'd live on humble pie for a month if it got her near the mother.

No need. Jenny Page loomed into view behind Colin's shoulder, eyes flashing distaste, lank hair in disarray. "What do you want?"

She ignored the spittle on the woman's chapped lips. "To help you."

"You've got a nerve."

"Damn right I have." It was out before she knew it.

"You as good as…"

"Get over it." She'd not got the hang of this humility lark. Jenny Page looked as if she'd been slapped in the face – and it crumpled.

Bev raised hands in surrender mode. "I am truly sorry." Then bit the humble bullet. "I was out of order. I've got a big mouth and no tact." She paused, willing the woman to open her mind as well as her ears. "But I'm not a bad cop, Mrs Page. And I swear I'm trying to do everything on God's earth to bring Daniel home to you."

She meant every word. Maybe it showed in her eyes and Jenny Page detected it. Without speaking, she gave a tight nod, retraced her steps. Bev nipped in before her mind changed. Everything else about Jenny Page already had. Scruffy and listless, she slopped about the place in a stained dressing gown, bare feet filthy. Her make-up consisted of stale mascara and a trace of eyeliner. There was no vestige of the immaculate ice maiden.

Bev shot a quick glance round. The posh sitting room had an impersonal feel, as if people just passed through. Jenny now sat in the middle of a massive settee, hugging her knees, looking lost. There was plenty of space. Bev took some close by. "Is your husband here, Mrs Page?"

She shook her head.

"He's looking for Daniel." Colin kept his voice low. "Says it helps to be out there."

Bev sniffed. It wasn't helping his wife a bunch. Jenny's glassy eyes gazed into the distance, seeing nothing.

Desultorily, she wiped a tear as it trickled down a hollow cheek. Physically she was there, but her thoughts were in the past, maybe the future, anywhere but the here and now. The woman needed support.

"Is there anyone you'd like us to call, Mrs Page?" Bev asked.

Maybe she hadn't heard. Bev rose, gestured the FLO to one side, asked him to get Richard Page back to the house. She wanted him there when the package was opened. Waiting a while longer would make no difference. Far as the kidnappers knew – assuming it came from them – the package was still languishing at the agency. As for what it contained, that was anyone's guess. Could be innocuous; could, God forbid, be a body part. Either way, Jenny Page was in no state to face it alone.

"How do you get through it?" Still staring ahead, Jenny could've been talking to herself. "The endless waiting. Hoping for the best. Fearing the worst."

The voice was unrecognisable. Bev had heard the question before. Most people who'd been there said 'take it a day at a time'. From what Bev'd seen of it, taking a breath at a time was problematic. She moved back to the settee, slid even nearer. The woman deserved more than platitudes.

"I can't begin to imagine what it's like, Jenny." Having kids had never been on Bev's agenda; she'd too often seen what it meant to lose them. "But I'm pretty sure I'd want the people I love around me." Her face softened as she pictured her mother, Emmy. "My mum…"

"My mother died years ago." Jenny turned her head, a catch in her voice.

Bev closed her eyes. Emmy could drive her up the wall but Bev couldn't imagine life without her. "I lost my dad a while back," she offered. "Hurts like shit."

She sensed Jenny's glance, sudden spark of interest. Bev bit her lip, milked the fledgling connection. "That's why I joined the police," she said.

The notion lit another spark. "Your father was a police officer?"

English lecturer, actually, but Jenny had opened her mouth, was engaged at some level. Bev busked it, made up stories on the hoof; she'd juggle bubbles if it kept the woman's attention, diverted her from the nightmare. Jenny might not be hanging on every word but at least she was listening, appeared slightly less lethargic.

Colin clocked the situation as he re-entered the room. From the doorway, he held up ten fingers, then left them to it. Ten minutes, then, till Page returned. Bev sneaked a glance at Jenny, brought her gently back to reality. She talked her through Operation Sapphire: the ongoing observation and surveillance strategies, the covert inquiries, the extensive interview programme, a possible Wayne Dunston link. "We're doing everything we can to get Daniel back, Jenny."

She nodded acknowledgement, gave a long shuddering sigh, clasped arms round her stomach. "God, I feel so sick."

Bev rose, held out a hand. "Come on, let's take a turn in the garden." The air inside was stale and stifling. "Blow away the cobwebs."

The strategy, such as it was, had the desired effect. Jenny hesitated, then pulled herself up reluctantly. "I'll put some clothes on."

Bev smiled encouragement and watched as she left the room. The high-speed rifle through Jenny's Prada handbag revealed nothing incriminating. Not that she'd really expected it. On balance, she tended to think that the woman was innocent of involvement in her son's kidnap. At least the trauma appeared genuine.

Still, a sliver of doubt remained in Bev's mind. What if the grief was down to remorse? Either way, she needed Jenny Page on side. And sweet.

She checked the time. Where the hell was Richard Page? The door opened as Jenny returned in casual slacks and t-shirt. A spot of exercise had the desired effect. The simple act of stretching the legs, taking in oxygen, feeling the sun's heat, added a hint of pink to her cheeks.

They circled the lawn a few times, then sat on a bench in the shade of an apple tree. Bev asked Jenny to talk about Daniel: his favourite film, TV show, superhero, football team, chocolate bar, breakfast cereal. What made him laugh, was he ticklish, did he like school? It hit the right buttons. Jenny smiled as she painted a word picture. The animation and the way the light hit her face evoked a shadow of the natural beauty that had so struck Bev at their first meeting.

Jenny halted suddenly. "Why do you need to know all this?"

It gave insight into the mother-son relationship and brought Daniel alive in Bev's imagination. But she gave Jenny a different reason. "So I'll know what to talk to him about." The meaning was implicit. Not put into a promise she might not be able to keep.

Jenny nodded, circled her wedding ring. "Thank you. I..."

"Mrs Page!" Colin hurried across the lawn, mobile in hand. "It's your husband. He's seen Daniel!"

18

Richard Page had seen his son in the back of a car on the Pershore Road, heading out of town. This much Bev gathered from a near-hysterical Jenny before putting a clarifying call through to Highgate. The guv was on another line, liaising with control, but according to the duty inspector Don Wainwright a city-bound Page had spotted Daniel in a Fiesta travelling south. Page had turned, tailed the vehicle before losing it at the Edward Road lights. He'd had the presence of mind to clock the number. The PNC had thrown up an address; the car was registered to a female owner in Longbridge.

"The guv's deploying the troops now," Don said.

"I'll hold, thanks, Don." Bev tapped impatient fingers, waiting for a word with the big man. Jenny paced the sitting room, barely able to control herself.

"Guv?" Bev said. "Where're we at?"

"Watching brief. No sign of the car. We're in position, ready to move as soon as it arrives."

It was eleven-fifteen. She could be there in quarter of an hour. "Want me out there, guv?"

"No. Mike's there with Carol." Powell and DC Pemberton. "I've got plain-clothes teams in place, couple of unmarked cars. Whichever way this develops, you'll be more use where you are."

She glanced up; Jenny was out of earshot. "Is it a goer, guv?"

"We'll know soon enough." She heard a voice beyond Byford: a police radio. "The Fiesta's just turned the corner."

The hasty covert operation centred on a modest

Edwardian villa in Regent Street: two pints of gold top on the doorstep, 'Troops Out' poster in the window. Having established no one was in the property, plain-clothes teams were in position front and rear. Powell and Pemberton were parked opposite, trying to get a good look at the kid in the back of a clapped-out Fiesta that was pulling up outside number seven.

"What you reckon?" Powell asked.

Carol shrugged. She thought he'd have a better idea himself without the aviator shades. From her position, only the youngster's profile was visible, but if the hair was anything to go by they were on a winner. The shaggy blond thatch, almost too long for a boy, was identical to Daniel's. Shame Richard Page wasn't here. It'd make ID easier.

As to the operation, she thought it was overkill. Page had glimpsed a kid who looked like Daniel and they were out here like it was the second coming. In a way she understood the rapid response. The inquiry was stalled, the squad frustrated. But a fleeting glance was hardly conclusive. On the other hand, if the woman behind the wheel had kidnapped the kid in the back seat, they had to play safe, take it gently. If she were culpable and caught wind of anything, the risks were incalculable.

Powell straightened his tie, made for the door. "Let's go have a little chat."

The sitting-room door flew open as Richard Page, oblivious to Bev's presence, ran to his wife. "It was Daniel, Jenny. His hair, his eyes – I'd know him anywhere." The couple stood a little apart, searching each other's face, the distance and brief silence saying more than a torrent of words. Page's conviction was absolute. Maybe Jenny was afraid to question it.

"Did Daniel see *you*, Mr Page?"

Richard, frowning, registered Bev for the first time. "And you are?" Had he poshed up the voice a tad?

She approached, hand out. "DS Morriss, Bev Morriss."

Richard shot a glance to Jenny, who nodded what must have been approval.

Page's palm was damp and clammy. "To answer your question, I think he might have seen me." Definitely a touch of the Bow Bells in there now, Bev reckoned. "Not a great answer, I guess. But I think he did. It's just that it all happened so fast."

He bore no relation to the mental picture Bev had built of Mr Smoothie Ad Man. His eyes were puffy, the chin stubbly and the hair lank.

"Understandable." She smiled. "Shall we sit while I run through what's happening for you?" She explained about tracing the number through the police national computer and that a team was now on the spot. "They'll call here soon as."

Jenny whispered, "So it'll be over soon?"

One way or the other. "Let's hope."

If the waiting was bad before, it was interminable now. Page's compulsive pacing left a track in the carpet. Jenny, back in her comfort zone of the sofa, buried her face in Daniel's t-shirt. Timing the mating calls between ardent wood pigeons in the garden was as exciting as it got. Bev sighed, wished she were in on the action. Hopefully it was superfluous now – but the parcel was still in her bag.

"Jenny." Bev showed her the plastic wallet. "This came to the agency for you. Can I take a butcher's?" Jenny nodded, detached, other things on her mind. Bev was already peeling on latex gloves.

As she eased the flap open, she struggled to mask her

shock. Her heart skipped a beat, then leapt two more. She glanced at the Pages, both unaware, still reason to hope. The sudden ring made her jump; she grabbed the mobile, took a deep breath before answering. But even without the call from Highgate, she knew beyond doubt the child Richard Page had seen couldn't possibly be his son.

As they neared the Fiesta, Powell issued instructions to Carol from the side of his mouth. "You concentrate on the kid. I'll take care of the driver."

A flint-faced woman, early thirties, observed the approach, made no effort to get out of the car. The fake tan, false nails and big hair were very footballer's wife – pub team. Powell showed a warrant card, mimed window opening. The glass dropped an inch.

"Morning, madam." He smiled.

Carol peered into the back. The little boy was rummaging on the floor, probably dropped a toy or something.

"Police harassment, that's what this is." She crossed fleshy arms over what looked like a boob job.

"Sorry?"

"You will be. I'm sick of you lot." The window descended another six inches. "It was speeding, for Christ's sake, not effing murder. Shouldn't you be out there catching real criminals?"

Powell had a vision and it was pear-shaped. "We're investigating reports of a missing child."

"So?"

"Boss." Carol tapped Powell's arm. "Don't bother."

He followed her gaze. The child was now kneeling on a back seat that was strewn with stray chips and Skittles. The golden hair was Daniel's but not the nose squashed against the glass. The crossed eyes and lolling tongue could belong to any cheeky kid. But this one wore a satin dress. And answered to the name of Britney.

Flint Face cracked a smile. "Nice one, Brit. Now tell the nice officers to fuck off and get a proper job."

Bev shielded the phone, lowered her voice. Byford was on the other end. Maybe her expression or tone let something slip. Without warning Jenny was on her feet and snatching the parcel. Bev watched, helpless, as the action unfolded seemingly in slow motion: a mass of golden hair cascading on to the green carpet, unspeakable shock on the Pages' faces, open mouths, no words. Then Jenny fell to her knees, gathering the tresses, screaming, crying, tears streaming down her cheeks. "My baby! What have they done to my baby?"

Richard tried to comfort her; furious, she shoved him away. "You said you'd *seen* him! You'd said you'd seen Daniel! How could you have seen my little boy? You *liar!*" She lashed out, but he grabbed her shoulders.

"I'm sorry, Jenny. I was so sure." He dropped his gaze, maybe couldn't bear the pain in his wife's eyes. "I wanted it too much."

Hysterical, Jenny ran from the room, colliding with Colin who was on the way in with a glass of water. Her footsteps echoed in the tiled hall, then became muffled as she reached the stairs.

"She'll go to bed, try to sleep. It's what she does when things get too much." Page's voice petered out.

Bev was vaguely aware of a discussion between the two men, something about calling in the doctor to take a look at Jenny. She wasn't really listening; she'd spotted a corner of white paper jutting from the parcel. Still wearing the gloves, she knelt, gently teased the rest out. The sheet had been folded in half to fashion a greeting card. Which in a sick way it was. She knew immediately there'd be prints on it. Again, in a way, there already were.

The drawing was a stick figure with yellow hair, crimson mouth and huge green eyes. There was no subject name or artist signature. There was no need. The equally childish scrawl said it all and raised countless unknowns.

Get well soon, Mummy. Love, Dan-Dan.

19

Ask a child to draw a picture of a villain, Byford mused, and they'd come up with something close to Harry Maxwell. Swarthy, heavy brow, squat body, he put Byford in mind of an ape who'd stolen a suit. And got the wrong size. The jacket seams pulled across the back and when he turned, Byford saw the same pressure on the shirtfront. Lardy flesh poked between the buttons, though the coarse red face had clearly been in the sun.

"Time you call this?" he snarled, delving into molars with a stubby finger.

"I got held up." Civil response: no mileage in anger at this stage. Maxwell was one of the few people who could get under Byford's skin. Like a filthy needle. He'd been mildly surprised the crime boss had waited. The so-called break in the kidnap case meant the DS was running twenty minutes late. Judging by Maxwell's beery breath, he'd spent it at the bar.

The venue was Maxwell's call. The Grapes was a run-down, half-timbered pub in Digbeth. Décor ran the gamut of brown, nicotine being the lightest shade. Maxwell added another layer with smoke from a fat Havana.

"Drink?" Byford asked.

Curt shake of the head.

The superintendent bought tonic water, indicated a corner table away from prying eyes and pricked ears. If he had hard evidence they'd be in Interview One at Highgate.

"What's this about, then?" Maxwell re-lit the cigar with a flashy gold lighter; leathery cheeks puffed like miniature bellows; hard, almost black eyes stared through blue-grey haze.

Rumour. Whispers. Hearsay. Byford started with the only tangible item he had. He opened an attaché case, slung Saturday's *Evening News* across the table.

"Jaswinder Ghai. What was he doing at Robbie Crawford's funeral?"

Maxwell pulled a fuck-knows face, then picked up the paper, turned it this way and that, brow creased in mock concentration. He gave a wide mocking smile, revealing crooked yellow teeth. "Know what? I reckon he was filming."

Byford clenched his jaw. "Why was he filming a police officer's funeral?"

"How should I know? You're the detective." Maxwell aimed smoke at Byford. "Ask him."

"I'm asking you." He'd had uniform searching all day, but Ghai had gone to ground.

"I'm not my *brother's* keeper." The stress was deliberate. Meant to menace.

"You're not his brother, you're his boss. He wouldn't shit without your say-so."

Maxwell leaned forward, spoke slowly and raised the volume. "Are you deaf? I don't know why he was there and couldn't give a fuck." The voice could sell gravel.

Byford swallowed more than saliva. "The hit and run? I don't buy it, Maxwell."

He shrugged. "What goes around comes around."

"Meaning?"

"You know what it means, copper." Maxwell slurped from a pint glass. "What you sow, you reap. Just deserts and all that."

"And Doug Edensor? What did he sow?"

"Fucking cop, wasn't he?" Maxwell spat.

"And did you make it happen?"

"In a manner of speaking." Only his mouth smiled. "It was the answer to a prayer. After my boy was killed, I prayed every night you bastards would die horrible deaths. Divine intervention, eh?" He lifted his glass. "Cheers, God."

Byford's jaw ached with tension. Maxwell's smug taunts were getting to him. The bastard was enjoying this; either he was innocent or the tracks were so well hidden he believed he was untouchable. Pointless, but he asked anyway. "Did you have anything to do with it?"

"Fuckin' wish I had."

Byford balled his fists. "I swear I'll find…"

"Evidence?" He smirked. "You won't. 'Cause there is none." He scraped back the chair. "If that's it…"

"Sit down," Byford snapped. "I haven't finished."

The crime boss took his time but resumed the seat. Not that he was taking orders; the patronising sneer meant he was taking the piss. He knew as well as Byford that he could walk any time. And time was in short supply; Byford moved on.

"I hear you're branching out."

"Always looking to expand." Spread arms.

"Into child pornography." Had he imagined the flicker in Maxwell's eyes? Byford's didn't waver. "And I'm investigating the kidnap of a five-year-old boy." A purple flush started at Maxwell's bull neck. "You've got the equipment," Byford said. "And the workforce. Ghai's not the only lackey handy with a camera, is he?"

"You bastard." The voice dripped hatred. "I don't touch kids."

"Your *brother* did." Maxwell's breathing was laboured; loathing seeped through every pore of his mottled skin.

116

Byford had one more goad. "And one of your errand boys delivered the ransom note. Wayne Dunston."

The barb struck but Byford couldn't define what it had hit: shock, fear, anger? The crime boss recovered quickly, stubbed the cigar butt in a heavy glass ashtray as he spoke casually. "Never heard of him."

"Where's the child, Maxwell?"

"That's it, copper." He slammed the chair into the wall. "You want to talk again? Arrest me."

"I'm close, Maxwell. Dead close."

"What you want? A medal?"

"I want the boy back," Byford shouted. Knew he'd blown it. The goading had backfired.

"And I want mine." Maxwell stormed across sticky mud-coloured lino, turned at the door, still breathing heavily. "You wanna watch it, copper. You know what they say: trouble comes in threes…"

Maxwell's dumpy silhouette – like a poor man's Alfred Hitchcock – waddled past the window. Byford drained his glass, wondered if he'd ever handled an interview so badly.

20

"Know the worst thing of all, guv?" Apart from an on-going kidnap, the fiasco at Longbridge, the victim's shorn hair, Richard Page drinking himself into a stupor, Jenny being admitted to the Nuffield overnight with nervous exhaustion. And she didn't even know about the Maxwell interview.

Byford stopped writing and glanced up from what Bev laughingly referred to as his captain's log. Except it wasn't a joke; it was a drag, yet more police-procedural paperwork. Accountability was still a big buzzword: officers had to keep a contemporaneous record detailing each operation's every strategy, every action, every decision. Obviously there were advantages, but it also made it well easy to point the finger when an incident went off at half-cock. Talk about thought police. If faced with the same admin demand, James T Kirk would tell the men-in-grey-spacesuits to boldly take a running jump.

The guv took one look at Bev's face and laid down his Parker. "You mean there's worse?"

She nodded, fiddled with the worry ball that would normally be gathering fluff at the bottom of her bag; the flexing was supposed to keep her calm. "Jenny Page lost a kid some years back."

Byford briefly closed his eyes. "No wonder she's in hospital."

"Her old man told me. Little girl. Stillborn." Without the booze, Bev reckoned Richard Page would never have breathed a slurred word. Apparently the subject was verboten. Jenny was in denial about both the birth and the

118

death. The worry ball was really getting it in the neck.

"Don't blame yourself, Bev. You weren't to know."

How did he do that? Maybe this thought-police stuff was contagious. The big man was right, though. She'd been royally beating herself up for giving Jenny Page a hard time. Any suspicions she'd harboured about the woman's guilt had been well scuppered after witnessing her collapse.

"Too easy, isn't it, guv? First impressions." She'd clocked Jenny Page as the sort of woman she despised, a stuck-up bint who traded on her looks and thought sisterhood was for nuns.

He stretched his legs under the desk, crossed his hands behind his head. "We all do it, Bev. Can't avoid it, in this job."

He sensed her misjudgment wasn't the only reason for the current mood. It was fifty-four hours now since Daniel Page was last seen. Her sigh lifted a loose sheet of paper on Byford's well-covered desk. "I keep thinking about that poor little kid, snatched from his mum and dad, kept by god knows who, god knows where."

He watched the worry ball as she tossed it from hand to hand. The hair-cutting aspect worried him. It worried everyone. Did it mean that the kidnappers had no intention of returning Daniel? If anything, it made Maxwell's involvement less likely. And the more he thought about it, the less Byford was convinced that Maxwell was in the frame. Either way, vice officers were keeping close tabs on the crime boss.

Byford's real fear was that Daniel's new look could equal a new passport, leading to a new life in a new country with a new family; the ransom demand a ruse to lead them down the wrong garden path. But who? And why? Control had circulated Daniel's description on day one as a matter of course; now ports and airports had been asked to step up vigilance.

"And the card," Bev said. The garish depiction was imprinted on her brain. "'Get well soon, Mummy.' What's that all about?"

"And why send it to the agency?"

"And why no instructions for handing over the money?"

Twenty questions or what? She shook her head. The ball shot through her fingers, bounced across the desk. The guv caught it one-handed, chucked it back.

"I'll confiscate it next time," he warned. His faint smile didn't register because she was deep in thought. She looked tired and tense. Byford reckoned she should get rid of the ball permanently; it didn't live up to the job spec. Thinking of which... "How's the media liaising going?"

The change of tack seemed to perk her up a bit. She smiled, recalling her hands-on approach with Jack Pope. "Wicked, guv." In fact the daily news-feed wasn't as bad as she'd feared. The hacks knew the score, generally accepted it would be meagre rations until the pig-out at the closure. As for Pope, she'd not yet replied to the reporter's e-mailed effusive apology. But she wasn't convinced of the guy's motives. Probably still regarded her as his personal deep throat.

"Bernie did a turn this afternoon." Byford saw her confusion. "Not the kidnap, Doug Edensor." The news chief's appeal for witnesses was being run on local radio and TV. It wasn't big enough for network.

"Anything back?"

"Early days." He sensed her indifference. Or maybe he was being unfair. He'd not exactly opened up to her about Maxwell, and there was still no proof of a link between

Doug's death and Robbie Crawford's. And obviously Bev's priority was the kidnap.

"So is some psycho bumping you all off, then?" The smile didn't reach her eyes. The jocular tone masked her concern. Byford chided himself: he should have known her better. And until he had proof either way, he had no intention of making it worse.

"You watch too many movies, young lady." The light tone hadn't worked. He injected some gravitas. "I can take care of myself, Bev."

She held his gaze for a several seconds, then appeared to take him at his word. She smiled, pointed a finger. "Better than you take care of that, I hope." The cactus looked as if it was facing the final curtain. "You watered it yet?"

"Yeah, but. No, but."

She shook an indulgent head. He sounded like Vicki Pollard in drag. "Shan't buy you any more."

"Promise?" He winked.

Bev rose, stifled a yawn. "Time to go home, boss."

Byford glanced at the desk. The procedure log lost what little appeal it had; anyway it might look different in the morning. "I'll join you," he said. "Amazing what a good night's sleep can do."

"Your place or mine?" She said it without thinking. It was a glib one-liner, a throwaway remark. Her cheeks would be pink; she could feel the heat. "Sorry, guv. Well over the line there."

She shifted her feet, studied the carpet, sensed his gaze on her. If she'd looked up, she might have seen disapproval in his eyes. Or was it disappointment?

121

21

Byford had come so close to saying *mine*. But what if she'd said, you're on, guv? Would he have run a mile? Fact was, he didn't know. He certainly no longer saw Bev as the daughter he'd never had. Fearless and fragile, she evoked a plethora of feelings in the big man, none of which was remotely paternal.

He'd skirted the issue, made some excuse about needing to pick up a file, then watched from his window as she crossed the car park. She must've put her foot down. The exhaust fumes lingered in the warm air when he left a few minutes later.

Now it was another Sunday evening, home alone, except for myriad unwanted thoughts impossible to switch off. He was plonked in front of the box with an empty plate and an almost empty bottle of Chianti. And still his head was full. *Midsomer Murders* wasn't doing it for him: he had enough of his own.

Leaning back, he flicked the remote, his interest as high as Bev's in line dancing. A smile tugged his lips as he recalled her words: "Sorry, guv, well over the line there." The smile grew when he imagined her in cowboy boots and Stetson, all guns blazing.

All guns blazing. Like the Longbridge fiasco, the false sighting of a child who wasn't Daniel. He sighed. Getting the troops out in force had been a knee-jerk reaction; it had cost a packet and he blamed himself. He'd wanted it too much. What Daniel's parents were going through was inconceivable. He wondered how he'd have played it if one of his kids had been snatched. A big concern was the kidnapper finding a way round the surveillance and contacting one of the Pages direct. He hoped to God the couple didn't try going it alone.

Did he seriously rate Harry Maxwell as a suspect in the kidnap inquiry? It seemed a hell of a coincidence. And a hell of a leap. They had only one anonymous tip-off that the crime boss was involved in child porn. Unless Maxwell had staged the kidnap as a distraction, to hamper police inquiries into Doug and Robbie's deaths? Byford shook his head; even to his ears that sounded far-fetched. There wasn't even proof that those deaths were down to Maxwell. If he were waging a personal vendetta against officers he blamed for his son's death, surely he wouldn't have agreed to see Byford? Unless he got some sort of sick kick out of it...

He felt for his glass on the carpet, searching fingers making contact with a file. It was the one he'd told Bev he needed to pick up. It had been a white lie to spare her further blushes. It contained everything Highgate had on the crime boss. With hindsight, he'd been woefully unprepared for today's interview. It wouldn't happen again. Only an idiot would underestimate Maxwell twice.

His copper's instinct told him Maxwell was involved in Robbie's death. But Doug's as well? As for the crime boss's throwaway threat about trouble coming in threes: bravado or bullshit? Whatever, he needed evidence to go on.

If he could prove that Crawford's death – like Edensor's – was no accident and establish a Maxwell connection, he'd take squad members off Sapphire. As it stood now, he couldn't justify that. Live cases took priority, and developments like those this afternoon demanded immediate decisions and actions.

So, meanwhile, he'd have to go it alone.

He had in mind a visit to the crime scene, to talk to people living nearby. They'd been questioned once but another session might unearth something new. He'd already spoken to Robbie Crawford's widow Josie, discovered the ex-detective's nightly routine of walking the dog. Had someone else established it was a regular pattern and worked out where was the best place to strike? Had Robbie been tailed on those nights?

Or was he becoming obsessed with Maxwell? Side-tracked and fixated? Deep into mountain-molehill territory? Either way, he couldn't let it go. It niggled away in a brain already overloaded. No wonder his memory wasn't what it was. Thinking of which… He'd forgotten yet again to tell Bev who her new partner was. He'd ring Highgate, get someone to leave a note. The name wouldn't mean anything to her but she'd be able to keep an eye out for the guy.

Byford had decided on Mac Tyler soon as he saw the transfer application. The superintendent had watched Bev walk all over Darren New in the last few weeks. She wasn't even aware of it but it was no good for them or the squad. On the other hand, during a recent West Midlands-Derbyshire operation he'd seen Tyler in action. The DC – a bit like Bev – didn't take any crap and didn't do doormat.

Byford gave a slow smile. Maybe in this instance the memory lapse was deliberate.

Bev drove straight home and headed for the kitchen. It was either that or a cold shower. Fanning her face with the fridge door open, she contemplated pulling an ice pack from the freezer. It was a sticky night and she was feeling the heat, particularly under the collar. She groaned. She'd as good as hit on the guv.

"You OK in there?" Frankie in concerned-lodger mode.

"Tickety." Another groan, *sotto voce*. OK, the come-on had just slipped out. No big deal. *But it was. She fancied him.* The startling revelation had dawned in the nanosecond between delivering the line and the apology. If he'd said yes, she'd have been in there. Then she recalled the guv's inclusion in her Desert Island Dicks wish list the other night. She'd thought it had been the wine talking. Maybe *in vino veritas?* Another groan.

"There's salad in the fridge," Frankie shouted. Bev grimaced, stomach flipping at the thought. Plate of chips, maybe... Actually she couldn't eat a thing. Felt a tad sick. Must be the heat, maybe a bug?

"Coming in?" Frankie'd get a sore throat if she carried on throwing her voice.

"Nah," Bev called. "Brought a bit of work back."

Frankie popped her head round the door. "Y'know what they say, my friend, about all work and no play?"

"Yeah, right." Bev gave a token laugh and carried on up the stairs. Dunno about dull boy; she felt dorky bint. *Your place or mine, guv?* How much crasser could it get?

The long shower was cooling in more ways than one. Ten minutes later, towelled and turbaned in front of the bathroom mirror, Bev tilted her head, practised her pout. *Christ, if the guv can't take a joke...* She was dead good at denial. Say it enough times, she might even believe it.

Where was her bag? On the carpet next to her cords and Docs. She'd downloaded a shed-load of stuff from newspaper websites that afternoon, local and national. Bit of light reading. Printouts fanned on pillow, she lay on her front on the duvet, tried to get a handle on the case.

Operation Rainbow was way before her time. 1986. The rape and murder of a little boy. The gangland boss Reg

Maxwell sent down for life. The story had been front-page across the country. Ugly scenes outside the court; Harry Maxwell and the family screaming stitch-up; the usual suspects demanding the return of the death penalty.

Her eyelids were growing heavy and she wasn't taking it all in. Not lack of interest, more sleep deprivation. And it needed looking at properly. Not in the context of the kidnap; she still didn't see Harry Maxwell having a hand in that. A tip-off that he used delivery-boy Dunston from time to time didn't do it for her.

No, it was more to do with the guv. Either he wasn't taking his mates' deaths seriously or he was deliberately making light of his concerns when she was around. She pondered that for a moment, then held up a copy of the photograph she'd first seen on the Byford's desk. Two of the police officers pictured there had died in the last two weeks. If that wasn't coincidence, it was scary.

Because if someone was killing cops from back then, Byford was in the firing line. And so was another face she'd recognised in the line-up.

Daniel was frightened. He didn't want to go to sleep. She'd cut off his hair last night. Actually he didn't know that for sure. It could have happened during the day. He had no way of knowing any more. Had no idea what he looked like now, either. A tear ran down his cheek and he dashed it away angrily. He'd be brave. It's just that Mummy loved his hair so much... Daniel ran his fingers over his scalp. A few tufts stuck up and the rest felt like tiny soft feathers, or like Smoky the kitten next door. He smiled, thinking of Smoky, then realised he didn't know who lived next door now.

Daniel stroked his head again. She'd said he had nits and cutting his hair was the only way to get rid of them, but he knew that wasn't true. He counted on his fingers all his school-friends who'd had nits: Laurie, Benjie, Matt, Eloise and the new girl who'd only just started. Their mummies just washed their hair in special shampoo and used a special comb.

There was a glint in the little boy's eyes. At least he knew now. Knew the woman wasn't a nice lady; knew she told lies. Mummy said only wicked people told lies.

Daniel wiped away another tear. He wanted his mummy very badly.

MONDAY

22

Bev knew where Bob Geldof was coming from. Even though she'd had ten hours' sleep, even though the sky was an unbroken azure, even though Oz had texted before breakfast, there was still something about Mondays she didn't like. Mind, some weeks she didn't go a bundle on Tuesdays, Wednesdays or Thursdays, either. She glanced in the mirror, flashed a bright smile. *Come on, Beverley, it's gonna be a cracking week.* Cracked case – with a bit of luck.

She was waiting for a green at the lights in Moseley Road. This early, the streets round Highgate had that down-at-heel out-of-season shabbiness. Post-weekend litter was strewn around: chip paper, vomit puddles, empty cans, the odd shoe. A mangy fox was ferreting in a bin liner outside a butcher's. The exhaust-and-excrement fumes made her gag. Summer in the city and no air conditioning. She patted the MG's dash. "Might have to trade you in, old boy." Fucking thing stalled.

Ten minutes later she strode into headquarters, shoulders back, head high. She'd bought an electric-blue power suit off eBay and was trying to live up to the new image. Even the Docs had been abandoned for a pair of blue suede kitten heels.

She liked getting in early. The nick never slept but there were fewer bodies around, less buzz. Gave her a bit of thinking space. She grabbed a coffee from the machine and took the stairs at a trot. The door to her office was open. She frowned, nudged it gently with her foot.

A bucket and chamois stood on the desk, a ladder was propped against the far wall. A burly guy displaying bum-crack was bent double, tying a lace. Given she'd passed the window cleaners' van in the car park, the scene didn't call for amazing powers of deduction.

"You've missed a bit." She pointed to a smeary streak, bottom right.

"Thanks, Sherlock." He was on his feet now, giving her the once-over.

Cheeky sod. An ostentatious removal of the cleaning gear was followed by the pointed positioning of paper-work. "Will you be long, love?" she drawled. "Got a stack to do."

"Sorry, ma'am." He tugged an imaginary forelock, wielded the chamois. "I'll try not to get in your way."

The whistling got on her tits. Not only did it make Dazza's sound like the Philharmonic, *When I'm Cleaning Windows* was so not original. Bev sipped the coffee and cast the occasional glance. Talk about Mr Bean in a fat suit. *Tad harsh, Beverley.* On slightly closer inspection, the brown eyes were warm and friendly and his mouth looked as if it smiled a lot. The wavy hair was almost too long and, apart from the silver threads, so dark that the six o'clock shadow was probably permanent. Still, at least he was happy in his work.

Sighing, she reached for a file. How long could it take to clean a fucking window? Two things happened almost at once: she noticed the tip of a yellow post-it under her keyboard, and a fit guy in overalls entered the room.

The note read: *Bev, Keep an eye out for DC Mac Tyler – he starts first thing. BB.*

The logo on the young guy's overalls read Stay-bright.

Bev closed her eyes, so she missed the new DC's wink as

he chucked the chamois at the window cleaner. *Could it get any worse?*

"Morning, both." Byford popped his head round the door. "I see you two are getting acquainted. Unless there's anything outstanding, Bev, you and Mac may as well team up straight away."

Oh yes.

"No, straight up, sarge, anyone could've made the same mistake. Me and George Formby?" Mac Tyler crossed two chubby fingers. "We're like this."

Even Bev knew Formby was a long-dead British actor who'd played a gormless window cleaner – and the ukelele – to perfection. Tyler winked. Bev smiled without moving her lips. He was taking the piss.

"I mean." The new DC shovelled black pudding down his throat. "I had you down as Margaret Thatcher's love-child when you walked in."

She glared. Fucking suit was going straight back on eBay. The new look had attracted a bunch of unwelcome one-liners and double-takes. Vince'd called it "very Dynasty" and Daz had asked if she'd got dressed in a power cut. As for Mac, he was digressing.

"You could've said something, mate," she pointed out.

"I was only having a laugh." He winked. "NHD."

"NHD?"

"No harm done." The wink was getting to her. Maybe it was a tic. She shrugged, took a sip of tea, tapped her watch.

After the initial misunderstanding, she'd given Tyler a lightning tour of the nick and they were now grabbing a quick bite in the canteen before the early brief. Correction. He was scarfing stroke-on-a-plate, she was keeping an eye on the clock.

The guy was a comedian. Literally. He'd been filling her in on a bit of his background, said he did stand-up in his spare time. Observational stuff. Fancied himself as a cross between Ross Noble and Ricky Gervais. Yeah, right. She so didn't appreciate the look she was getting when he informed her he got most of his material from people at work.

Come back, Daz, all is forgiven. Nah. It was early days; she'd not be making any more snap judgments in a hurry. The new DC could do with shifting a few kilos and smartening his act. Loud plaid shirts and denims didn't do any favours for a guy in his late forties, especially when the face looked as if it had squatters. But he could be a fine cop for all she knew. She hadn't got a handle on him yet.

"So tell me about you, sarge?" Mac asked. "Married, are we? Any kids?" He was mopping his plate or he'd have seen her face.

Nosy bastard. "Yeah." Dead casual. "Six."

"Husbands?"

His timing wasn't bad. Her mouth twitched. But it was time to nip a few buds. "Let's get some things clear." She watched as he laid the eating irons on a now pristine plate, fixed her with an attentive gaze. "My personal life's exactly that. We work together. Nothing else. And we're not a double act. I don't need a straight man, and the last thing you need's a feed." She gazed pointedly at his belly.

He swallowed a burp. "Fair enough. Long as I know where I stand." He rose, checked his watch. "You'll be late, love. Best get a move on."

It was early days to pull rank. Bev let Tyler's remark go. Probably a lame attempt at a joke, anyway; there was ample time for what she needed.

The photograph outside the law courts had been preying

on her mind. She headed for the office, left voice mail on a couple of numbers. Hopefully she'd have answers later in the day. By the time she hit the early brief it was standing room only.

The guv was at the front introducing Tyler to the squad. Matey smiles all round, a few hands casually raised in welcome. Bev watched from the back. It was clear Mac would be accepted from the word go: he was a bloke. The observation was statement of fact, not sour grapes. Women cops had to prove they had balls before being treated as one of the lads. Not that she was bitter or anything. Fact was she could have a sex change and still never be accepted by some of the older blokes.

And what about DC Mac Tyler? She watched him bask in the metaphorical backslaps and bonhomie. Wondered how he'd take to a woman nearly twenty years younger dishing out the orders. Come to think of it, she'd no experience working with an older sidekick. Dream team? Or partnership made in the pits? Whatever. They'd find out soon enough.

Mainly for the new guy's benefit, Byford up-summed Operation Sapphire. Where they'd been, where they stood. It was day four, sixty-eight hours since an unknown woman not so much snatched as led a little boy away from his school. Lamb to the...

Bev closed her eyes, saw Daniel's shorn hair strewn across the carpet. Shit thing to do to a kid.

"Door-to-doors have thrown up nothing." The guv gestured at one of the white boards behind him. A map of the area around Daniel's school was virtually covered in colour markers. A board on the right displayed the streets round the Page home in Moseley. More pretty patterns. Loads of shoe leather; sod all to show. It was the same blank picture with the CCTV footage. And it was ditto with well over forty interviews among the family's friends, colleagues, contacts.

Slumped shoulders and shit posture said it all; the squad knew what was coming.

The guv said it anyway. "We're going to have to go back, revisit every property, speak to everyone again. Someone must have seen something."

It was the cop's mantra. And it was probably true. And nine times out of ten what they saw was as much use as chocolate sunglasses. The problem in this instance was that the only way of eliciting information was on a one-to-one basis, costly in terms of hours and officer power. The news blackout was a two-edged sword. OK, they didn't have a flood of nut calls to wade through; Balsall Heath's Jack the Ripper wasn't going to surface again this time. But media appeals could also produce the occasional real-deal gem. With no press coverage feedback, they weren't spoilt for choice. But neither did they have a lot to go on.

"Got to be worth another chat with Stephen Cross," Bev said. Posh Cross from Priory Rise. Mr Not-Have-A-Go-Hero and the source of the only even vaguely useful information they'd uncovered since the boy's disappearance. It wasn't unusual for wits to recall a detail or two after an initial interview. She'd left numbers but her faith in someone like Cross getting back was not high.

"As soon as you like," Byford said.

"I take it the boy's family's pukka?" The new guy wasn't backward in coming forward. He was on his feet at the front asking a question, making a point.

"Bev?" The guv, presumably bowing to her greater knowledge.

She nodded. "Far as I can tell."

"Background checks pan out." Powell offered; Pembers nodded agreement.

They were still following the Wayne Dunston line. Daz and Sumitra Gosh were heading out to Winson Green prison later that morning see if they could flush out any more of Dunston's dodgy associates.

"The kidnappers are bound to make contact soon," Mac said. "Longer they hold on to the kid, the greater the risk."

"Of?" Byford asked.

Mac spread his hands. "Some nosy bugger seeing something."

"I wish," Bev muttered.

"Who wants to be cooped up with a five-year-old longer than it takes?" Mac said. "If they want that half-million, I'm surprised they haven't dropped hand-over instructions by now." The new guy was clearly keen to make an impression, mark his territory.

"So why haven't they?" *Mr Smart Arse.*

"I'm a cop, sarge, not a clairvoyant. But if they don't get in touch PDQ, you have to question why they're holding the kid."

Sounded good, meant nothing. She tried to recall something someone else had said in the last day or so. It was one of those mental silverfish moments, darting and difficult to pin down. When she tuned in again Byford was gathering his papers. "Right, everyone," he said. "Let's get on the phones and on the road. Stay focused. Stay positive. We'll get there. It's just a question of time."

As a rallying cry it wasn't his best. What everyone wanted to know was how much time. And where exactly they were going.

April 1997

Holly dreamt of escape, fleeing from the man who abused her, the man she now called Satan. At first her plans had been childish, unrealistic, born out of despair and ignorance. But as she had grown older, her ideas became more focused, more workable.

She no longer blamed her mother for the hell she endured. During her blackest hours, Holly's greatest fear was that her birth mother was dead. It would explain why she'd never returned, why there'd never been even a birthday card.

Still, Holly tried to keep faith, told herself there was a reason for her mother's absence, assured herself she'd find out in time. Her adoptive parents, the Pipers, said they knew nothing about her background. Holly didn't believe them.

In a few years she would run away, trace her mother – and then together they'd wreak revenge on the man. Those were Holly's only thoughts on the nights when the bedroom door was inched open.

23

"We stopping for a bite?" Mac was in the Midget's passenger seat. Bev cast a sideways glance. No wonder the guy's seat belt was straining. In the interval between the canteen fry-up and the fruitless visit to Priory Rise, he'd seen off a packet of crisps and a Twix.

"Peckish, are we?" Like she cared.

"TFR."

"Uh?"

"Watch the red!" He gave a too-late shrug. "TFR. Too fucking right."

Bev ran a finger along her eyebrow, not sure what pissed her off most – the whistling, the winking or the initial-speak. Benefit, doubt, and all that. Maybe Mac was an acquired taste. Not that she was hungry; she'd been biting her tongue all morning.

At least Mac had moved on from thinking about the next pit stop, and was now gazing through the window, people-watching. Keep him going for a while, that would. Moseley's multi-ethnic mix was colourful in more ways than one. Place had a stack of flamboyant characters and in-your-face attitude. Bev, who'd never set foot in Mac's old stamping ground, bet rural Derbyshire was pale in comparison. She was a second-city girl through and through.

"What you make of this Cross geezer then, sarge?" He'd clearly been exercising brain as well as eye-movement. The new DC hadn't had the dubious pleasure of making Stephen Cross's acquaintance. Cross hadn't been at home, neighbours hadn't seen him around for a couple of days.

She waggled a hand. "Sexist, arrogant git."

"Don't hold back."

"I don't."

"Seriously, was he straight up? Or after his fifteen minutes?"

Good point. She pulled the visor down, struggling with retina flash from the noon sun. Tyler had already come up with a couple of valid points that morning. Like kidnap not being a woman's crime. She'd been playing with the gender thing herself. A woman had collected Daniel from school, so obviously a female was involved, but to what extent? Almost invariably, in big-boy crimes, women played the minor roles: the often willing, occasionally unwitting accomplices. There were exceptions: the *folie à deux* exemplified by the evil coupling of Myra Hindley and Ian Brady. Bev shuddered. Didn't want to go there.

As to Stephen Cross being Mr On-the-Level, she'd no real reason to believe otherwise, except... "It's weird no one else saw anything. No corroboration anywhere."

"Like you say, he's worth another chat. I'll keep chasing, if you like."

Taking initiative, not control. "Nice one, mate."

"DMI." He winked, flashed a smile. "Don't mention it." His head whipped round. "Hey, sarge. Wasn't that a KFC?"

Bernie Flowers strode into Byford's office without knocking. Not a wise move. Everyone at Highgate knew the super-intendent had a thing about people bursting in unannounced. Bernie had either a death wish or breaking news. "We've got a witness, Bill."

The guv laid down his pen. "Go on."

The news-bureau chief stood across the desk from the big man. "That turn I did for the telly?" The appeal for information in the Doug Edensor inquiry.

Byford nodded, felt a faint tingle on his scalp.

"Call just in. Geezer in the right place, right time, says he saw three men in the car park."

"Three?"

"Yeah. The witness thought nothing of it till he saw the appeal. Reckoned they'd been on the jolly juice. The men's arms were linked, lot of staggering about. Thinks now the two younger guys could've been forcing the other bloke."

"Forcing?"

"As in frog-marching." The witness had seen the men go through the door that led to the car-park roof, assumed their motor was up there. It was late, so he didn't stick around.

"Descriptions?" Byford asked.

"Two Asians, early twenties, cargo pants, hoodies."

Byford forced himself not to overreact. Maxwell wasn't the only crook in the city who hired Asians. Just the biggest. "And the third?"

"Dead ringer for Doug, guv."

Bernie had arranged transport: the eyewitness was on the way to Highgate, where he'd work with e-fit specialists to come up with decent likenesses, which in turn could prompt more wits to come forward. "The street the garage is on?" Bernie said. "The locals call it Muggers' Row."

Byford wasn't convinced. Since when had the average mugger started carrying insulin? Was Maxwell into pharmacy now? There was one way to find out. Christ, he wished he'd known this earlier.

The news chief turned at the door. "It's Doug's funeral Friday. You going, Bill?"

He nodded. "I'll be there."

Bev's desk looked as if a pack of giant confetti had been dumped on it. A quick skim through myriad messages revealed the person she wanted to hear from most hadn't replied. She hit a number, cradled the phone under her chin and tackled the wrapping on a Prét à Manger prawn-mayo sarnie. Multi-tasking, they called it. There was no answer so she ditched the phone, but the cellophane was still impregnable. Ready to eat? Yeah, right. It finally yielded after a stabbing from a letter opener. As for Andy Quinn, why hadn't he got back?

Feet on the desk, she bit into a prawn, recalling the first time she'd met Andy. She'd been a rookie on basic training at Ryton and Quinn one of the best lecturers there, acerbic and a bit of a loner. They'd hit it off from day one. Now, though, he was no longer a police officer, instead made a living as a private detective in Brighton. It was a bit seedy for Bev, mostly end-of-the-lens marital work, wandering husbands, flighty wives, dirty weekends. But when Andy had been photographed on the steps of the law courts, he'd been a young detective. Like Edensor, Crawford and the guv.

Apart from the odd call and occasional postcard, she'd not hooked up with Andy for years. She gave a wry smile. He always sent cheesy shots of donkeys on the beach; she responded with Birmingham's Bullring. Not much of a contest, really. She wasn't even sure why she felt the need to talk. Just knew she'd feel better when she'd touched base.

She pressed redial. Still no answer from his mobile. Didn't mean anything, of course; he was probably doing his Jim Rockford bit. She left messages on Andy's home and office numbers. He'd get back.

24

By early afternoon, two e-fits lay side by side on Byford's desk. He'd leaned on the technicians and the job had been fast-tracked, but the witness was satisfied: these were the guys he'd seen with Doug Edensor. Byford studied the likenesses. Two Asian hard men. He recognised neither, but by God he'd know both again.

Did Maxwell know them already? He'd despatched a squad car to bring the crime boss in for questioning. The pretext was flimsy but Byford didn't care. He wanted Maxwell under pressure.

The detective's voice was sharp when he answered the phone. Regretted it instantly: Robbie Crawford's widow didn't deserve that.

"Sorry, Josie." He injected a warm smile. "Caught me at a bad time. What can I do for you?"

He listened carefully; it was difficult to catch every word, her voice was breaking. She'd been bagging Robbie's clothes for Oxfam when she found letters in a jacket pocket. Death threats.

"They're vile, Bill," Josie sobbed. "Poisonous." He pictured the pain twisting her pretty features. Josie was a petite blonde with a sharp mind, quick tongue. Robbie had worshipped the ground she walked on.

"How many?"

"Twelve."

"Anonymous?"

"They're not signed," she said. "But I can guess who they're from." They'd been sent on the same date each year: the anniversary of James Maxwell's death. Ditto the threats sent to Byford, though they'd dried up six years ago.

"I'll get someone over, Josie." The letters would have to go to forensics. Though if Maxwell's prints were on them, he'd eat the fedora.

"Why didn't he tell me, Bill?"

Why didn't he tell me? "He wouldn't want you worrying, Josie."

And Doug? What might he have hidden from his wife?

Byford rang off, reached for his hat and keys, decided to make a quick call to control before leaving. Patrols were still searching, he was told. It looked as if Maxwell was in hiding too.

Bev put her head into the kidnap room. "Anyone know where the guv is?"

Twenty other heads popped up or round, seemingly glad of a distraction, however brief, from pushing paper and bashing phones. Powell, who'd been leaning over DC Sumitra Gosh's shoulder, lifted his gaze from her screen. "He's in town. Auditioning for the Grant Young show."

Bev tapped the toe of a kitten heel shoe. "Meaning?"

"He had a meeting with Young. Something to do with a TV programme. We all reckoned you'd gone with him." The sly grin said more than the DI's words. Mind, it must be the royal we. Every face in the room was as blank as Bev's.

He was clearly waiting for her to take the bait. Should she give him the satisfaction?

"Hey! Where you off to?" he yelled. "There's a stack of stuff needs checking here."

Like she'd been painting her toenails? She popped her head back. Powell was standing now, hands in pockets, dead casual.

He looked her up and down. "So when's the interview?"

Bev sighed. The DI clearly had some snide gem he wanted off his chest. "Go on. Spit it out." She could live without enlightenment but the squad was clearly dying to know.

"The suit." He smirked. "Either you've got an interview or there's a royal visit."

She shook her head: how many cracks like that had she heard today? Actually, most of them were a good bit sharper. "Nah. I'm wearing it for a bet." Her smile was sweet, too sweet.

Powell's turn to look blank. Least he had the nous not to ask what the bet was.

"Hey, sarge?" Mac Tyler, the newbie, had slipped in behind. The subtle wink meant he'd cottoned on fast. "What's the bet?"

"Which loser'd be the first with a shit-for-brains cheap shot. And guess what?"

The new DC turned his mouth down. "You just won?"

"Got it in one."

Byford wasn't in town. He'd cancelled the meeting with Grant Young. As a sop, the detective had agreed to take a look at the media man's programme treatment and get back with an early answer. Apparently Mansfield and one of the Birmingham Six had already signed contracts. Young had been full of it; Byford thought he'd never get off the phone.

And the big man needed to get away...

He sat now in the chintzy front room of a large Victorian villa in Harborne. The florals and frills, heavy furniture and low light added to his discomfort. Opposite, arms hugging waist, a painfully thin woman rocked herself slowly to and fro. Grey roots showed through faded auburn hair. Sylvie Edensor was in her late forties, looked a decade older. An agoraphobic, she hadn't set foot outside the house in seven years; a bundle of neuroses. Doug would never have added to her worries.

Since speaking to Josie Crawford, Byford had tried calling Sylvie, but knew Doug's widow rarely answered the phone. She looked a wreck, much worse than he remembered. Not that he'd seen a lot of her in the seven years since Doug left the force. Her welcome had been frosty and a thaw hadn't set in.

She was aware that Doug's death was being treated as murder. Byford told her he was following a line of inquiry. Given her fragility, he was working out how best to broach it.

"I knew it wasn't suicide all along. Doug would never have killed himself." She twisted a strand of hair, the movement compulsive, probably unwitting.

"Sylvie, did Doug ever mention… enemies?"

"No."

"Threats?"

"No."

"Letters?"

"No. No. No. How many more times…?"

"Sylvie." He leaned forward, elbows on knees. "I know this is difficult, but have you gone through his things?"

She rarely made eye contact. He noticed, for the first time, flecks of yellow in the hazel pupils. Until tears welled and she turned her head.

"Sylvie, I need to take a look." He took her silence as assent.

Upstairs, he checked obvious hiding places first: pockets, drawers, wardrobe, floor-boards, suitcases, bookcases, CD racks. But Doug hadn't hidden it. The old tobacco tin was part of a collection on display in a glass cabinet on the landing. Inside were twelve cards, the kind found on funeral wreaths. All were black-edged, all bore the same message.

I'll be pissing on your grave, cop.

Jenny Page's overnight hospital stay had been extended for at least twenty-four hours. Bev and Mac were on the way to the Nuffield. Mac was honoured: he was in the Vauxhall's driving seat. It normally took weeks before Bev would relinquish the wheel to a partner. And never her MG's. Maybe it was because he'd stuck up for her in the exchange with Powell. Mac could obviously think on his feet and the impromptu stand-up had put him in her good books, unless he overstepped the mark.

"Does he always try and wind you up, sarge?"

She considered the question carefully. Before the attack, she'd have had no hesitation saying that Powell saw it as part of his job spec. But she'd seen another side since. In the immediate aftermath, he'd been painfully polite. Not so much skirting the issue as erecting wardrobes round it.

But who was she to talk? Or not. She'd not discussed the rape in detail with a living soul, including her therapist. "You're in denial, Ms Morriss, yadda yadda. Not dealing with it, Ms Morriss, blah-de-blah." True, though. And if it was difficult for her to cope with, it couldn't be easy for the people around her, especially an emotionally stunted guy like Powell.

Initially he'd gone for the kid-glove treatment. Like that would work. It was the last thing she needed and she'd hit back hard. In the last month or so, she'd detected his attitude gradually toughening. She smiled and shook her head. Ironic or what? The DI goes in for a few gratuitous

144

piss-takes and she welcomes the change.

"I give as good as I get, Mac."

"I'd heard that."

"Next left." She looked away, smile on her face. It froze as she spotted a familiar figure. Was that Stephen Cross? And who was the blonde? Had Bev seen her before? She swung in the seat but Mac was a member of the Morriss school of driving, fast and furious: the couple were almost out of sight. "Turn round, mate."

He pointed at a road sign. "One way."

"Sod it." At least they knew Cross was back in town. Edgbaston, no less. The Nuffield was only a few blocks from his home. They'd pay a house call after the hospital visit.

Being private, the place looked more like a rest home or a health farm. A nurse showed them to the room and left them to it. Bev hoped Jenny Page didn't feel anywhere near as bad as she looked. Slumped listlessly on top of a single bed, her sallow skin co-ordinated with the sepia décor, the blonde hair was matted to her scalp. A silver-framed photograph of Daniel stood on the bedside table. Perhaps she'd drifted off staring at the smiling image of her son.

"Sedation's kicked in, then?" Mac stood at Bev's shoulder.

She glared but the guy was right. Jenny Page didn't even know they were there.

"What'd she want to see you for, sarge?"

Bev shrugged. The message, buried under all the others on her desk, hadn't specified. "I'll leave a note so she'll know I dropped by."

She was still scrabbling at the bottom of her bag for a pen when Mac's phone shrilled. He turned, head hunched, voice so low she only caught the odd word. There were a zillion notices telling people to switch off mobiles and she was about to give him a bollocking, until he turned back and she saw his face. The eyes rendered the words almost superfluous.

"They've found a kid's body." He jammed the phone in a pocket. "Wasteland in Selly Oak."

25

The wasteland was close to a council playground, primary colours bathed in golden sunlight. Bev registered the bright tableau as Mac drove past, carried the pictures in her head. Little kids playing happily on a slide, beaming toddlers on the swings, a roundabout standing empty. Paradise Row, it was called.

The children were out of sight now but the soundtrack of excited laughter mixed with high-pitched squeals carried across the crime scene. A scene as bleak as any Bev had attended. The wasteland abutted a row of pebble-dashed council houses, twitching net curtains and trailing trellis. Similar properties had stood here not that long ago; building rubble littered the site, rusting bedsprings poked through a stained mattress, two supermarket trolleys locked handles as if in weird sexual foreplay. Here and there nature staked claims with colonies of nettles and dandelions, daisies and dock. It was eerily quiet: voices were hushed, movement slow, even the streamers of police tape hung motionless in the still air. Foul smells lingered: dog mess, cat pee – and something sweet, sickly sweet.

Bev stood a few metres from a shallow grave that partially covered the body of a little boy. White-suited SOCOs were standing by and uniforms who'd fingertip every inch of the land were waiting for a green. Everyone was hanging fire for the pathologist, except the police photographers who'd already shot stills and videos. They'd take more once the body was turned.

"Poor little man." The words were trite but Mac appeared genuinely moved. He was kicking grit, head down, hands deep in pockets. She'd watched him brush a tear from his eye. Some officers never showed emotion. Wasn't macho, was it? Maybe later they did. Over a sixth pint or second bottle. Bev sighed, gave a sad nod. Poor little man was probably as good an epitaph as any. Words didn't exist that could cover a child's death. It was the ripple effect across an ocean.

"Is it Daniel?" Mac asked softly. No one had the answer.

A tarpaulin sheet lay to one side where, according to the jogger who stumbled across it, a dog or fox may have dragged it. The little boy lay face down, blond hair cropped close to the skull. The body was fully clothed apart from shoes; skinny little legs were crossed at the ankle. One Dennis the Menace sock was higher than the other. Bev bit her lip; recalled Jenny Page burying her face into her lost boy's t-shirt.

It had to be Daniel, didn't it? Who else could it be? Since day one, she'd tried to ignore the stats but they were compelling. If abducted kids are murdered, seventy-six per cent die within six hours of being taken; within twenty-four hours that shoots to ninety-six per cent. After three days, none survive.

She raised a hand in greeting as a grim-faced Byford picked his way across the site. She knew he'd blame himself if Daniel were dead. They all would, to a certain degree, but the guv would take the lion's share. It wasn't just professional can-carrying, it was in the big man's nature.

"Where's Overdale?" He scowled. Bev shrugged. The pathologist had got a call same as everyone, but wasn't best known for her time-keeping. "Get the bloody woman here now, I'm not having…"

"Guv." Bev tilted her head. Dr Overdale's Range Rover was looming into view.

"About bloody time." Unlike Byford, this. The guv didn't often swear and was Mr Cool in a crisis. Who or what was rattling his cage?

"Superintendent." Gillian Overdale's tight smile wasn't returned.

"Let's get on with it."

Apart from pursing permanently puckered lips, Overdale ignored the rebuke. Kneeling close to the little boy, she snapped open the locks on a steel case and peeled on surgical gloves. The first examination was visual, external. Her expert gaze swept the body, searching for signs of injury. As everyone knew, the real work came later in the morgue.

How did they do it? Bev wondered. She hated being close to dead bodies. Best advice she'd ever had was *don't look*. The brain's a camera. Once seen, an image is imprinted forever, so don't take the pics in the first place. Easier said than done. Her head was full of the bloody things.

"Get those ghouls out of my sight!" Byford's sudden verbal explosion startled a colony of crows in nearby tree-tops. Branches cracked as wings beat and the huge black birds took off, circling and screeching overhead. Both the birds and Byford's outburst had shattered Bev's thoughts, jerked her back from the distance she'd deliberately created. She looked in the direction of the guv's accusing finger.

A gaggle of thirty or so locals lined the police tape at the edge of the site. Teenage mums with babes in arms, kids in school uniform, middle-aged women with fags in their mouth. Better than daytime telly, this was. Two uniforms were already on the way to disperse the audience.

"I take it your people have done their thing?" Overdale asked without looking round.

"Finished half an hour ago," Byford said.

Gently the pathologist turned the little boy's body, her

own shielding it from Bev. Not that she complained. An occasional burst of radio static and a dog's almost non-stop barking disturbed the silence as Overdale continued her examination. Still kneeling, she delivered her initial observations.

"Can't give you a cause of death. Nothing obvious. No apparent injuries. Given the state of the body, he's been dead hours rather than days. I'll run the post mortem this evening. Seven o'clock. Can't tell you anything more until after that."

But Bev could. As Overdale rose, Bev had a clear view of the body. The little boy lay on his back, wide eyes staring sightlessly into a cloudless sky. She shot a hand to her mouth, felt the colour drain from her face.

"Sarge?" Mac reached out an arm as she swayed forward.

"It's not Daniel." She breathed. "Look at his eyes."

Big beautiful eyes – almost as blue as Bev's.

Any relief in knowing Daniel Page might still be alive was tempered by the fact that an unidentified child lay dead on a steel slab in the city morgue at Newhall Street. DI Powell and DC Pemberton were on the way there. The guv had assigned Mike Powell senior investigating officer to the new inquiry that had been codenamed Operation Hawk. It was seven pm, three hours since the body's discovery.

At Highgate, Byford paced an incident room that was still in the throes of being set up. He sidestepped technicians as they carried in gear and walked round electricians installing it. A mobile IU and most of a hastily appointed squad was already active at the Paradise Row site. With two major criminal investigations plus regular smaller-scale inquiries, they were short on space and – more important – personnel.

Bev and Mac were on hand, with Seth Gregson, the information officer who was running the admin show. Short and stocky, Seth did more than shuffle papers; IOs were human hard disks. Scanning, logging, prioritising, cross-referencing, updating hundreds of witness statements, police reports, messages, phone calls, every scrap of information that could have a bearing on an inquiry. Gregson was one of the best. The top man was on Sapphire.

"A child can't just go missing," Byford said. "Why hasn't it been reported? Where are the parents, for Christ's sake?"

His complexion was tinged with grey, sweat dampened non-designer stubble. He looked as rough as Bev felt. Her throat and chest were still sore from throwing up. The nausea had kicked in back at the nick. It didn't often happen these days. Delayed shock, perhaps. Plus the heat, and the smell of rotting pork that clung to her hair and skin. As for the electric-blue suit, she was getting shot of it anyway.

"Bound to get a steer soon, guv." The search team and dog handlers were still at the location, officers were canvassing passers-by and uniforms were on the knock. Christ, a whole row of houses backed on to the wasteland. Surely no one could dump a body without being seen.

As well as the police activity, the press boys had been busy. The story had been running on TV and radio for a couple of hours. The media circus had set up camp while the body was still on site. No big surprise, given how many of the locals had mobiles clamped to their necks. There'd been no police news conference but plenty of press speculation: sad-faced, mournful-toned pieces to camera all milking the Paradise Row name. As in hell on...

Byford finally came to rest on the edge of a desk. "I wish

I had your faith, sergeant."

Sergeant? Bad as that? She shrugged. She was doing her media-liaising bit in a minute, conveying what little they had on Operation Sapphire with the even leaner offerings on Operation Hawk. The news hounds might be content with the occasional titbit on the kidnap but they'd be chasing every crumb on the dead child. "What if they want you on camera, guv?"

"Saying what?"

She spread empty hands. "Appeal for witnesses? Help identifying the body? Usual stuff."

"You do it." He rubbed a hand over drawn features. "I can't see the point."

Bev took in the slumped posture, the flat tone, reckoned there was more than one point the big man wasn't seeing.

26

In his office a few minutes later, Byford was seeing so many points he felt dizzy. A five-year-old boy was in the hands of kidnappers and now the mystery death of another child. Two major on-going inquiries that demanded a hundred per cent of everything from everyone, in particular a fully focused SIO.

So why couldn't Byford get Harry Maxwell's ugly smirk out of his head? Patrols had failed to locate either the crime boss or his right-hand henchman, Jaswinder Ghai. Uniform had been out much of the day trawling massage parlours, casinos, clubs, pubs – all Maxwell's usual haunts. His home, a detached Tudor pile on the outskirts of Alvechurch, was under surveillance. But for how long?

Operations Sapphire and Hawk had to take precedence. The detective couldn't afford to waste valuable resources on a case still based more on instinct than evidence. Death threats and a penchant for hiring Asians weren't proof of anything.

He rose, paced the space, hands deep in pockets. He kicked himself for giving Maxwell an easy ride the other day in The Grapes. It wouldn't happen again. The cocky bastard thought he could walk on water.

And get away with murder?

"Boss always like that, sarge?" Mac offered her something that reeked of cheese and resembled a bright orange slug. She was starving, not suicidal. He munched as they walked along the corridor.

"How'd you mean?" The question was unnecessary; she

knew where he was coming from. The guv had been uncharacteristically negative, leading from the back.

"Wasn't exactly Braveheart in there, was it?"

She turned, hands on thrust hips. "Fuck you know, Tyler?" The benefit-of-the-doubt shop was empty. "He's a bigger man than you'll ever be." OK, she knew it was childish: "Fatso."

"Charmed, I'm sure." He casually licked orange fuzz from his fingers.

She wasn't expecting that; she threw him a life-threatening glare. "The guv's got a lot on his plate, right now. Fucking dinner service full."

Mac shrugged, shoved the empty pack in his pocket. "Goes with the job. Know what they say about kitchens and heat?"

Finger jabbing, she let rip. "Don't slag the guy off. You haven't got a fucking clue. He's forgotten more about policing than you'll ever pick up. Constable."

"Know the workings of the great man's mind, do we, sarge?"

She moved in, caught a whiff of cheesy breath. "Back off, fuckwit."

"Everything OK, Bev?" Vince Hanlon's head poked round the corner.

She nodded, held eye contact with Tyler. "As your senior officer…"

"Act like one then, Bev." She flinched. Not because Tyler had used her name but the way he'd spoken the words. No hint of aggression or defiance; well-meant advice gently administered. "I'm the new guy, remember? I asked a reasonable question. Your loyalty does you proud, sergeant. But not your attitude."

Tears blurred her eyes and she turned her head. She'd

heard it before, never really listened. But there was something about this guy... OK, they weren't going to be instant best buddies – and there'd certainly be no kiss-and-make-up-session – but maybe she'd try to find another benefit-of-doubt place to shop.

He touched her arm; she didn't pull back. "OKM?" he asked tentatively.

Easy peasy. "OK, mate," she said. His eyes lit when he smiled. There was mischief in hers. "FOF."

He worked it out fast. "You swear too much." Then wagged a finger in mock admonition. "And I'm not fat."

DI Powell slumped next to Carol Pemberton on a wooden bench in a narrow corridor at the Newhall Street morgue. The busy black-and-white floor was marginally less nauseating than the bile-green walls. Neither held a candle to the gut-wrenching odours all around them. Disinfectant hadn't been invented that could mask the smell of death. A hot shower and a change of clothes would get rid of most of it, but not the stink at the back of the throat. That would be trapped there for days.

"Is this the short straw, or what?"

Pemberton raised an eyebrow. Given why they were here, others were a damn sight shorter.

"Inspector?" Overdale in green scrubs, mask slung round her neck, beckoned to them. Appropriately booted and suited, they followed her into the dissection area. Powell breathed slowly through his mouth, carefully timing each inhalation and exhalation if only to concentrate on something other than the corpse. He hated post mortems with a passion. It was about the only time in his professional life that he found the bravado almost impossible to sustain. It would be infinitely harder now. Until this evening, he'd managed to avoid attending a child's autopsy. Maybe if he closed his eyes…

Worse. He saw Sam in his mind's eye. The DI's brother had died at about the same age as the little boy on the slab. Sam had been swept to sea off a Greek island, his body never found. It was the Powells' last family holiday. After Sam's death, there was no family. Not to speak of. His father walked out, his mother never really recovered. It was no cliché to say her death five years ago had been a release.

Powell rarely thought about any of it, never talked about it. But his mind was currently running the movie. What was the saying? What doesn't kill us makes us strong? He'd played the tough guy so long, he'd forgotten the tender part.

Until now.

Maybe it was the tag round the tiny toe: a little boy reduced to a number. Or those dead eyes, the shade of the sea on a summer's day. Powell steeled himself as the pathologist selected a scalpel – passed out as she made the first cut.

"We've all been there, sir." Pemberton sat next to Powell in an anteroom next to the path lab. He was clutching paper towels to a fair-sized gash on his forehead. The DI had been out cold for several minutes after hitting the edge of a steel trolley on his way down.

"Dodgy burger," he muttered. "Felt ropey all afternoon."

"Sure." Poor guy. Carol was genuinely sorry for him. Why lie about it, though? He wasn't the only cop to faint at the first sight of blood. Though they normally stayed on their feet till the Y incision.

"All over in there?" Powell asked.

"Yeah. Just the tidying up."

He made to stand. "I'd best have a word."

"She's gone. Called out. Stirchley way. Fume-filled car."

Good. The pratfall would be history next time they met. "Top line?"

Pembers rubbed the back of her neck. "Doesn't know."

"What!"

"Don't shoot the messenger, boss."

"Sorry. Go on." He dabbed the cut, grimaced at the blood.

"No signs of abuse, no broken bones, bruising, bleeding. Something might show up on the tox results but Overdale's stumped. The guv wants…"

Powell jerked his head up, regretted it instantly. "What did you…?"

She raised a palm. "He rang. Wanted to know what was happening. Wants pictures circulated like yesterday." Obvious action. Once they had an identity they'd have a better idea where to look for answers. "I had a word with the news bureau," Carol said. "They're sorting the visuals. If you're OK, boss, I'm gonna get off." She wanted a cold shower, a hot bath, then a long cuddle with her kids.

"No prob. I'm outa here." He rose, waited out a blood rush. As they left, they talked priorities for the morning, assuming nothing broke overnight. There should be forensic follow-ups; and surely a lead or two from the good folk of Paradise Row.

It was like stepping into a wall of heat outside: high temperatures trapped by tall buildings. Powell felt a tad light-headed. "Carol?"

"Sir?"

"When you spoke to the guv… did you mention…?" No need to spell it out.

"Not a word." She smiled. "Could happen to anyone. Dodgy burger."

Good girl. He'd never hear the last of it if it got back to Morriss.

Carol turned to leave, hesitated. "Who's Sam, sir?"

He tensed, couldn't respond.

"You mentioned the name a few times while you were out. I thought..."

"Well, don't." The smile was meant to take the edge off the words. "It's nothing," he said. "Just someone I used to know."

27

The hacks were restless tonight. Hunting in a pack, they scented blood. Bev reckoned it was hers. Seated behind an ebony table on a dais at the top of the conference room, she did a quick head count. Thirty-two. Even with big Mac on side, the odds weren't brilliant. She glanced up. Make that thirty-three. Jack Pope was putting in a late appearance. She'd not clapped eyes on him since their brief encounter at The Prince. He raised a casual hand, slipped into a seat at the back. He hadn't missed much.

Operation Sapphire had been dealt with summarily. It went: any developments? No. She sensed a keenness among the reporters to move on. The *Evening News* crime correspondent Matt Snow was centre front. She'd noticed Snowie exchange pointed glances with other sharp operators. There was a stir in the air that wasn't down to the kidnap inquiry.

She raised an eyebrow at Mac, then indicated a carafe of water. Considering she'd not said much, her mouth felt like the Gobi. "Ta, mate." She used the sipping time to try to work out what was afoot. In the absence of hard fact, the journos had been on site at Paradise Row in Selly Oak pulling together vox pops and colour pieces. Most people spout off when there's a camera in their face. Occasionally, it's worth hearing.

"Heard of Monks Court?" Matt Snow asked.

Natch. It was a halfway house for ex-offenders, parolees, what were nowadays called the socially challenged. *What's this?*

"Sorry? Say again?"

"Monks Court. Locals aren't happy." Snow riffled pages in a dog-eared spiral notebook. With a less than natty line in shiny brown suits and dirty blond Tintin tuft, he put Bev in mind of something short and snappy. Like a shitzu.

"Oh?" She drew out the word, wished it were longer. There'd never been any trouble at Monks Court; vetting was tight. But it was in a neighbouring street to Paradise Row. *Tread carefully, Beverley.*

"Residents are forming a pressure group," Snow said. Peripherally she registered other hacks nodding sagely.

"Since when?" A cool pool of sweat was forming at the bottom of her spine as she sensed the potential minefield.

"This afternoon." No wonder the fringe was vertical; he couldn't stop fingering it. "Don't you read the papers?"

Yeah. While Paul Burrell peels me grapes. "Pressed for time today, Matt."

"The group's calling itself SOAP."

"SOAP?" 'Course it was.

"Selly Oak Against Perverts."

Shit. "The residents of Monks Court aren't…"

"People aren't happy. They want it shut." More nods and mutters.

"There's nothing to suggest a link between the boy's death…"

"And there's nothing to suggest there isn't." She'd started but he'd not finished. "They plan to picket the place till they get a fair hearing." He tapped his pen on the notebook. "Or till you lot catch the killer."

She met his gaze. "There may not be a killer." The media were aware of that; she'd disclosed the PM wasn't conclusive.

"Oh, of course. Natural causes, then?"

Smart arse. Not worth pursuing. Not with serious stuff

around. "You said a fair hearing, Matt. What about the men in Monks Court? Do they get one?"

"Best ask SOAP." He shrugged. "I just report the news."

"Tell me about it." The tabloids were full of it: stabbings, unprovoked attacks, motiveless murders. She was a cop and the level of violent, almost casual crime pissed her off royally. The streets weren't safe because of a shit system. And Selly Oak certainly had its fair share of mindless thugs. There was no discipline; yobs got away with terrorising decent people. Courts didn't crack down and prisons couldn't cope with the numbers anyway. And what puerile goodie had that Tory tosser come out with: hug a hoodie? Pass the crusher.

She held the glass to her forehead. It wasn't cold enough. Christ, there were plenty of issues to get worked up about. But a bunch of losers in what amounted to a care centre?

"I need a quote," Snow said. "What's the police take on it?"

Thin ice. Freeze. Except this was potentially inflammatory: hot nights, hotheads, volatile vigilantes. "No comment at this stage."

Not till they'd been there, assessed it properly. If it stood up, there'd have to be a police presence at the property till things cooled down. Great. Like they were awash with bodies right now. On the other hand, Snow could be stirring.

"Is the *senior* investigating officer available?" The stress said it all.

Nice one, Matt. She shook her head. "Operational duties."

He muttered something that sounded like *bollocks* but let it go.

"OK, if there's nothing else..." She started gathering papers, tried to look busy as opposed to bushed. It was gone eight, she was starving, knackered and a shite day wasn't over.

"Bev…" Pope made to stop her as she swept out.

"Not now, mate." The curt dismissal felt good at the time.

It was gone nine before Bev had struggled through the reports, writing her own and skimming the latest offerings from others. She wished a paper fairy came in every night to look after the words. Give her action over admin any day. By now she had a thumping head and a grumbling stomach. No surprise. A plate at her elbow bore the greasy outlines of a brace of sausage rolls. Sod school dinners, Jamie Oliver should kick up a stink about police cuisine. When was the last time she'd eaten something green? Or cooked a real meal? As for her mental stove, pans were bubbling and the burners full. Too full.

The Sapphire and Hawk inquiries had shoved less pressing stuff to the back. She checked her to-do list, picked up the phone. No answer on both Andy Quinn's numbers. She left messages again, then transferred the task to tomorrow's list. When she'd spoken to Andy she'd tick it off. Why hadn't he got back to her? She scribbled a note to Byford; he needed to know about the SOAP bunch. But they hadn't got their act together yet; according to uniform, there was no sign of picketing outside Monks Court. As SIO, Powell had ordered extra patrols on the place.

Bag and bits hoisted, she headed for the superintendent's office. OK, she shouldn't have looked. The folder was nothing to do with her but the title, *Hard Time,* piqued her curiosity. She glanced at a few pages, registered a couple of names. If anything, she was a tad miffed that the guv hadn't mentioned it. She laid her own note on top. Jumped a mile when she caught someone watching from behind.

Wally. She laughed out loud. Not someone, something. The cactus she'd given the guv as a peace offering. It was more like a sodding triffid lurking in the corner. And it looked decidedly sorry for itself. *Join the club.*

Mac Tyler had dropped in to the Hurst Street glee club on the way home. Home? A grotty crib in Balsall Heath, a cheap bed-sit in a multi-occupancy gaff more suited to penniless students than DCs past the first flush. He was never in a hurry to get back. It wasn't as if anyone was waiting for him.

Standing at last in what was laughingly called a kitchen, he scoffed his last few chips, chucked the paper in the bin and stepped all of two feet into the living space. It was like a shoebox and the beige anaglypta walls put him in mind of porridge.

The club hadn't been a bundle of laughs, either. He'd heard the material before, used some of it. But he loved doing the comedy, standing up and making people laugh. Or not. Either way, it kept him going, made him feel good, compensated for the nine-to-five crap. He snorted: would that the hours were that regular. And some of the shit nothing would compensate for. Like the image of that little kid.

Mac emptied his pockets on a wonky bedside table: wallet, keys, warrant card, gum, loose change. He told himself not to, but picked up the wallet again anyway. He'd taken the boys' picture just before he kissed them goodbye on Saturday. George was seven, Luke eight. Mac was supposed to have access every other weekend. Like that was going to happen, living in this dump and his ex ensconced with Prince Fucking Charming up in Matlock.

He ran a finger over the kids' faces. Thank God they'd inherited their mother's looks. Despite himself, he returned a grin with identical dimples. He sighed, propped the photograph against the wall. No point moping. He was a glass-half-full bloke.

Maybe he should cheer the place up a bit, buy a few posters and a telly. Or get a goldfish or a budgie. Something he could talk to without getting a load of verbals. Unbidden, an image sprang to mind: Bev Morriss. Prickly or what? He gave a slow smile, loosened his belt, and sat on the edge of the bed. She called a spade a fuck-you shovel and she'd definitely be a handful, but he hoped they'd get on. He patted his paunch. And maybe she had a point: he probably was a fat old fart.

"You have to eat, little man." There were runny scrambled eggs in the bowl. Daniel didn't think much of the lady's cooking and he'd stopped being polite. She brought the spoon close but he clamped his lips together so tightly his teeth hurt. He wasn't hungry and he didn't want her food. Didn't want anything from her. All he wanted was to go home and be with Mummy and Daddy.

She placed the bowl on the arm of the chair and forced his head round to face her. "I'm getting angry, Daniel. You don't want me to get angry." The smile wasn't friendly, not like when nice people smiled. "Trust me on that, little man."

He didn't trust her on anything. She didn't even lie about Daddy coming to visit any more. And she wouldn't answer any questions about Mummy. Just told him to shut up, be quiet, stop acting like a baby.

Tears filled his eyes. He was a baby. Mummy's baby.

"Stop snivelling." She picked up the bowl and placed the spoon to his lips. He took a mouthful this time. "There's a good little boy." It was the silly voice she used when she tried to make him do things. But he wasn't a good little boy. He spat the egg in her face, then grabbed the bowl and hurled it against the wall.

He cowered, convinced he'd get a slap, but she rose, walked to the door. "That was very silly, Daniel. Mummy's outside and she's going to be very upset, isn't she?"

He raced across the room, clutched at her skirt, clung to her legs. "Where is she? Where is she? Can I see her? Please let me see her."

"Oh, dear me, no. You should have thought of that before, Daniel."

"Please, please, let me see Mummy." He sobbed hysterically. "I'll be a good boy."

She gestured at the eggs running down the wall. "Eat, little man. And I'll think about it."

28

Broad Street it wasn't. At least there was a bit of nightlife in the city centre. OK, lowlife. Binge drinkers, blokes on the pull, birds on the pill, clubbers on whatever they could grab before hitting the pavement. Kept you on your toes. Not like being on traffic, especially in the not-particularly-mean streets of Birmingham suburbia.

PC Simon Wells stifled a yawn, opened the window an inch. Selly Oak's pubs, chippies and eating-houses had closed a couple of hours earlier. Apart from Dosser Jo kipping in the job-centre doorway, the place was dead.

Truth to tell, lates didn't do anything for Si. They were same-old-same-old: drunks, druggies, domestics. He preferred day shifts when more people were around, anything could kick off. Fact was – or fantasy – he fancied himself as a Tom Cruise, *Mission Impossible* kind of guy. Rescuing the blonde, saving the world, nothing too taxing.

As it was, he couldn't even have a smoke. Not with Ram riding shotgun. Ram Karimjee, his sergeant, was in the ASH camp. Talk about smoke police. He could detect the slightest whiff at a hundred metres with his nostrils taped.

Ironic, as it turned out. Because it was Simon who spotted the flames.

Weird, the notions that go through the head when the eyes and brain are out of sync. Simon Wells saw flashing lights behind the glass-panelled door at Monks Court and for an instant – no more than half a second – thought it was a disco. Except the movement was dancing flames and they were all shades of red.

Simon leapt out as Karimjee hit the brake. "Fuck's sake,

Ram. Call it in: fire, control, Powell."

Neck. Block. Bollocks. They'd driven past the building three or four times every hour since coming on shift. How could a fire-raiser have slipped under the radar? Simon had no doubt the blaze was deliberate. Apart from not buying an astronomical coincidence, the petrol fumes made him gag as he approached. What he couldn't be sure of was how long it had been burning and how far it had spread.

Karimjee shouted his name as he reached the door. The young constable looked back briefly – just before the blast blew apart the front of the building.

Mike Powell made it to the scene as a fire crew brought out a body. They knew it was male because Monks Court had no female staff or residents. The corpse gave no clues.

The DI weaved a wary path through emergency vehicles, snaking hoses, puddles of greasy water. He needed a word with the chief fire officer. No point pissing round with minions. It looked like a shoot from *London's Burning*: six fire appliances, two ambulances, four squad cars, flashing blues, TV lights, cameras. Controlled chaos.

At six-five, Chief Fire Officer John Preston was easy to locate. He continued directing operations as he fed top lines to Powell. Thirteen men had escaped through the back before the flames took grip, but it wasn't yet known whether that was all the occupants. A team wearing breathing apparatus was in there searching.

The noise was intense: engines, pumps, generators, barked instructions. Powell had to shout to make himself heard. "Any more good news?"

Preston ignored the comment, turned anxious eyes on the building. The tall Geordie wouldn't relax until the outbreak was under control; thirty of his men and women were fighting to stop it spreading. The neighbouring properties were business premises; empty, thank God, in the early hours.

Powell tapped the fire chief's arm. "Sorry, mate. It's a bit much to take in. We had patrols keeping an eye on the place."

"You knew there was a risk?"

"Of picketing." Shadows flickered on the planes of the DI's face. "Not this."

Death and destruction. He shook his head in sorrow and anger. Were there more bodies inside? As for the halfway house, it would be a charred shell by first light. Even as the thought formed, a huge cloud of sparks shot into the night sky, sounds of cracking timber added to the frenetic vocal chorus.

The DI felt the heat, turned his head. An office block over the road reflected the flames, every window a screen showing the same movie, a poor man's *Towering Inferno*. Powell's eyes smarted and his forehead throbbed; the cut must've opened again. He dabbed it with a tissue. Should he have ordered a 24/7 police guard at Monks Court? He'd taken the budget and lack of police bodies into account but it could be a costly mistake. In his favour, the risk had seemed minimal, flimsy almost. In his experience, action groups were mostly all mouth, and this one had only been established the previous afternoon. It was a hell of a jump from waving a placard to lobbing a petrol bomb. Unless mindless cretins looking for senseless kicks had hijacked the bandwagon conveniently provided by SOAP.

Either way, there'd be an inquest. He sighed. Too soon to apportion blame, but where the hell had his patrol officers been? And where were they now? They should be briefing him. Powell already had squad cars cruising the neighbour-hood but anyone who had a hand in this would have to be brain-dead if they were still out there.

"Seen Hughes anywhere?" he asked. Gavin Hughes, manager at Monks Court. Bald, ex-boxer, Captain Bird's Eye beard. Wasn't as though you'd miss him in a crowd. Not that there was a crowd. The DI took a confirmatory glance round. It was the only crime scene he could recall where there wasn't a band of gawpers taking perverse pleasure in other people's personal tragedies. Maybe SOAP fans didn't give a toss what happened to Monks Court clientele.

"Probably on the phone somewhere," Preston said. "Trying to organise emergency accommodation." The CFO nodded at the pavement opposite where dazed-looking men wearing nightclothes huddled in foil blankets. They put Powell in mind of refugees, except the shelter they'd been given had been snatched away. An old woman moved among the men, offering hot drinks from a tray. Salvation Army or local do-gooder? Powell shook his head. Unbelievable. Everything those poor bastards owned was going up in flames and an old biddy was dishing out PG Tips.

"I'd best try and find him," Powell said. "Thanks, mate."

Preston tapped his helmet. "Sorry about your man, Mike. Shit thing to happen."

"Say again?" He'd heard nothing about a police casualty.

"Young officer, first on the scene? I heard the door blew in his face. He was whisked off to the burns unit."

Bad, then. No wonder Karimjee and Wells weren't around. Jesus, thought Powell, could it get any worse?

TUESDAY

29

Death messages, they're called, when a cop breaks bad news. Bev had delivered an unfair few in her time, hated getting them even more. She was woken just after six by a call from Brighton CID. They'd found Andy Quinn's body late the previous night; he'd probably been dead a week. The pathologist couldn't be more precise because the July temperatures had accelerated decomposition.

DI Paula Ryland was calling in response to Bev's messages on Andy's machine. Bev sat up, wide awake but barely able to take it in. And there was more. When Ryland realised Bev was a cop, she didn't hold back. Andy Quinn had died from multiple stab wounds. The DI had never seen anything like it in twenty years' service.

Shock. Grief. Anger. Disbelief. Tears welled in Bev's eyes. It wasn't as though she and Andy had been particularly close. But at the end no one had been there for him. The guy had lived alone and died alone – unless the killer had hung around to watch.

"Dangerous line of work," Ryland said. "Private eyes make a lot of enemies."

Got that right. "So do cops," Bev muttered. In her mind's eye she again saw the photograph taken twenty-odd years before, on the steps of the old law courts. Andy Quinn. Robbie Crawford. Doug Edensor. And the guv.

Still out at Monks Court, Mike Powell was slumped on the kerb, knees drawn up, head cradled in both hands, weak with exhaustion, as a huge red sun emerged against a lavender and violet background. The DI was oblivious, mind on other matters. Most firefighters had been stood down, a five-man crew was damping down; there was still a danger the fire would re-ignite. Hoses were directed at occasional wisps of smoke that drifted from the wreckage. The stink was everywhere. It clung to the DI's clothes and hair. Even if he noticed, he was past caring.

When it was safe, a fire investigation team would move into what little remained of the building, to confirm or otherwise John Preston's conviction that there'd been more than one petrol bomb, more than one seat of fire, maybe more than one arsonist.

Powell glanced up as a car pulled into the street. He shielded his eyes from the glare of the sun. Still rising, it was reflected now – blood red – in the windows of the office block. Not that it would rise for everyone. The fire had eventually claimed two lives.

Powell stared at his hands. The first victim's burns had been so severe identification was impossible at this stage. The second victim was the manager, Gavin Hughes. He'd gone back into the burning building, succumbed to the dense acrid smoke. The DI closed his eyes.

"Sir?"

Ram Karimjee knelt beside Powell nervously jangling car keys. The sergeant's soft brown eyes were red-rimmed and held a message Powell knew he wouldn't want to hear. Ram swallowed. Powell watched the bob of the man's Adam's apple, studied the sweat on his top lip, the stubble on his chin, the grey streaks in his hair, the amber flecks in his irises – any damn inconsequential thing so he didn't have to acknowledge what the sergeant couldn't bring himself to say.

"Simon…" Ram spread his hands – nothing there.

"When?"

"Twenty minutes ago."

The Monks Court arson attack had claimed its third victim. PC Simon Wells had died in the burns unit at the Queen Elizabeth Hospital.

The second Ryland rang off, Bev hit the shower, grabbed a navy-blue trouser suit from the rail and headed for the kitchen. Thoughts racing, she slung two slices of Mother's Pride into the toaster. Was it too early to call the guv? He had to know about Andy soon as. The dithering lasted all of two seconds before her hand went for the phone; it rang before she picked it up.

"Bev. Vince here." Terse. Dead serious. Not the affable Sergeant Hanlon.

Hand over mouth, she listened as he told her Simon Wells and two other people had died in an arson attack at Monks Court.

"If you're near a TV," Vince said, "they'll be running it on the next bulletin."

Stunned, she flicked the remote, watched without seeing the end of an interview with a vacuous blonde selling the latest volume of her life story. The fire deaths led the news.

The Beeb had got hold of an old photograph of Simon from somewhere. Might've been taken during his gap year. The hair was long, the tan deep, the laughing eyes crinkled against the sun. Fucking incongruous, seeing him like that, knowing he was dead, knowing how he'd died. She often wondered how grieving families coped when happy snaps of loved ones were plastered time and again over the media. She had a damn good idea now.

Feeling sick and light-headed, she binned the toast, scribbled a note to Frankie and drove to Highgate in a blur.

Along the corridors, officers huddled in twos and threes discussing the night's events. Every cop had a favourite story about Simon. He'd been a popular guy, twenty-five years old, engaged to a nurse at the General. Never a harsh word to say about anyone.

She overheard a DC mention that Byford was addressing the troops at a special meeting before the brief. There was just time to grab a machine coffee and check her desk for messages.

And dry her eyes and blow her nose behind closed doors.

A couple of minutes later, sitting beside a crumpled-looking Mac Tyler in the conference room, Bev reran the news footage in her head, this time focusing on what had looked like snatched shots of Powell. The DI had appeared pale, gaunt, almost shell-shocked. Might be because of the harsh lighting. But not the gash on the forehead. She wondered how he'd picked that up.

She glanced round, not surprised he wasn't there. Powell would've been on the go most of the night. Every available officer was there, though: seats were full, walls lined, windowsills perched on as they waited for the latest. Word was that Byford was still with the brass on the sixth floor. No worries, Bev thought; the big man could hold his own.

She felt sorry for Powell. If the DI had ordered a police guard, would there have been an arson attack? Had it been her decision, she'd be asking herself the same question. Along with everyone else, judging by the mutterings doing the rounds.

Event. After. Easy. Wise.

The conversational buzz halted abruptly when the doors flew open and the superintendent stalked to the front. With Powell, who strove to match the big man's stride. So the DI hadn't gone home. And no, the harsh lighting hadn't been responsible for his drawn features. As for the guv's appearance, were the salary and perks of rank worth the burden? Everything bowed from the eyebrows down. And she'd yet to tell him about Andy Quinn.

There were a hundred ways to start. Byford chose the one that meant the most. "Simon Wells was a fine officer and a good man." His glance took in every cop before he delivered a dignified tribute in dispassionate tones. The silence was absolute, expressions grim. Bev sensed fury, too. Every man and woman in the room wanted to get their hands on the fire-raisers, wanted justice. Rightly or wrongly wanted revenge. Observing, gauging reactions, Bev almost missed the guv's next words. "DCS Flint will lead the investigation, codename Phoenix." She frowned; thought she'd misheard. Byford glanced at his watch. "He should be here within the hour." She hadn't.

The brass were bringing in a senior officer.

Detective Chief Superintendent Kenny Flint headed up Wolverhampton CID. A sharp disciplinarian who didn't suffer fools full stop, the man was well named. He was known for playing it by the book. No one doubted his ability; but no one was happy about an outsider investigating the murder of one of their own.

"He'll bring in a small team, and supplement it with some of you as and when needed," Byford added.

Using his own people as well? With huge difficulty Bev kept her face neutral, exchanged bland glances with Mac and Daz; tried to catch Pembers' eye but Carol was concentrating on the DI. It was patently obvious the move had been dumped on the guv from a great height. Like the sixth floor.

"It's no slur on anyone here," Byford said. "It's an

operational decision. Don't read anything into it."

Yeah, right. Bev folded her arms, crossed her legs, swung a foot.

"I mean it, Bev." Message received and understood, then. "We're already stretched to the limit."

Two major ongoing inquiries: one small boy kidnapped, suspicious death of another. And now the fire. She gave a brisk nod of grudging acceptance.

"DI Powell will continue as Operation Hawk SIO. He'll take the early brief, then get off home for a few hours. I'm still senior officer on Sapphire. We'll reconvene in the kidnap room in ten minutes."

Could be worse. Flint was investigating the arson attack. Nothing else.

"There may be overlap," he said. "Whatever. We're in this together. Everyone will co-operate. Clear?"

Chairs were scraped back as people rose to get on with it. Byford hadn't finished. "Just before you go. In case there's any doubt, DI Powell has my full confidence." The guv must've heard mutterings as well. "What happened last night was tragic. It should never have happened. But it was down to a criminal act, not a bad call. Given the circumstances, given what we had to go on, I'd have made the same decision."

Bev nodded. Good on you, guv. How many bosses stood next to the fan when there was so much excrement flying around? Powell was lucky; they all were. Thank God the big man had knocked the early retirement idea on the head last year. The very thought of him not being around sent a shiver down her spine.

30

Where was the guv? Bev had checked the other incident rooms and now leant, ankles crossed, against the wall outside his office. There was a pile of stuff to do but she was going nowhere till she'd told him about Andy Quinn's murder. When there were so many inquiry balls in the air, it was easy to drop a communication bollock.

She straightened when Byford appeared at the top of the corridor with a steaming mug in his hand. She could smell the peppermint from here; his irritable bowel was about to turn nasty.

"Guv." She held the door open. "A word."

"Not now, Bev." Uniform had pulled in Jaswinder Ghai, Maxwell's heavy, an hour earlier. Byford was about to interview him. Bev's request was bad timing, given everything else that was going on.

"It won't wait, sir."

The 'sir' alone was enough to make Byford change his mind. "Two minutes." He pointed at a chair.

It took less. The guv's face rarely showed his thoughts. She'd no idea what he was thinking.

"Is anyone in the frame?" he asked when he'd heard her out.

She shrugged. "They're going through Andy's files. Ryland seemed to think it might be some client he pissed off. But…" She shouldn't need to say it.

"But what?"

"Come on, guv. Crawford, Edensor, now Andy Quinn. It's got to be connected."

He considered for a few seconds. "If there is a pattern,

Andy's murder doesn't fit. You say it was a violent attack. No attempt to make it look like an accident."

"Your mates are dying, guv."

"I'm aware of that."

"And you doubt there's a pattern?" Her fists were clenched. "You're the only cop in that line-up who's still alive."

"Do I look stupid?" Her face – unlike his – said it all. "Hasn't it crossed your mind I might be looking into it?"

No. Her mind was brimming already. She hid concern behind truculence. "Yeah? And?"

"Listen. And don't interrupt." He gave her the edited version: the stolen BMW that killed Maxwell's son, the police pursuit, the death threats, the interview with the crime boss, the fact that Maxwell had gone into hiding.

"Fuck didn't you bring him in earlier?" she exploded.

She flinched when he slammed the desk. "Don't tell me how to run an inquiry! Maxwell knows more about the law than most briefs. What was the point of dragging him in with no evidence? Watching him walk away waving two fingers in the air? Even now there's no proof. Just a stack of questions I want answered."

"You're right. Sorry." She swallowed. "Guv, the stolen car, the police pursuit – were you involved?"

He couldn't lie to her. He rose, reached for his jacket. "I've got work to do."

Getting rhesus negative from a small stone would be easier. Byford stared at the man mountain that was Jazz Ghai, willing him to open his eyes let alone his mouth. He reckoned *heavy* was the right word for Maxwell's chief goon. The Asian sprawled, ankles crossed, brawny arms folded, massive thighs encased in denim overhanging the edges of a metal chair. Sleek blue-black hair was pulled taut in a long ponytail, incongruous alongside such overt machismo. Ghai was a giant – without the gentle gene. Hence the two bulky uniforms on the door.

It wasn't that Ghai wouldn't talk; he had words to say. Two of them, repeated ad nauseam.

Byford knew he was in danger of losing it; made a huge effort to stay calm. "Let's try again, shall we?"

Eyes still closed, Ghai flapped a hand as if bestowing permission.

"Why film Robbie Crawford's funeral?"

"No comment."

"Where's the camera?"

"No comment."

"Where's your boss?"

"No comment."

Byford slammed his chair back. He'd had a bellyful. Every question had provoked the same response. Ghai knew nothing – or was saying nothing – about Doug Edensor, Robbie Crawford, death threats, Maxwell's alleged foray into child pornography; Wayne Dunston's delivery round or Daniel Page's kidnap.

The detective hadn't even mentioned Andy Quinn's murder. The MO wasn't Maxwell's style, and it didn't fit the pattern of the other killings. He'd keep an open mind – but as far as he recalled, Quinn hadn't been involved in the crash that killed Maxwell's son.

Byford paced the small airless room, Ghai's after-shave more than a match for the stale smoke and sweat. They were both going round in circles – again. Ghai's stonewall technique was an interview nightmare. Byford had no chance of catching him in a lie, throwing words back in his face. Ghai wasn't suddenly going to trip up. Not over three syllables. No wonder he'd refused a brief. He was brief without a lawyer.

The routine had been going on for more than an hour: sixty precious minutes down the pan as vital inquiry work backed up outside. Byford could hear it: Highgate's corridors buzzed with urgent voices, quick footsteps. And Ghai now feigned sleep.

The detective slipped the e-fits of Doug's alleged assailants into a file. Not surprisingly, Ghai had dismissed them early on. "Right, you're free to go..."

Incredible so much flesh could move so fast. The Asian was bouncing on Reeboks before Byford opened his mouth to finish the sentence. "On condition you let us search your property."

Ghai stiffened, every molecule rigid, face suffused with colour – even the pockmarks. Black granite eyes glittered; Byford caught the merest glimpse of what he was capable of, what lay beneath the skin. For a second, he thought the Asian would lash out. So did the uniforms; they stepped forward smartly.

The heat faded almost as fast. Ghai slowly, deliberately, started cracking his knuckles as a thin smile twisted his mouth. "Be my guest." The sound was surprisingly loud. Byford refused to wince. Not impressed by the hard man. Nor the offer. If Ghai was happy to let them take his place apart, anything they'd want to find had already been removed.

Mike Powell was still at Highgate. The gash on his forehead throbbed and he was so knackered he could barely walk straight, let alone think. What he had to do would only take a minute, then he'd nip home for a few hours' sleep. He dry-swallowed a couple of paracetamol, picked up a pen, mentally reviewed Operation Hawk as he wrote.

He had sensed a level of hostility at the brief but had just about held his own. The squad knew what had to be done anyway; establishing the identity of the dead child was priority. Without a name they had nothing. Hopefully they'd get a steer from the media. The boy's picture had been widely circulated and was getting national coverage, according to Carol Pemberton. Uniformed officers had been out at Paradise Row since first light, knocking on doors, stopping traffic, canvassing people on the streets. Powell briefly closed his eyes. Please God, let there be a development by the time he got back. Maybe the boy's death was one case he could close.

Gently the DI ran a finger along the wound at his temple. It would undoubtedly scar. Not just physically. Every time he saw it, he'd remember. Remember the night he fainted at a post mortem that revived the trauma of his brother's death, the night three lives were lost in an arson attack that could have been prevented.

The decision to bring in Kenny Flint as investigating officer didn't tally with the guv's public vote of confidence. However Byford couched it to the troops, it must be a blow to the big man's professional pride. It had certainly shattered Powell's. He wouldn't even have the satisfaction of nicking the bastards who'd done it. And whatever anyone said, he blamed himself.

The DI sighed, laid down the pen. His resignation letter just needed a signature.

31

The charred hulk that had been Monks Court squatted in the middle of a row of seedy three-storey business premises on Friars Road. As Kenny Flint took his first look at the building where PC Simon Wells had perished, it put the normally prosaic DCS in mind of a blackened rotting tooth. And it would have to come out – or down – as soon as the council made arrangements. The tape closing off both ends of the road wasn't just protecting evidence, it was preventing further casualties.

After a six-hour operation, fire investigators had declared the property unsafe, a verdict confirmed by a local surveyor. It didn't stop a stream of stroppy property owners banging on about access. The uniforms posted at either end did.

Flint paused before ducking under the police tape to have a word with a constable who looked about twelve. It was a bad place to stop. The detective had been spotted by a roving pack of reporters, desperate for a sound bite, and camera people looking for something marginally more interesting to shoot than the exterior of a burned building. Flint certainly looked the part: a hard-nosed copper straight out of central casting, late forties, close-cut greying hair, cool blue eyes and craggy features. A suit-and-tie man, he'd look equally at ease, and in command, in a bomber jacket and jeans.

Half a dozen journos had broken away and were actually running down the road to grab a few words with him. He glanced round at the noise, sighed and masked a scowl. Did he want to talk to the media? He knew the news bureau had issued releases with the official police line on the fire and the tragic loss of lives. Flint hadn't known Wells. Anything he added would sound trite. And he couldn't feed them any new lines until he'd liaised with the fire investigation team who were still on site.

"Superintendent…?"

"Sir…?"

"What's the…?"

"Have you any…?"

"Is there any…?"

They weren't going anywhere. He waited until the bombardment petered out. He needed them on side but was acutely aware that yesterday's reporting on the Selly Oak protest group might have fanned the flames. He'd assigned a couple of DCs to trace and talk to SOAP members. No point getting heavy with the messengers till he knew the score.

"First off," he said, "there's nothing new to add to what you've already got. I'd just reiterate that we're anxious to talk to anyone who was in the vicinity of Friars Road prior to and in the hours following the arson attack at Monks Court."

In Flint's broad Wolverhampton accent, the police-speak sounded stilted, even slightly comic, like something out of Monty Python. His grim features reflected in the nearest TV lens were anything but amusing. "They may have seen something or someone suspicious without realising the significance. I'd ask those people to contact us at the earliest opportunity."

"What times are you talking?" A hack shoved a mic in front of his face.

"I'm not tying it down," Flint said. The arsonists would have recced the place at least once, could have been hanging round for days, weeks even. He didn't want a defined time-frame to deter potential witnesses from coming forward. He wound up with an appeal for the perps to turn themselves in. Everyone knew the likelihood had less chance than a snowflake on a red-hot hob. Flint's raised hands dismissed a chorus of further questions, then he turned his back and walked away in search of answers.

Nigel Blackwell, head of the fire investigation team, stood on the pavement opposite Monks Court surveying the remains. Even as the two men watched, timbers creaked, debris crashed down into pools of black greasy water.

Blackwell was in his late thirties, tall, thin, nervy. His sweaty hand left dirt streaks across his pale face. "I'll tell you something. We're bloody lucky the body count wasn't higher."

The tone was inappropriate, almost upbeat. Flint stiffened. "There's nothing lucky about three dead." There was steel in the voice and the unblinking stare was lethal. "Tell me something else."

Blackwell's thin lips tightened. "I'm telling you: it was luck, not judgment, that no one else died. These people knew what they were doing: they were out to kill. The more the…" Either a belated sensitivity or Flint's incredulity stopped Blackwell in his crass tracks. "Sorry. But the evidence is there."

Flint listened, face impassive, as Blackwell ran through what the team had uncovered. At least four petrol bombs had started four separate outbreaks – two on the ground floor, two on the first. The fires had been located to prevent egress, designed to endanger lives. It looked as if furniture had been shifted to hamper escape further and to provide fuel for the flames. The top floor may have been set alight too; there wasn't enough of it left to determine.

"Evil bastards." There was ice in Flint's voice.

There was more. According to Blackwell, the killers had disabled smoke alarms, dismantled security cameras.

"How come the noise didn't wake anyone?" It was a question for himself as much as Blackwell.

"It did, eventually, or we'd be looking at double figures." The fire investigator brushed off ash that had settled like grimy dandruff. "I'd say there had to be two arsonists, maybe more. And timing was crucial." A few seconds out and a perp risked being trapped in the burning building.

Flint's nod acknowledged the observation. This was no one-man operation. It was team-work, well planned and all too ably executed. On the other hand, all the residents had now been accounted for – but one of the bodies had yet to be identified. Maybe, Flint thought, that's where the bastards' luck ran out.

Byford had spent most of the morning flitting between incident rooms trying to keep on top of an unprecedented workload. The decision-taking and task-assigning was seemingly endless, as was the tsunami of calls and information from officers on the ground. Christ. He was getting too old for all this. Three major ongoing inquiries: three overall pictures to try to maintain in a head that pounded.

He'd just popped back to check his desk and was now eating a cheese sandwich in the comparative quiet of his office. His other hand clutched a report from the search team that had gone through Jazz Ghai's Balsall Heath flat. It looked as if the cleaners had been in. Byford scowled. No surprise there. Half the city's criminal underworld knew the police had been on the Asian's tail; someone would have tipped him the wink.

And Maxwell?

Byford was on the point of calling off the search. Sapphire, Hawk and Phoenix needed every available police body. He couldn't justify allocating cash or resources to flush out Maxwell. Not without something more substantial to go on.

It came in a phone call. He swallowed a mouthful of lunch, lifted the receiver and listened. Then he tossed the rest of the sandwich aside and headed for the control room.

There had been something vaguely familiar about the voice. He asked the officer to play it again, tapped an impatient foot and ran possibilities in his head as the tape was re-cued. The caller was male, sounded local, middle-aged, ill-educated. Whoever it was had also watched the lunchtime news, had seen the e-fits of Doug's assailants.

Them fellows you're after...? Ask Mad Harry...

No one called Maxwell a maniac. Not to his face. Certainly not more than once. Only criminals and cops even knew the nickname.

"Can you trace it?" Byford asked.

The officer shook his head. "Phone box, sir."

"If he calls again, try and keep him on the line." Like the man would call. Grassing up Maxwell was equivalent to suicide. Not that the snitch had given more than a blade or two. But it was enough. Byford decided to keep the search going, see what else might crop up.

The last thing Julia Tate wanted was for other people to classify her as a nosy old biddy, with twitching net curtains and a nose forever stuck in other people's business. Miss Marple she was not, thank you very much. But.

Keeping a polite distance was one thing; it was something else entirely to maintain aloof indifference or, God forbid, criminal neglect. If there was – how should she put it – a *problem* next door, she'd never forgive herself.

Julia poured Earl Grey into a porcelain cup, took a genteel sip. Tea always helped her think. Maybe she was just feeling piqued; she'd always been rather over-sensitive. But Julia had so hoped to make friends with her new neighbour. Not live in each other's pockets or anything vulgar like that. But the occasional morning coffee would be rather nice, wouldn't it?

She sank large yellow teeth into a slice of home-baked granary bread thickly spread with homemade marmalade. A retired librarian, living alone, she perhaps had too much time on her hands. She drifted into the sitting room, munching the remains of breakfast on the way. Look, she thought with a smile, I don't even possess a net curtain. She drew back the wooden shutters and basked for a moment or two in the warmth of the sun.

She also happened to notice that the rather ostentatious motorcar wasn't on next-door's drive, so she dismissed the idea of popping round with one of her Victoria sponges. Maybe later… She ought to try to elicit information before deciding whether to take action.

It must be a month now since the woman had moved in and Julia still didn't know her name. Rather a good-looking blonde with striking green eyes; younger, but surely that didn't matter. Julia thought the woman would have welcomed the kindness an older neighbour could offer. Taking in post? Admitting tradesmen? Keeping a protective eye on the place? Julia hadn't even mentioned baby-sitting, because back then she hadn't seen the little boy. Well, she thought it was a little boy – it wasn't always easy to tell these days, was it? Such lovely hair, though.

Julia sighed. She'd not spoken at all with the woman

since that first time. So she'd had no opportunity to ask if anything was wrong. But surely it wasn't normal for a little one to cry so much… And not just during the day; the sobbing woke Julia at night as well. She'd held a tumbler against her ear and pressed it against the bedroom wall. She couldn't be sure, but thought she heard the little boy cry for his mummy. It couldn't be right, leaving a child so young alone in the house, could it? Julia shook her head. She didn't even think it was legal.

But one was so afraid to interfere nowadays, wasn't one?

A quiet word, the very next time she saw the woman. That's all it should take. Calling social services at this stage seemed so heavy-handed. And yet… the crying haunted Julia. It really needed some more serious thought.

She turned from the window, drifted back to the kitchen. There should be more tea in the pot. She always made enough for two.

August 2000

Holly had known early on not to expect help from her adoptive mother. At thirteen, she'd threatened to tell Satan's wife. He'd laughed in her face. Said his wife had known from the beginning. It was her idea; didn't want him bothering their own daughter. Bothering? Holly had spat in his face.

After that, Satan started to bring other men, other perverts, to Holly's room.

Satan told her she was lucky she wasn't in a kids' home. They'd only adopted her because they thought they couldn't have children. She'd cast her mind back to when Amy was born, how the bitch had doted on the new baby, how the abuse had begun not long after.

Now a few months off her sixteenth birthday, Holly had started to notice how Satan looked at his daughter, how he stood too close, touched too much. Amy was only six. Holly would try and leave her out of the reckoning but Satan's bitch was definitely included.

She lay back on the bed, running the plan through her mind for the umpteenth time. Everything was almost in place. The fire was a last-minute inspiration. But as soon as the idea struck, she realised how appropriate it would be. He'd been Satan to her for so long. She pictured him burning until he was no longer distinguishable from the flames.

32

"Oh joy," Bev drawled. "Another brick wall. Let me beat my head again."

Bev and Mac Tyler were drawing blanks. They'd been mopping up house-to-house inquiries in Windsor Avenue, one of the streets near Daniel Page's school. Bev had shoved notes through several doors, asking the occupiers to get in touch. Then they'd driven round the corner and were now outside Stephen Cross's place. Several birds – one stone – same story.

"Put another card through, sarge. We know he's around. He'll get back to us."

She wasn't convinced, wasn't even sure re-interviewing the guy was worth it, but what the hell. The call came as they headed back to the car, arguing the toss over the best place to grab a late-lunch sandwich.

"They've made contact." Byford's effort to sound casual had the opposite effect. Bev froze, mid-pavement, heart racing. He told her a telecom officer monitoring the Pages' incoming calls had picked it up: a mobile phone in the Kings Norton area. And the signal was on the move. Covert squad cars were out there now, guided by data from comms.

"Where d'you want us, guv?" she asked. Mac had registered the urgency in her voice. The motor was already running as she slipped in beside him.

"With the parents," Byford said.

"'Kay." It was a tad reluctant; being in on the action had a lot more going for it.

Maybe the big man caught the inflection. "I haven't heard

the tape, Bev. But from what I gather, they need all the support they can get."

The voice was distorted, metallic, menacing; the message chillingly clear: *Dan-Dan thinks his mummy's dead.* A click on the tape, then a little boy crying his heart out. It would have shattered stone; it was tearing Jenny Page apart. The woman had only been home from hospital a few hours when the call had come. She was now under sedation upstairs, Richard at her bedside. Bev had spoken briefly to them both; unsurprisingly, neither had recognised the caller's voice.

She and Mac sat uneasily round the kitchen table with Colin Henfield, the family liaison, and the telecom officer Pete Marr who'd monitored the call and issued the alert. Wheels were in motion. Literally. The signal from the caller's mobile was still coming in loud and clear from Kings Norton; comms were still passing information to officers on the ground. After three days' silence from the kidnappers, the police activity would be frenetic, adrenalin levels stratospheric. They weren't the only reasons Bev would rather be out there. Rather be anywhere.

Dark thoughts filled the sunlit room as Marr replayed the tape. Daniel's gut-wrenching sobs were completely at odds with the bright surroundings. The fridge door was covered in gaudy pictures, all in a child's hand: a house with smoking chimney, a grinning fat cat, Mummy and Daddy, Batman, Daleks, daisies. A huge yellow sun appeared in every one. Bev shivered; saw them all through a gauze of tears. Her fists were tight balls as she tried to imagine the little boy's anguish, what she itched to do to his tormentors.

The cries stopped abruptly. Excited laughter drifted in from next-door's garden. It sounded as if the neighbours' kids were splashing round in a paddling pool. The heat was stultifying. Bev rose, closed every window.

Marr leaned forward, hit rewind. "What they've done is record the boy, then play the tape down the phone. There's a distinct click after the voice, then the quality drops off." He made to play it again. Bev laid a hand on his arm, shook her head. Enough already, they'd heard it four times. Voices, screams, sounds stay in the brain as long as visual images. Like forever.

She half-listened as Marr ran them through the intricacies of tracking: it was techno-babble to her. She had a vague idea how it worked anyway, didn't give a stuff about co-ordinates and triangulation, DSM and GPS. All she cared about was the end result – whether Daniel Page would be there. And in what state.

But then Marr's words finally made more sense. Or she thought they did. She frowned, tuned in properly. "Say again, mate."

"The guys at base reckon the signal's still moving." Marr stretched back in the chair, hands behind his head. "Whoever they are, they'll be in a car." He said it like it was a done deal.

"How accurate's all this stuff?" she asked.

"We can track to within fifty metres."

She nodded, thought so. "Long as the phone's switched on?" And the battery didn't die. And it hadn't been nicked. And there wasn't an r in the month. But assuming the best, why make the trace easy? The kidnappers weren't stupid. It didn't make sense.

"What've we got on the phone?" she asked. Every Sim card sends a unique IMSI number, an International Mobile Subscriber Identity. In theory, the police – working with the service provider – should be able to establish who bought the phone almost immediately.

"They're checking now," Marr said. "We'll have a name any time. And the billing address."

She nodded, wished she shared his confidence. The way their luck was going, the purchaser would be Ms Madonna, or if the kidnappers were really imaginative, Mr Mouse. She rose, paced the room, mobile frustration. Everyone was out there doing things and she was sodding baby-sit... She stopped the train of thought.

Colin offered tea; refusals all round. The atmosphere was tense, sombre, claustrophobic. It was like waiting for Godot. At Christmas. The hands of a huge station clock ticked in the silence. It was three-fifteen. Bev did the math: five days, sixty hours, since Daniel's disappearance. Why was he still being held? Why no mention of the half-million quid? What the hell were the kidnappers playing at?

Even Marr jumped when a mobile cheeped. Bev took it from her pocket, held it to her ear. It was comms with an update. She listened, made the right noises. A grim smile tugged her lips as she shook her head. Fucking unbelievable. She'd been well wrong about the name.

According to the data, the cash buyer of the pay-as-you-go phone was a real person and alive, if not particularly well. She was upstairs now – at the billing address – and despite what Daniel had been told, his mother wasn't dead. She just looked it.

"Talk about taking the piss..." Bev took a swig of shandy, ran the back of her hand over her mouth. It was getting on for seven pm. The Prince was providing a late-lunch-early-dinner. After the events of the last few hours, it felt more like the last supper. But it was actually a quick pit stop; there was still a bunch of stuff to check back at the nick.

"Pass the vinegar, Mac."

Tyler shoved the Sarson's across the scarred tabletop. A vigorous shake on to a basket of pallid chips, then Bev said, "Can you believe they used her name? Bastards." And that wasn't the half of it.

Mac, munching pasty, shook his head in rapid response. Bev bit on a chip, glanced across at Byford who was running his index finger round the rim of a pint glass. Distracted or what? She'd bet a pound to a penny she knew what was going on in his head. She'd heard most of it at the evening brief. The kidnappers had run rings round the covert operation in Kings Norton. Literally. It had taken four hours for the circular tracking pattern to emerge. It was spotted eventually by a sharp-eyed operator on the ground who put two and two together and came up with seventy-eight. The number of the double-decker that was taking the mobile – and the cops – for a long ride round the leafy suburbs.

The phone had been shoved down a gap at the side of the bus's back seat. It was with forensics now but if there were prints, Bev'd take a vow of silence. And celibacy.

"They're making us look like prats." Byford could've been talking to himself.

Bev took another chip. Couldn't argue with that. "They'll cock up sooner or later, guv."

"Great. Perhaps they'll be kind enough to let us know when." He raised his glass, sank a mouthful of bitter. A guy who didn't drink on the job and didn't do sarcasm.

By now, he'd heard the recording of the phone call. The tape had been played to a squad already reeling at being given the run-around and with its collective adrenalin rush long gone. If the mood had been rock bottom before, Daniel's cries had hit previously unheard emotional depths.

The contrast between the little boy smiling down from the posters and the pitiful wailing emanating from the tape had made not just uncomfortable but painful listening. Officers had shifted uneasily in their seats, shock etched on stone faces. Bev had sensed more than compassion: there was white fury too. And an absolute determination to get a conviction.

"I've been thinking about the timing." Mac dabbed at the crumbs on his plate, licked his fingers.

"And?" Bev asked.

"We wait, what, three days for any contact. And the minute the mother sets foot in the house…"

Bev nodded. "Almost as if they knew, as if they were waiting."

"And no mention of the ransom," Byford said. "They were demanding half a million at one stage."

"Unless…" She pushed the bowl away. Sick? Or a stir of excitement?

Mac picked desultorily at the leftovers. "What?"

"What if…?" Christ, she could do with a baccy; it always helped the old brain cells. Should never have told the guv she'd quit. She frowned as she thought it through: Richard Page frequently left the house on his own, ostensibly searching for his son; Jenny had been isolated in a private room at the hospital…

Byford was there already. "One or both of them's dealing direct?"

She leaned forward, elbows avoiding spillages on the table. "It's possible, isn't it?" The blue eyes sparkled as she expounded. "Richard Page is never around. He's either looking after the missus or in his study. As for Jenny… how do we know what she was up to, tucked away in the Priory?"

"Has she had any visitors?" Byford asked.

"Leave it with me." She grabbed a biro from Mac's shirt pocket, made a note on a beer mat.

"Come on, sarge. She was away with the fairies last time we were there."

"Was she, Mac?" Bev tucked the beer mat away. "Was she *really*? How do we know?"

"The point is," Byford said, "they've both been in a position where it's a possibility."

"'Xactly." Bev folded her arms. "The Pages could be keeping their distance in case…"

"One of them gives the game away." Mac was finishing sentences now.

"Makes sense," Byford said. "Everyone knows we never give in to ransom demands. If they think paying out's the only way they'll see…"

"I'd do it." She registered the men's shocked looks. "I would." A tad defensive? "Any parent would."

"Reckon they could both be in on it?" Mac asked.

She shrugged. "Dunno." Was it possible Jenny's hysterics were part of an elaborate charade?

"What about the hair and the tape?" he pushed.

"Could've been a lot worse," Byford murmured. "Think about it…"

Of course it could. Body parts: bits that don't grow back. "Could be window-dressing, then?" she asked. Cooked up with the kidnappers to convince the cops there was nothing going on behind the scenes?

Byford sighed. "Anything's possible."

She sank back; suddenly deflated. It was all sodding ifs and maybes. And the scariest bit of all: whether the Pages paid or not, covertly or not, there was absolutely no guarantee they'd get their son back.

33

The evening sky was a flawless blue, more Mykonos than Moseley. High-spirited drinkers had spilled out of the Prince, and were now propping up the walls watching the world, or the female half, go by. Bev sighed. Several hours' graft still lay ahead for her.

"Need a lift?" Byford cocked an eyebrow as he chucked his keys in the air.

Yeah, but not in a motor. "No, ta, guv," she said virtuously. "Fancy the exercise."

"Where you going?" Deadpan. "Worcester?"

She gave him an insincere ear-to-ear smile. Highgate was a five-minute walk. If that. Mac was joining her soon as he'd powdered his nose.

"I'd better be off," Byford said. "I need to catch Mike before he goes."

"How is he? Haven't seen him since first thing."

"He's been better."

She nodded. Not surprised. There'd been zilch progress on Operation Hawk. The DI's teams had been at Paradise Row all day. Daz and Pembers had been going round schools with the dead boy's photograph.

"Bit of movement on the Phoenix inquiry would help," Byford added. "Mike's not said anything about the arson attack, but..."

"What about the CCTV stuff?" She already knew several cameras had captured youths hanging around the Friars Road area; knew the faces were hidden under hoodies. So why ask? Then it hit her. He looked so damn tasty. If she had the bottle, she'd ask him for a date.

Byford was oblivious. "By the way," he said as he put the key in the lock. "There's a collection going round Highgate for Simon."

Passion killer if ever there was one. "Right, ta, guv." The young constable had been in her thoughts off and on all day, like a stack of other things: Operation Sapphire, Operation Hawk, the fire, the SOAP protesters, Andy Quinn's murder.

Thank God they could probably cross that one off the list. Paula Ryland, the Brighton DI, had left her a message during the afternoon. They had a suspect in custody. She'd promised to keep Bev in the loop. Bev had passed it on to the guv soon as she heard. He'd not been surprised.

She gave a mock salute as the big man pulled into a line of traffic, watched until his Rover disappeared. Most likely he was right, and Andy's killing wasn't linked with the other police deaths. She'd not really got a handle on all that; the kidnap took up so much headspace.

Lost in thought, she leaned on the nearest lamppost, lit a Silk Cut, frowned uneasily. There was too much going on, too many snatched conversations, hurried thoughts, half-baked ideas. Not enough time to think things through. A tap on her shoulder made her jump.

"Looking for business, love?"

She glared, then stamped off. Mac struggled to keep pace. He had no idea how lucky he was to be walking at all.

Grant Young had called. More than once. Byford frowned. The media man wasn't normally a time-waster, and it wouldn't be to do with the programme. He'd already told Young he was up for it, assuming he was free when filming began. He slung his fedora on the cactus, checked the time on the messages, dialled back. They'd come in while he'd been out at Kings Norton, liaising with officers on the ground. He hated being stuck at a desk when there was action going on. Action? Bloody fiasco, more like.

"Bill. Thanks for getting back."

"I take it you've got something?"

"Not on Wayne Dunston." Byford wasn't heartbroken. Dunston wasn't going anywhere anyway; he'd been remanded in custody.

"It's more for your porn people. I keep hearing the same whisper…"

Byford froze. Three separate sources had volunteered the same information to the media man. Harry Maxwell was moving into kiddie porn. "People don't like it, Bill. Even the bad guys."

"I owe you, Grant. Thanks a lot."

Was a case against the crime boss beginning to come together at last? He felt a stir of excitement. He'd give a lot to make Maxwell toast. And it was time to turn up the heat.

The phone rang before Bev sat down. She juggled print-outs, shoulder bag, bottled water, and a tub of M&Ms before picking up. "Detective Sergeant Morriss."

"I love it when you talk formal."

"Oz! How goes it?" She smoothed her hair, licked her lips, thanked God it wasn't a videophone. He talked her through Fulham, his flat, thumbnail sketches of colleagues. She ignored a niggle that a female name got more than a fair share of mentions. She pictured his lips moving, those dark chocolate eyes. It was great to hear the dulcet tones, a welcome break from the grind.

"When you up next?" She wasn't begging but he knew it

198

was her birthday soon.

"One of the reasons I'm calling, Bev." Not good. She could hear it. "I'll be away last weekend of the month. Only just found out and I wanted you to know."

Fuckety-shit. "No prob, mate. What you up to?"

"Diversity awareness course."

"That'll come in handy." She scowled, more gutted than she'd admit. "Someone on the other line, mate. Catch you later."

She broke the connection, slumped in the chair, leaped a mile when the phone actually rang. Maybe he'd had a change of mind. "Oz?"

"Bev, it's Jack."

As in Pope. Is there no end to the joy? Mind, she'd wanted a word anyway. "And?"

"Might have something for you."

"Yeah?"

"Can we meet?"

"Not tonight, mate. Up to my neck in it. Before you go..." She stretched a hand to reach the bin. The local rag was in there somewhere. She'd jettisoned it in disgust after a fruitless search for information on the protest group, SOAP. The *Evening News* was the only paper that mentioned it. But even the *News* hadn't named names. Which meant either it didn't have them, or they didn't exist.

"You seen Snowie today?" The paper's crime correspondent stared from the front page in a single-column smug shot: Matt Snow looked pretty pleased with himself. She'd tried calling him a couple of times but he'd gone to ground.

"He was in the Jug earlier," Jack said. "Liquid lunch."

Jug of Ale: Moseley pub. Snowie would need more than a stiff drink if he'd been pissing in the wind.

"Why? What's up?" Jack asked.

"Just wondered." The arson attack wasn't her baby, of course. Maybe she saw it as a way of helping Powell. Either pointing him in the right direction or eliminating a line of inquiry. No point wasting precious time if the SOAP angle wasn't going anywhere. OK, Kenny Flint was SIO, but the DI could do with a break. Anyway, when had she ever kept her nose out of other cases?

"He had a few names for me."

"Oh?"

"Yeah, the SOAP groupies." She crossed her fingers, not for luck; she was telling whoppers. "Said you had them as well."

He snorted. "Maybe if I wrote scripts."

So it was fucking fiction? "How d'you mean?"

"Nothing. Forget I said it."

"Jack?" One word, a million wheedles. She waited, breath bated. He was probably weighing up if he still owed her.

"Sorry, Bev. Can't do it."

"What?"

"Drop a mate in the shit."

"What'd you chuck me in? A bed of sodding roses?" She came out in a cold sweat every time she remembered that news conference. She was still Deep Throat to a few Highgate wags. She pricked her ears: had he hung up?

"Off the record?" he asked.

"Aren't I supposed to say that?"

"If you're gonna piss about…"

"Sorry."

"Snow was flag-flying."

She scored out the reporter's eyes with a biro. "That the same as making it up as you go along?"

"If you like."

"I don't fucking like." She scrawled *tosser* across Snow's forehead. OK, the reporter hadn't started the Monks Court fire but he might have distributed the matches. The story had brimmed with emotive phrases, verbal incendiary devices. "How's the scumbag live with himself?"

"Come on. He wrote a story. End of."

"Yeah. Three lives."

"Fuck's sake. You can't blame Matt for that."

'Course not. Not directly. But didn't Snow's sort of coverage add fuel to all sorts of metaphorical fires? A constant drip of anti-this-anti-that – surely it had to feed a culture of fear and suspicion. And people like her picked up the pieces. She was sick of it. And she couldn't be arsed to argue with Pope. She slammed the phone down before she said something she wouldn't regret.

It was getting on for ten pm before she was ready to hit the road. The M&M tub was empty and the office stank of smoke. Standing on a chair near an open window for a crafty fag or two hadn't really worked. Good job she kept a can of air freshener in the drawer. Tropical Glade. Yeah, right.

She flicked the light, headed for Powell's office. The note she'd scribbled made it clear SOAP was a non-starter. It didn't further the investigation but was worth knowing for elimination purposes. She gave a crooked smile. Knowing the DI, he'd tell her not to stick her nose in anyway.

The light was on, so she knocked. No answer. She slipped in. The paper fairies had been busy in here. Only one A4 sheet on the desk. How come hers was still covered in the stuff? She shouldn't have read it; certainly shouldn't have shoved it in her pocket. She wasn't thinking straight. Like Powell. Must be the bump on his head. Obviously he needed time to mull it over. Something serious as resigning.

November 2000

For years it had rarely been out of Holly's thoughts: getting away, fleeing from Satan and the bitch wife. Escape was so close now. Just another few weeks and she'd be sixteen, legally entitled to leave. Then nothing would keep her here.

She moved to the mirror, gazed critically at her reflection, knew she would more than survive. Tall and slender, she'd grown in other ways too. These days Satan and his evil side-kicks weren't the only men who wanted her. They all looked at her that way. Her beauty turned heads in the street; seemingly natural, though her every sensual move was controlled, every casual gesture calculated. Under Satan's malign control, she'd developed a power of her own. And under his obscene tutelage knew how to use it.

Holly was wise beyond her years, but then she'd had no childhood since the age of ten. Not since Satan snatched it. She gave a knowing smile. She'd been systematically robbing him as well, ever since. Every penny she ever found she squirreled away for her new life in London. With her mother.

She scowled. She hadn't quite worked that part out yet.

The money was concealed beneath a floorboard in Holly's bedroom; every now and then she'd count it, fantasising. She lived in a dream world to keep out the nightmare.

The temptation was to act too hastily. Burn Satan and the bitch on her birthday. Set fire to the house and sling her hook. The best present she could wish for. Almost. Except there'd be too many questions.

No. Patience and planning. She'd steal back one night, after escaping to London, and serve her revenge. But it wouldn't be cold.

WEDNESDAY

34

Hey, my friend! Leave a photo – I forget what you look like!!!
FP xxx

The note in Frankie's distinctive diva scrawl, all loops and curlicues, was propped against the toaster. It was the first thing Bev saw when she popped her head into the kitchen, hair damp from the shower. Would that there was time for breakfast. On the other hand… A smile played on her lips as she grabbed the scissors from a drawer and flicked through Frankie's latest copy of *heat*. That'd do it: Keira Knightley in strapless backless little number. She clipped it to the note and was still grinning when she left the house.

Frankie had a point, though. Bev had hardly been around of late. Baldwin Street felt like a hotel. Shame it didn't have room service, breakfast in bed served by a tasty bloke. Perhaps she'd pick up a bite on the way in. It wasn't that she was running late, she wanted to get cracking.

As she eased into the MG, her cotton dress, the coolest blue in her wardrobe, was already sticking to her skin. Sauna in the city. And it wasn't even seven am. She wondered vaguely how much weight a body lost through sweating. She looked down. Not enough.

She reached for the CD, briefly closed her eyes. Every sodding day she did it, every sodding day forgot. There was no player. She'd had it stripped out, couldn't listen to music in a car any more. Before the attack, it had always been her way of switching off, singing along at the top of her voice, driving a tad too fast. Not now. The rapist had taunted her with tapes played in her home and a police motor.

203

Move on, Beverley, move on. She gripped the wheel, put her foot down. Christ, there were plenty more productive thoughts to keep her going. Her brain had been working overtime in the early hours, compiling a list that would occupy an army. It had been nearly three before she finally drifted off. She stifled a yawn just thinking about it.

Three early birds, all slap and sundresses, were waiting for a bus on the Alcester Road. The women were about Bev's age, shop workers, office staff, maybe factory hands. They were having a giggle, nattering about last night's telly or where to drink at the weekend. Did she envy them? People who didn't take their job home, whose heads weren't crammed with killers, whose lives weren't haunted by death?

Yes. No. Maybe. She turned her mouth down. A few years back she'd not have given it a second thought. Now?

Focus, for Christ's sake, Beverley. She lit a Silk Cut, dropped the window an inch. Current priority was pinning down any possible collusion between the parents and the kidnappers. Mac could check the Priory, find out who'd visited Jenny. As for Bev, she had a financial avenue to explore. Half a million pounds might not be a lot of cash to the Pages but if the handover went pear-shaped it could turn into the costliest mistake of their lives. One that Daniel could end up paying.

Byford's office smelt of peppermint and Pledge. The cleaners had left the polish fumes, and a mug of mint tea stood at his elbow. He'd brought in a flask of the stuff from home to try and combat a flare-up of IBS. Byford had hit the Laphroaig last night, hoping it might help him sleep. Big mistake. The guv was now as irritable as his bowel. There'd been no overnight developments on any of the inquiries – nor the Maxwell case. That could change. He'd told the news bureau to issue a picture to the media and a release about man-wanted-for-questioning. He hoped the hotline number would melt in the heat.

At least, coming in early, Byford had caught up on most of the other paperwork. He skimmed yet another crime-scene report. And heard a faint alarm. He read it again from the top, seeing a line of spinning plates. One lay shattered on the floor.

On Monday, a man and woman in their thirties had been found dead in a stolen fume-filled car in Stirchley. The attending officers had written it up as a suicide pact. Or written it off? The big man pictured a child's body lying in the city morgue, unidentified, unclaimed. Wondered if there was a connection and why no one else was thinking along the same lines. He dialled an internal number. "Mike? A word..."

Powell arrived a minute later, tie askew, looking as rough as Byford felt. Byford noted mauve shadows under the eyes, blood beading from a couple of shaving cuts on the DI's jaw. In all the years he'd known Powell, he'd never seen the DI less than perfectly groomed. "You OK?"

Powell nodded; didn't elaborate. Byford pushed the report across the desk, curious to see if he would read it the same way.

The DI's frown deepened. "Rings a bell, actually." He ran a finger gingerly along the gash at his right temple, still an angry scarlet. "I was at the lab when Overdale got the call-out."

The guv sat back, a tad annoyed that Powell hadn't mentioned it, simultaneously relieved it hadn't been over-looked in the welter of other work. "It's been checked, then?"

"Sorry?"

"The suicides. No connection with the boy's body?" The sites were less than two miles apart, the couple found within hours of the child. Uniform at Stirchley may not have made a link but Powell was SIO, paid to think further.

The DI shook his head. "Never occurred."

"What?" Unbelievable.

"Other things on my mind."

"Tell me about it." It was a sneer, and meant to be. The guv rose, walked to the window, fists clenching at his sides. The car park at the back of Highgate was nearly empty. "Two days you've had squads out there, chasing leads going nowhere." The angrier he was, the quieter he spoke. Powell strained to catch the words.

"Come on, guv. I'm not the only..." The DI's petered out as Byford spun round. Powell had a point, he wasn't the only cop not to spot it. The guv was furious with himself as much as anyone. It wasn't that he'd taken his eye off the ball: there were just too many balls in play. But Powell had been right there on the pitch - knew the pathologist had been called out, knew about the deaths, hadn't acted.

There might be no connection, of course, Byford realised that. But not to have checked was slack. *Like not mounting a police guard at Monks Court?* He'd backed Powell at yesterday's brief, but was there a part of him that sub-consciously thought the DI had fallen short? Byford shook his head, wasn't sure. "Forty-eight hours down the pan."

Powell stiffened, voice raised. "You don't know..."

Byford lifted a hand. "No. I don't. Not yet. But *you'd* best find out. Fast."

"Seen this, sarge?" Mac barged into the office waving a printout. He stopped suddenly, sniffed suspiciously. "God. It stinks in here."

Bev gave a weak smile. "New perfume, mate." She'd only just walked in and was standing at her desk, steaming coffee in one hand and a Subway BLT in the other. She read the report over Mac's well-covered shoulder: a missing person. Then joined a few mental dots. "You thinking what I'm thinking?"

"I checked the A-Z," he said. "Lords Drive's in the next street."

From Monks Court, the scene of an arson attack that had claimed three lives – one body still not identified. And here was a misper from round the corner.

"It came in last night," he said. "No action assigned."

Bev nodded, not surprised given the current workload. And like any cop she knew the stats: two hundred and ten thousand people go AWOL every year in the UK. Most come back safe and well. A tiny number are never seen alive again. Police act in the vulnerable cases, concentrate on the under-eighteens. This guy was twenty-two.

The mother had phoned it in Tuesday evening. Liam Fallon had gone for a drink with mates on Monday night and since then… nada. Early days, but Bev's tingling scalp said otherwise. She sniffed, off-loaded her bits, picked up the phone. "Prob'ly nothing in it."

"Shouldn't we pass it on to Flint's team?" DCS Kenny Flint, the SIO on Operation Phoenix.

"Sure should." She shushed him with a finger. "Mrs Fallon?"

Where the hell was it? Powell riffled through in-tray, out-tray, top-to-bottom drawers, even checked the bin. He could've sworn he'd left the letter on his desk. If he'd had any doubts about chucking it in, he had none now. The guv had looked at him as if he was shit on the bottom of a shoe.

Was he justified? The DI cradled his head in his hands as he recreated the scene in the pathology lab. The pain as his thumb grazed the cut at his temple acted as an unwitting prompt. He'd been out of it when Gillian Overdale got the call. Literally. Carol Pemberton had mentioned it in passing after he'd regained consciousness.

How the hell was he supposed to...? He slammed his fist on the desk. Byford was well out of order. Then the DI saw the little boy's body on the slab. No. Powell was culpable. He should've been thinking on his feet. He just wasn't up to it. Like with the police guard at Monks Court.

For a second, he considered walking. Leaving without a glance back. Knew he couldn't do it. Knew that until the case was sorted, the boy's dead eyes – like his brother Sam's – would follow him, however far he went.

"Has Liam ever taken off before, Mrs Fallon?" Bev twirled a biro, listened for the silences that could say more than words.

"Oh no, bab. Never. He's a good boy. Knows how I fret, does Liam." The Birmingham accent was thick enough to grate. There was something else in the voice: it sounded older than Bev expected. She skimmed the notes she'd made since the start of the phone conversation. Liam lived at home, was unemployed, hoped to go back to college to do A-levels. "Has he ever been in trouble with the police, Mrs Fallon?" Mac was running a check with criminal records anyway.

"Oh no, bab. Never."

"Was there any sort of an argument, misunderstanding?" Bev mouthed along with what had become Mama Fallon's mantra: *Oh no, bab. Never.* "You've checked with his friends? The rest of the family?"

For the first time there was a pause at the other end. "It's just Liam and me. I don't really know his friends."

There was a good deal she didn't know. In Mrs Fallon's maternal eyes, Liam was angel made flesh. But the criminal record Mac had just slipped on Bev's desk suggested Liam's halo had slipped. It was mostly minor stuff – shoplifting, criminal damage, a TWOC or two.

She stiffened. According to the files, Liam hadn't just taken vehicles without consent. He'd torched them.

The Morriss scalp tingled again; her voice gave nothing away. "Right-oh, Mrs Fallon. Leave it…"

"But what will you do?" Bev heard a sob. "If anything's happened…" She pictured a crumpled face, wished she had the answers. She told Mrs Fallon they'd get back soon as and hung up deep in thought.

It might not stand up, of course. Liam could be on a bender or a coach trip to Blackpool. She punched another number. If in doubt, check it out. But someone else would have to take over now. She'd point it in Kenny Flint's direction, just hoped it went somewhere.

May 2001

Holly had arrived in London a few weeks after her sixteenth birthday. She was under no illusion about streets paved with gold. No illusions, period. She had money in her pocket and hatred in her heart. Satan was behind her but still festered in her mind. Soon the poison would be extracted.

First, she had needed a roof over her head and a job to pay her way. Never again in her life would anyone exert control or abuse power over her. For years the beast had taken her body. Now, if need be, she would sell it to strangers. It would be no hardship, she had thought cynically. Needs must, when…

But the devil didn't drive. For once, Holly had an easier ride. She had barely stepped from the train at Euston when a youth worker approached, offered her temporary accommodation, a shabby room in a rundown tenement in Hackney.

The real break had come three days later when a fashion photographer stopped her in the street, said he could get her modelling work. Yeah, right, she'd said. Not that she doubted it. She was well aware of the openly admiring glances, whispered asides. As many heads turned here as at… No, she had thought, not home. Home – like her mother – was a place she had yet to find.

Holly attended her first shoot that week. Three months later, she appeared on the cover of a teen magazine. In demand for her fresh-faced innocence and breathtaking beauty, only Holly knew the canker behind her smile, only she knew the poison in her soul.

35

Bev put the phone down, worked the timings in her head. Should make it before lunch. Having got the bum's rush from the Pages' bank and building society, she'd just had a word with the ad agency. Maggie Searle was the bean counter there and was expected back in ten minutes. She'd certainly know if there'd been any large movements in the account. 'Course, whether she'd be saying…

"Follow the money… Who said that, Mac?"

He glanced up from a monitor. "Deep Throat, wasn't it?"

She glared but he was all innocence; maybe he'd not caught that particular piss-take doing the Highgate rounds. She jumped to her feet, eager for fresh air and a fag. "Right. Come on. Let's hit it." They were dropping by the Priory on the way back from the agency. Mac's phone entreaties to the hospital had been less than fruitful. He'd not elicited a name, let alone a visitors' list. At least if they were face to face the female frost on reception couldn't hang up. Again.

The car keys were at the bottom of her bag. "Shit."

"What's up?"

"Nothing." The DI's letter lay crumpled at the bottom. What the hell had she been thinking? Must've been stark raving mad. Couldn't even put it back now, not with lipstick on it. She scrabbled round for the errant tube top, clamped it down hard.

"Not having a hot flush, are we?" Mac asked.

"Wasted in this job, you are, mate."

Saint Paul's basked and baked in the almost midday heat. The square was a suntrap, the green an anaemic dustbowl. A couple of chirpy sparrows took an impromptu shower under a dripping hanging basket. Bev smiled. "Aaah. Look at that. Cute."

"I'd rather look at that."

She followed Mac Tyler's lecherous gaze. "No chance, mate. Brad Pitt'd be hard pushed to pull a bird like that."

The woman wasn't flaunting it but she oozed sensuality: silky black hair, porcelain skin, bone structure that subtly enunciated class. Bev suddenly realised she'd seen it all before. "Well, well," she said. "If it isn't the lovely Laura." La Foster wasn't wearing the glasses or Bev might have spotted it earlier. It helped that the vision of loveliness had just turned into the ad agency.

Mac arched an eyebrow. "You didn't say she was a hottie." She'd brought him up to speed during the journey, but La Foster in the flesh had the DC's pulse racing.

"Watch it." She winked. "Man your age…"

A brass lion wedged the door open, a couple of electric fans were in evidence as well. Maybe the air conditioning was on the blink. Laura was leaning across reception, revealing a perfect rear profile. She was consulting with the new girl: Chelsea, was it? Bev gave a discreet cough.

Laura turned. "Sergeant? This is a surprise."

Before Bev opened her mouth, Mac had offered a hand. "DC Tyler," he said. "Mac Tyler."

She nodded, slightly uncertain. "How can I help?"

"We're here to see Maggie Searle," Bev said. "I did call…"

"No problem. I've only just come in, so I'm a little out of touch."

Chelsea lifted a tentative hand. "Maggie's not back yet. Held up in traffic."

Laura nodded, glanced round. A well-dressed man, presumably a client, was in the seating area, flicking casually through GQ. Mac was hitching his denims when Laura looked back. "Why not wait in my office?" Bright smile. "I have to go out again anyway."

Least she was polite about it; police were bad for the image business. She ushered them through reception. "Have a seat. I'll get Chel to rustle up some coffee." Bev masked a wry smile; thank God the new girl wasn't a Clapham. She watched as Laura exited, leaving a discreet trail of vanilla.

Mac flopped on to an ivory leather two-seater sofa but the chances of Bev sitting when she could be on the snoop were zero. She prowled round, trying drawers on the desk and the filing cabinet. All locked. She sidled over to the wall, cast a glance at framed letters and photographs. Beaming grins, grateful customers. Boring. Her eyes lit when she spotted Laura's glasses on the desktop. She'd always fancied a pair like that.

"What are you doing?" Mac's bemused smile was reflected in the glass as, stern black frames perched on the end of her nose, she posed in front of one of the picture frames.

"What you reckon? Intellectual, or what?"

"Or what." His glance shifted to the side and he jerked upright.

"There they are." Laura was framed in the doorway, holding out a palm. "I wondered where I'd left them."

Bev's blush was bright red as she snatched off the glasses, handed them over with a faltering smile. "Nice bins."

"Nice bins?" Mac's withering tone matched the look on his rumpled face. He was behind the wheel, Bev jotting notes at his side. She shrugged. More pissed at not getting a steer out of Maggie than being caught red-handed by Laura.

The formidable Ms Searle had been adamant. Without authorisation from Richard Page, her lips were sealed. Bev hadn't really expected much else, even though she'd played every emotional card in the deck. She tapped the pen between her teeth. "What d'you make of Maggie Searle?"

"Seemed straightforward enough." Mac checked the mirror, overtook a kamikaze cyclist. "She was being loyal to the boss."

What about the boss's son? Shame they hadn't done the interview in Richard's office. Daniel's picture gallery might have loosened the accountant's tongue. Bev had got into the habit of carrying the boy's picture round; she slipped it from her bag, studied it for a few seconds. "Sod the Priory – let's hit the Pages. Straight to the horse's mouth."

Mac nodded. "Fine by me."

They drove in silence, apart from forty-mile-an-hour boom boxes – convertibles with mega-speakers blaring music so loud it made your ears vibrate. She caught snatches of reggae, bangra, James Blunt. Yeah, well. She closed the window. "Shall I get a pair, then?"

Mac's frown gave way to enlightenment. "Glasses?"

"Nah. Skis." She rolled her eyes. "Reckon I looked cool?"

"Cool as in…?"

"Classy chick."

"Not quite." He dodged pre-emptively. "I was thinking Nana Mouskouri. On medication."

"My wife's not well."

Bev and Mac were shuffling their feet in the hallway. The reluctant invitation had extended no further. Richard Page looked none too brilliant himself. Greasy hair flopped into

214

his troubled eyes; a hand worried a flaky patch of skin round his unshaven jaw.

"A few words. That's all we need." Bev glanced at Colin Henfield but the FLO had no chance of voicing support.

"I said no." Page's folded arms and planted feet reinforced the message. Short of Colin pinning the bloke down while Mac and Bev legged it upstairs, they'd not be questioning Jenny today.

"OK, Mr Page. But we'll speak to her sooner or later."

"That'll be later, then." It was the way he said it that riled Bev. "Hey! Where are you going?"

The sitting room. She didn't look back. Sun spilled across the carpet through french windows, picked up dust, the odd cobweb. Bev took an upright chair, adopted similar stance, let her body language talk. The prickly silence did the trick, or maybe the fight had gone out of him.

"I'm sorry." Page actually sounded it. "There aren't any how-to books when it comes to your child being kidnapped. Half the time, I don't know what I'm doing or saying. I'm out of my head with worry. I've lost Daniel. And I'm losing my wife..." He turned away. The raw emotion was at odds with the arsy attitude of a minute ago.

It moved Bev but Daniel's ordeal moved her more. "One question, Mr Page, then we'll..." *Leave you in peace?* Hardly. She waited, willing him to turn round, wanting the eye contact. "Mr Page?" It was a gentle prompt. She rose, moved nearer, almost reached out. "Mr Page, I need an answer. And I need the truth."

Upstairs, Jenny was crying, the faint sound an echo of her husband's sobs. The kidnappers were slowly destroying Daniel's parents. God knew what they were doing to the boy. Page was listening but still not looking. She couldn't wait any longer and there was no point pussyfooting round the privet.

"Are you dealing direct with Daniel's kidnappers?" He muttered something she couldn't quite catch. "Sorry?"

He was inches from her face when he turned, squared up to her. "I only wish I were!" Again the mood switch was sudden, unexpected; the voice dripped venom.

She stood her ground. Just. "I'd strongly advise…"

She flinched when he flung out an arm. "I don't want your advice. Six days he's been gone. And what have your lot done?"

"We…"

Like a child, he clamped hands over his ears. "I don't want to know. Get out of my house. Don't come back till you've got something worth saying."

"Never asked, did he?" Bev was driving, needed to feel in control. Page's verbal attack had left her trembling. Initially she'd put her response down as scared, but she wasn't. She was fucking furious.

"Never asked what?" Mac lifted his glance from *The Sun*. Sports pages.

Her hands squeezed the wheel. "If we had any news."

He gave a one-shouldered shrug. "We'd've said straight off."

"Not the point, mate. If you had a kid and it was snatched, it'd be your first question." She ignored his wince as the gears crunched. "Christ, Colin's one of us and he asked before we'd set foot over the door."

"Maybe Page was being protective." He glanced at the speedometer.

Protective of who? His wife? Himself? Who was protecting their son? She slammed the wheel with a fist. "What if he was just dodging questions? Deflect us with a show of emotion?

We got his Mr Mad-With-Grief and a bit from Mr Angry. Guy did the whole sodding gamut, didn't he?"

"He's going through it, sarge. Cut him a bit of slack."

"I'm fresh out of slack, mate. Daniel's hidden away God knows where…" She was welling up. The fury and frustration was aimed at herself and the entire police operation as much as the parents. Six days they'd been at it and were as far from a result as on the first. There'd not been the slightest move, let alone the sense of an imminent break. They were short of witnesses, suspects, forensics. "And we haven't got a sodding clue."

Compared with what they had got, smoke and mirrors looked like bricks and mortar.

The wall had a few dents, dirty smudges and the paper was flaking. Daniel collected the tiny white scraps each time so they didn't stand out against the dark carpet. The nasty woman hadn't noticed, or he'd have been smacked. But had anyone else noticed? The little boy had no idea who lived next door, or if they'd heard him knocking.

He always waited till he was alone in the house. Before leaving, the nasty woman would come to the bedroom and tie his hands and feet with a rope. She used a scarf like Mummy's to gag him. He would wait until he heard the two doors close before shuffling across the floor on his bottom. The knocking wasn't loud because he couldn't work his hands properly. But he had to do something.

If he got out of here, Mummy would be so proud. He tried not to think about Mummy too much. It made him cry and hurt inside. The nasty woman seemed to like it when he cried. He sensed she was losing patience. She snapped at him more and more.

Daniel knocked on the wall as hard as he could, five

knocks, then a count to five, then five more knocks. He repeated the pattern again. And again. And… The little boy pricked his ears, held his breath, then shuffled a little closer to where he thought the noise had come from. Maybe he'd imagined it.

He tried again: knock, knock, knock…

Suddenly the bedroom door flew open. He banged his head against the wall. Or had the nasty woman slammed it? It happened so quickly he couldn't be sure. Like the five muffled knocks he'd thought he'd heard. Were they real or had he imagined them?

36

The seedy house was in a row of condemned terraces in a Stirchley back street. The sash windows were grimy, and grey weeds poked through the brickwork. SOCOs had already searched the property. DI Powell had spoken briefly to one of the officers before driving over to take a look. He left the Vauxhall straddling the kerb, waited as DC Pemberton joined him on the narrow pavement.

The place had been home of sorts to the couple who'd died in a stolen fume-filled car half a mile away. A scrawled note on the dashboard had led police here; led them to believe that the deceased were Irina and Josef Kupiek.

Powell glanced round. The couple had clearly been squatting. The houses were due for demolition and there was an air of squalor and neglect. Previous occupants had probably left the few bits of tatty furniture. Faded daisy-patterned paper hung off the wall in places; bare floor-boards creaked underfoot in others. The electricity had been cut off, so burnt-out candles and used matches were in evidence. Little of the couple remained – no personal documents had been found – so why had the note pointed the police here? And how long had they been holed up? According to the housing department, the last actual tenants had been re-housed six months ago.

"Why stay in a dump like this?" Carol asked. "The council…"

"Hasn't heard of them. They're not on record." Social services, job centre, immigration, national insurance, DVLA, you name it, the DI had been there but the Kupieks hadn't. Officially they didn't exist.

The two detectives wandered, looked round as they talked. "Do you reckon they were illegals?" Carol asked.

Powell had been thinking along the same line. Human trafficking was big business, especially across parts of Eastern Europe. The couple could've fallen off the back of a lorry, shoved by some ruthless bastard who saw them as nice little wage earners. It would explain the lack of documentation. It was a known fact that gang masters withheld passports, official papers, anything valuable as insurance till debt bondage was cleared. Like some time never. And until then, their human cargo was as good as slaves. Unless this pair had done a runner.

"More than likely," Powell said. "Maybe they were hiding here."

"From?"

"Whoever brought them in." Organised-crime fat cats who feed poor suckers a pack of lies, backed up with violence and intimidation.

"Wonder where they came from?"

Albania? Kosovo? Moldova? Lithuania? "Probably never know," Powell said. Photographs and details were being faxed to European emigration officials. But if the couple had come in by the back door, the authorities would never get a hit.

"What about the little boy? Think he was their kid?"

The DI nodded. The search hadn't uncovered anything definite but circumstantial evidence pointed that way. He was pretty sure the relationship would be confirmed once they had the DNA results back. He couldn't work out why the couple had left a note with this address in the car. And he was struggling with another mystery. Why did the child die? Why was his body left on waste ground two miles away?

Unless the gang boss had tracked down his parents and they'd paid the ultimate price. If the boy had been snatched, maybe the couple thought life wasn't worth living, saw death as the only permanent escape. Was the note a final pathetic act of defiance against their masters? Did they want to leave a fuller message, but didn't have enough English? A million thoughts jostled: what a fucking mess. He turned, brushed a finger under his eye.

"You all right, sir?"

"Cut the Spanish inquisition, Carol."

There was a shuffling noise outside. They spun round; the DI ducked as a brick hurtled through a window. Carol took off like a bat on a rocket. Powell was hard on her heels until his foot struck a rotten floorboard. The wood gave way under his weight, pain shot up his leg. He was thigh-high in flooring when Carol returned, breathing hard, swearing softly.

"Fucking little toe-rag got away on a bike." Her eyes widened as she watched him prying himself loose. "Jeez, sir, you all right?"

"Hurts like shit. I'll need a tetanus." He winced as he gently lifted the ruined trouser material. The pale skin was broken, oozing blood.

Carol handed him a tissue. "Kid was this high." She raised a hand four feet in the air. "Probably doing course work for the next ASBO."

Her forced smile faded. She'd spotted something as the DI struggled to his feet. She knelt, reached a tentative hand down through the gap in the wood. The search team had done a crap job.

"What is it?" Powell asked. She shook her head, carefully untied a frayed pink ribbon from a few crinkled yellowing papers. As they were released, a stale smell wafted into the air. Human sweat. The DI picked up on it, pictured one of the couple strapping the bundle next to their skin. A make-shift body belt for items more precious than cash.

Handwritten letters, presumably from loved ones, and a photograph. The picture wasn't recent, was badly creased and the light was poor. But it was unmistakably of a little blond boy with a sunny smile and sea-blue eyes. Powell had last seen his lifeless body lying on a steel slab.

Julia Tate only used the guest bedroom for sewing nowadays. Needlework was not a great passion; truth was, she didn't really care for it. She was in there now, sitting in a wing chair, attempting to thread a purple silk for a fire screen. It would be a raffle prize for the WI Christmas bazaar. Julia gave a wry smile. Given the speed of her handiwork, it might just be ready for next year.

No, when it came to pastimes Julia preferred baking, or sitting down with a good detective story, a crossword, perhaps Sudoku. Enid always called it Sudafed. Julia laid her work down for a minute or so as she pictured her old friend. Her fond smile was tinged with sadness. Enid had died seven months earlier and Julia missed her greatly.

It was one of the reasons she'd hoped to make friends with the new people next door. Julia was sure now that it was a little family, not just the rather pretty young woman and the small child. Julia had heard a man in the house. And it wasn't a voice on the television or the radio. The blush-making noises she'd also heard were not for public entertainment. Certainly not daytime.

Julia picked up her needle again. She'd hate to be thought of as an interfering old busybody but actually it was rather embarrassing. She wondered if she ought to mention how thin the walls were. Naturally she couldn't make a direct reference; that would be so coarse. But a subtle hint?

Not that there'd been any opportunity. Sometimes she thought the new neighbours were deliberately avoiding her. A sudden noise made her jump. Her hand jerked and a bead of blood appeared on her thumb. She sucked it, frowning. Her hearing wasn't what it was but she thought the sound had come from next door.

Yes. There it was again. Someone knocking on the wall. Then silence. Then another knock and another and… Julia struggled to her feet, laid her work on the chair, hobbled across the room. Having sat in the same position for so long, she was stiff. She lowered herself gingerly to her knees, ignoring the complaints from ageing joints. A pattern emerged. Five knocks, five seconds' silence, five more knocks.

Was it the child playing games? Did he want her to answer? She gave a little smile, then rapped the wall with her knuckles – once, twice, three times, four, five…

The scream made Julia's blood run cold. And the loud thump. Had the little one fallen? Was he hurt? Julia covered her mouth with her hand. The woman's voice sounded very cross. Had she smacked him?

Clutching the wall for support, she struggled to her feet, torn with indecision. Maybe she was a just a lonely old woman letting her imagination run away with her. Maybe they'd been hanging pictures or something. But not once had she seen the child leave the house or a playmate visit. And surely he should be in school? It wasn't healthy to be cooped up all the time. And the cries still haunted her.

The uncertainty had drifted too long. Julia headed for the stairs, mind made up. If the woman didn't answer the door this time, Julia would phone the authorities.

Better safe than sorry, as her old friend Enid would say.

"Come in, come in. Sorry about the mess. You'll have to take me as you find me."

Darren New and Sumitra Gosh exchanged bemused glances as they followed a scrawny little woman through an immaculate hall into a pristine front room. Nell Fallon's council house in Lords Drive was a minuscule palace. Darren almost offered to take off his shoes.

The detectives were currently on loan to Operation Phoenix and DCS Flint had assigned them what Daz regarded as a particularly short straw. Long one was Sumitra. He'd clutch on to her any day. Sumi had the whole Bollywood thing going for her – blue-black hair, café-latte skin, dark chocolate eyes. Best of all, he reckoned, she was smart without being lippy. Well, she didn't answer back. Much.

"I take it you've not heard from Liam, Mrs Fallon?" Daz's glance took in spotless surfaces and hoover tracks in a speck-free carpet. Plastic sheets squeaked as he and Sumi perched in synch on a gold brocade settee. The air smelt of pine forests, sweet peas and bleach.

"Not a word, bab. It's not like Liam. I can't understand it." Neither could Daz; he needed a phrase book to decipher her accent. The old woman's hand signals were lucid. She was running bony fingers with bitten nails through lank greying hair.

Mrs Fallon clearly spent more time on the house than herself. Washed-out and weary, there was a slight though constant wobble to the cast of her head. It put Darren in mind of a cheesy nodding dog in the back window of a car. Poor old dear was either wired or in the early stages of Parkinson's. He watched as she jammed pink chapped hands in the pockets of a blue nylon overall.

"Sit down, Mrs Fallon." The hovering made him uneasy.

"There's tea in the pot." She edged backwards towards the door. "Shall I...?"

"I'll get it." Sumi smiled. "You stay and talk to DC New."

There was a matching armchair, gold velvet, clear plastic. Reluctantly she took a seat, wringing her hands in her lap. "He never goes off. I worry, see..."

Darren nodded; certainly did. "Who does Liam knock round with, Mrs Fallon? Can you give me his mates' names?"

"I would if I could. But you know what kids are. It's all nicknames these days."

He took out a notebook. "Tell me what you can, love."

She ran through what little Darren already knew. That Liam had left the house on Monday night and she'd not heard a word since.

"Did he say where he was going, who he'd be with?"

She rubbed the back of her neck. "I've been racking my brains but I can't seem to think straight."

Senior moments? She was certainly getting on. Looked old enough to be Darren's gran. "Is he seeing anyone?" The blank look was probably genuine. He prompted. "Has he got a girlfriend?"

She hesitated slightly, circling a thin wedding ring. "Not that I know of."

The generation gap still bugged him. How to broach it? He turned back a page or two. "Can I just check Liam's age with you, Mrs Fallon?"

She looked down at her hands. "Twenty-two. Just."

"Only child, is he?"

Casual delivery but she stiffened, appeared to be debating whether to answer at all, let alone what to say. Darren opened his mouth but she spoke first, confirming his suspicions.

"He's not mine. His ma did a bunk when he was a nipper. I'm his nan."

It clearly gave her grief talking about it. Who else hadn't she told? "Liam knows, does he?"

She bit her lip. "Found out a couple years back." Her hands would be raw if she didn't stop rubbing. "He's OK about it. Still calls me Mum and everything."

Darren nodded. "Can I take a look in his room, Mrs Fallon?"

"Oh no, bab. He wouldn't like that." She placed a hand against the side of her face. "I never go in there." She jumped up, took the tray from Sumi and bustled about sorting cups. Her hands shook so much he thought she'd chip the china.

"Liam's room?" Darren persisted. "It might point us in the right direction. Help us know where to look."

"Maybe in a day or two." Still playing mum, she couldn't or wouldn't meet Darren's gaze. "If he hasn't turned up."

Sumi asked if she could use the loo and the old woman's relief at the distraction was obvious. Darren could've forced the issue but the woman was a bundle of nerves. More pressure might push her over the edge. And there was more than one way to skin a cat. "Have you got a recent photograph of your grandson, love?"

A smile, the first since they'd walked in, lit her drab features. He waited as she searched the drawers of a heavy oak sideboard. "Here you go." Liam Fallon didn't take after his grandmother. Blessed with preppy clean-cut looks, he could do male lead in a soap – the Australian variety, not *EastEnders*.

"Good-looking boy." He studied it a few seconds before slipping it into a breast pocket.

"What will you do?" She lifted a cup to her lips but was

shaking so much couldn't drink from it.

"It's early days, love, and Liam's an adult…"

"But he wouldn't just go off. I know him, officer. He wouldn't do that. He'd call, let me know where he was."

"You've tried his mobile?"

"Of course."

Darren rose as Sumi returned. "We'll look into it further, Mrs Fallon. Try not to worry. Let us know when Liam gets in touch."

"Anything?" Daz's question was out before the door closed.

"Kitchen was clean." Sumi was dead serious, but when Daz burst out laughing she pulled a face as it dawned. "You know what I mean. Not so much as a mug with his name on." Let alone a signed confession.

A brace of teenaged mums barging buggies two abreast down the middle of the pavement forced the detectives to give way. Both girls had a fag on the go and were yacking into mobiles. Daz shook his head. "And they say conversation's dead."

Sumi waited until they were in the Peugeot, then slipped an evidence bag from her pocket. The hairs were blond and plentiful.

Daz's eyes lit up. "Nice one, Sumi. Not just a pretty…"

Her glare cut Daz off at the pass. "And this." She held another evidence bag aloft. Daz could see her smile through the plastic – and a toothbrush.

"Don't do things by halves, do you, Sumi?" With saliva and hair, they could probably fast-track DNA results.

"What now?" she asked.

"Get the samples to the lab. See if Flint wants it taken further."

They had a few names to go on, teenagers who were on

record as Liam's partners in crime. They could maybe shed light on his whereabouts. Daz reckoned any decision would depend on the DNA results. If there was a match between Liam and the unidentified body from the fire, the inquiry would shift a gear or five.

Cannock Advertiser, 12 June 2001

Fire kills family

Three members of the same family perished when flames swept through a detached house at Cannock in Staffordshire last night. Thirty fire-fighters tackled the blaze that took the lives of Hannah and James Piper and their six-year-old daughter Amy.

One fire-fighter broke down in tears as he described hearing terrified screams from upstairs. But intense heat and thick black smoke prevented rescuers from entering the property.

ALARMS

The cause of the blaze is not yet known but arson has not been ruled out. Smoke alarms were fitted but unconfirmed reports suggest they failed to operate. The tragedy has led Staffordshire police to issue this warning. "It's vital smoke alarms are checked regularly. Had the alarm been raised earlier, this appalling loss of life might have been averted."

Mr and Mrs Piper were teachers at the town's high school. Amy was a pupil at Lea Bank Primary where prayers were said for the family at assembly this morning.

Neighbours told the *Advertiser* that Mr and Mrs Piper's elder daughter, Holly, had left home several weeks ago. One woman who didn't want to be named said: "Thank God she was away – or the entire family would have been wiped out."

37

Eight pm, Highgate. Bev stood in her office, forehead cooling against the windowpane. She watched a couple of police cars take off in a flurry of squealing tyres and hot rubber, shook her head and sighed. Traffic cops were so *Top Gear.*

Her emotions were less heated since the earlier stand-off with Richard Page. Several hours' phone-bashing and paper-pushing usually had that effect. Shame there wasn't more to show for it. The absentee home-owners from Edgbaston had been in touch and were now eliminated as potential witnesses. But the Stephen Cross box had yet to be ticked; their only witness still couldn't be arsed to put in a call.

On the personal front, her mum had phoned, wondering if she'd emigrated, and Frankie was threatening to swamp Moseley with missing posters as in *Have you seen this woman?* A big case took precedence over family, friends, food and the other f-word. She sniffed. Chance'd be a fine thing.

Turning back to the office, she pulled a face. The waste bin said it all, circled as it was by screwed-up balls of paper and crushed Red Bull cans. Too much caffeine quaffed, too many theories bitten the dust.

One idea hadn't been discarded. She'd already bounced it off Mac. Time to share it with the guv. 'Course, she could have floated it at the late brief but then she'd have no excuse to drop in on the big man. She combed her hair with her fingers and pinched a bit of colour into her cheeks.

For a second, she thought he had someone in with him. Then it registered: the guv was using the cactus as a hat stand. The fedora hung at a jaunty angle. The man himself had his feet on the desk, hands clasped behind head.

"Hard at it, then?" She smiled; wouldn't be surprised if he'd been catching a few zeds. His eyes were bloodshot and the skin underneath matched the smoky grey irises.

"Are you just here to have a go?" He swung his legs down, stifled a yawn. "Good thinking, by the way."

"Oh?" She perched opposite.

"The Liam Fallon angle?" The Selly Oak misper she'd pointed in DCS Flint's direction. "There could be something in it. Kenny's pursuing it, he's put Darren New on the case tracking down Fallon's associates."

"Tickety." A few credit points could come in handy. Not that she was crowing. "Makes you wonder how much slips through the net, though." Actions not taken, statements not followed up, calls not returned.

"You heard about Mike Powell, then?" Byford asked.

Hadn't everyone? Talk about kicking a guy when he was on the carpet. It was so easy to point the finger. OK, he'd been a bit slow off the mark but given the same circs, it would be 'there but for the grace of God' for most cops. Herself included.

She bristled on his behalf. "He's well made up the lost time." She'd read his report. The dead couple's relatives had been traced through the letters, and arrangements were underway to fly the bodies back to Albania for burial. He'd established who, where, when, what. The biggie was still elusive: why.

"You're very supportive all of a sudden," Byford said. Powell had never been Bev's flavour of the month; nasty taste in the mouth, more like. But he was like an old pair of slippers; she hated the thought of having to wear in another pair.

"Better the devil you…" She left the implication hanging.

"Do you know something I don't?"

Should she tell him? Break a confidence? That was a laugh. Like the DI had shown her his resignation. "No way. Just... he's up against it. If I were you, I'd have a word."

"I have." Byford picked up a pen, initialled a sheet of paper. "He's not about to disappear, if that's what you think." He glanced up before she had time to close her mouth. "Mike had a bad day. We all do. He offered to resign, then changed his mind."

Been there, done that. "So the letter..." Game. Away. Given. Shit.

"The letter on his desk? He's furious. Thinks some idiot stole it for a laugh." Byford paused, locked glances with her. "I told him no one would be that stupid. What do you think, Bev?"

She giggled like a schoolgirl on helium. "Honestly. As if. What is he like?"

He raised an eyebrow. "You tell me." She had the grace to drop a sheepish glance; he wasn't asking for a thumbnail sketch of the DI.

"Anyway, guv." *Moving on.* "We need a tail on Richard Page." Moved too fast, she could see the guv wasn't with her. She'd had more time than him to consider. And the more she did, the less she liked the fact that Daniel's father disappeared whenever the fancy took him. Even if he wasn't colluding with the kidnappers, the guy could be up to all sorts of dirty tricks. In this business it was either follow the money or *cherchez la femme.* If Page was playing away from home it raised a zillion questions.

"Have you any idea of the cost?" The big man stroked an eyebrow. "We're already over budget, running three major inquiries plus the bread and butter stuff. And you want surveillance on a man who happens to rub you up the wrong way."

"Below the belt, guv." She hadn't needed to pinch her cheeks, the remark was like a slap in the face. "Give me a bit of credit."

"You're asking for a blank cheque." He pointed at the door.

"Nice to see you're thinking about it." She sat back, crossed her legs.

"Good night, sergeant."

She folded her arms. "That's what I like about you, guv – open mind."

He tightened his lips. "We're keeping an eye on Page." The voice was menacingly soft. "You know that." Just not 24/7.

Like Simon Wells had kept an eye on Monks Court? She swung a leg. "I don't think that's enough." His expression was difficult to read. In one way, she conceded, he was on the money: Page had got right up her nostrils. But it was more than that. Six days the kidnappers had held Daniel, six days without hand-over instructions, six days without any sign of closure. It stank. Like rotting fish.

Byford shook his head. "No can do."

She shrugged. "OK." She could tell by his eyebrows he'd expected a harder time. She also sensed he'd not budge, weighed down by pressure from top brass and bean counters. Balance sheets? Boy's life? Close call. Over-harsh, ludicrously simplistic, she knew that. It didn't stop a cynical snort.

"What's that supposed to mean?" he asked.

She held out empty palms. No mileage arguing. It wasn't a battle she'd win. She needed more ammunition. Maybe get hold of a few rounds by keeping unofficial tabs on Page's movement? She wondered if Mac would be up for it as well.

"Whatever you're thinking," he said, "don't."

"You don't fancy a pint, then?"

Byford didn't fancy a pint. He was dog-tired and there was little to celebrate. It had been another frustrating day: pushing paperwork, monitoring reports, liaising with Powell and Kenny Flint. Developments in the Hawk and Phoenix inquiries highlighted the lack of success in Sapphire. As for the Maxwell hotline, it might as well be ex-directory.

He opened the bottle of malt he kept in a filing cabinet and poured an inch into a paper cup. He hadn't eaten since lunch; the scotch burned a path to his gut. Reluctant to return to an empty house just yet, the detective adopted his habitual thinking pose: head back, feet on desk. Bev's gibe about an open mind had hit a raw nerve. He'd been unwilling to authorise a round-the-clock tail on Richard Page, but had ordered search teams and surveillance on Maxwell. Not that she was aware of that.

Like the rest of the squad, she was wrapped up in the Page inquiry. If she regarded Maxwell at all, it was as a side issue. And maybe she was right. Byford feared he was in danger of becoming obsessed with the man. He'd barely discussed the case with Bev or anyone else. He felt he was ploughing a solitary furrow.

Except for the media. Maxwell's ugly mug was still getting a fair share of exposure. A last resort, maybe. Byford hoped it'd pay off. He raised the cup, sank the contents, half-smiled at the thought that popped into his head: here's looking at you, Harry.

The water sloshed over the sides of the glass as Jenny Page's hand jerked. Desperate for sleep, she swallowed the pills one by one. Staring in the mirror, she barely recognised her reflection. And didn't care. Didn't care either about the fine house, the gleaming cars, the designer clothes – none of it meant a thing. All she wanted was her son. And he was beyond her reach. Jenny Page, so accustomed to being in control, was at the mercy of faceless monsters. Since Daniel's disappearance, she'd existed in a state of absolute constant terror, had never imagined such mind-numbing fear existed.

With pale slender arms stretched out to maintain a precarious balance, she drifted to the side of the bed. She was dizzy; her face felt on fire, her hair plastered to her scalp. She'd burned the other notes – taunting, torturing threats – flushed the charred flakes down the toilet. She retrieved the latest message from where she'd hidden it inside a satin pillowcase, read the instructions again. Where she should go, what to do with the money. And what would happen if she failed, or involved the police.

He'd be killed in forty-eight hours if she didn't do what they said. But could she trust them? How could she be sure they'd return Dan-Dan?

Jenny pictured the woman detective she'd so nearly confided in: DS Morriss, was it? Bev? The wooziness was getting worse, her forehead felt clammy, she had to lie down. Maybe Richard was right. Bringing the police in could be a fatal mistake. How had he put it? Ruthless professionals against a bunch of amateurs. Poor Richard was a pawn too, making the pick-ups, sneaking the vile notes back to the house. If only she could sleep for more than a couple of hours at a stretch. It could clear her thoughts. Maybe make a decision a little easier.

Daniel's t-shirt lay on top of the duvet next to her. Jenny buried her face in it, though all trace of the little boy's scent had gone. She broke down, sobbed herself into troubled sleep, oblivious of the tears that soaked into the soft cloth.

38

Emmy Morriss wiped the tears from her eyes. She'd not laughed so much since last dropping by Baldwin Street. Not that Bev was back yet. "Eeh, you should be on stage, girl."

"Darlink, I am." Frankie tossed a glossy curtain of ebony curls, slapped theatrical hand to forehead. She had singing gigs lined up for months but it was her miming talent that was creasing Emmy. "Your turn, Mrs M."

"Y'know what I mean, lovie." Emmy plucked a card from the box. "You should be a star. Get yourself on one of them shows."

"*Sky at Night?*" Frankie delved into a family pack of liquorice allsorts. They were playing Charades. Bev's mum was a games freak: she'd play Battleships on the *Titanic.*

"I'm serious," Emmy sniffed. "*The X Factor,* something like that. You'd run rings round that lot."

"Don't give her ideas, Mum. Head the size of a planet as it is." The twinkle in Bev's eye softened the barb. A twinkle the spit of Emmy's.

"Bev!" Mrs Morriss rushed over, drew her daughter into loving arms. Frankie fixed her best friend with a stare and pointedly bit into one of Bev's favourite sweets. "Do I know you?" she asked, deadpan.

"Funny girl." Bev ambled over, snatched the pack. "That was the last one!"

"Get over it, muppet."

"Moose."

"Ming…"

"Girls, girls." Emmy called them to order just as she had

for twenty-odd years.

The banter continued, good-natured, familiar; it gave Bev a rosy glow, like the warmth of the welcome from two people who mattered in her life. They were as far removed from the arse-wipes she came across on the job as chalk from mature cheddar.

Even without the gales of laughter, Bev had known the second she stepped in the house her mum was there. Wherever she went, Emmy trailed a signature scent of orange shampoo and peppermint. The chocolate cake and cheese scones on the kitchen table gave the game away as well. Bev's quick peek in the freezer had confirmed the mercy-dash nature of her mum's mission. There was enough comfort food to keep her and Frankie going for a month. Chili, shepherd's pie, lasagne, stews, soups. Eat your heart out, McDonalds. There was an opened bottle of frascati too. Silly not to, wasn't it? She'd grabbed it and headed for the sitting room, but rather than wade straight in had stood and eavesdropped on the two women for a moment.

The girlish giggling was infectious; an unwitting grin had spread across her face. It gladdened her cynical cop's heart to hear them joshing round. Christ, sometimes Frankie got on better with Em than Bev did. Not that Bev minded. Frankie had lost her mum when she was a kid. If Em wanted to play surrogate, that was fine by Bev.

She'd been taken aback for an instant, though, when she'd peeped through the half-open door. People always said she and Emmy were two peas in a pod but this was the first time Bev saw where they were coming from. She sniffed. Em must've had a facelift. Bev couldn't possibly be showing her age.

Now she sat round with them drinking wine, chewing

the cud, snaffling a bowl of nuts. Frankie's latest demo CD played in the background as they talked birthdays, books and blokes. When Frankie slid over with the frascati, Bev held out a glass but Emmy covered hers with a hand. "No thanks, sweetheart. I'd better get home."

Bev hauled herself to her feet. "Gran OK?"

Emmy screwed up her face, searched for her keys. "Not brill." It was two years since the vicious attack on Sadie. The old woman rarely ventured out now and was nervy staying in alone. "Vi from next door's with her."

Bev nodded, unsmiling. Her spiky feisty gran reduced to needing a sodding babysitter. Bev had reduced the scumbag attacker to a bloody pulp. His wounds would be healed now; Sadie would take her scars to the grave.

"She'd love to see a bit more of you, Bev." It was gentle but an admonition nonetheless. Fact was, it pained Bev to see the old lady. Sadie's way of coping was to talk about it, relive the trauma over and over. It revived memories Bev desperately wanted to let go. "I'll do my best, honest."

Emmy paused in the hall, studied her daughter's face. "Looking a bit peaky, sweetheart. You OK?"

"'Course I am." Felt like shit, had for a couple of days. Went with the bad-diet-lack-of-sleep territory. She let Emmy get to her Punto at the kerb, then called, "Thanks for the grub, mum."

Emmy blew a kiss. "You're welcome."

"Did I tell you I'd gone veggie?"

"Yes, dear. And I'm Linda McCartney."

Maybe it was the nuts or the slab of chocolate cake, but there was a storm brewing in Bev's gut four hours later. Staggering to the bathroom, she vowed never to let food pass her lips again. After sluicing her face and brushing her teeth, she stole to the kitchen, helped herself to a bowl of Frankie's cornflakes.

Sneaking cereal upstairs and scoffing it under the bed-clothes reminded her of illicit midnight feasts when they were kids. Mind, the orthodontically aware Emmy would've had a fit had she known. Bev sat cross-legged on the duvet, feeding her slightly guilty face. She smiled fondly as she pictured her mum. She loved the old bird to bits, couldn't imagine life without her. It was inconceivable, going through life without a mother's love. Look at Frankie. OK, Gio Perlagio would die for his daughter. But Bev knew Frankie would give her right arm to have her ma back.

The spoon froze halfway to Bev's mouth. Jenny Page had lost her mother too. A daughter had died at birth. And now her son's life was in danger. Bev closed her eyes. How much of a battering could the maternal bond take?

How far would Jenny Page go to get her son back?

The cornflakes lost their appeal. Deep in thought, she slipped the bowl on to the bedside table. Jenny hadn't said a word to Bev about the stillbirth; she'd not exactly opened up about her mother's death. Then again, Bev hadn't been able to get near Daniel's mother for days.

She reached for a notepad next to the lamp. A minute later, the to-do list had a new top line. If the Pages were deliberately keeping the inquiry in the dark, a few checks first thing might just shed some light.

THURSDAY

39

Edgbaston wasn't on the way in to work for Mac Tyler, but he generally followed through on what he said. He had an eye for detail and despite the borderline scruffy appearance was a sharp cookie. The lumberjack-wannabe look was deliberate. People often underestimated him; it was well sweet when they came a cropper.

Mac had no reason to suspect the elusive Stephen Cross was anything other than a witness, a pretty unreliable one at that. But the fact he'd not bothered to make any return calls bugged the DC. Showing a bit of common courtesy didn't hurt, did it?

He cruised past Cross's pad a couple of times to suss signs of life. One more lap and he'd pull over, pay a personal call. He'd finish the bacon roll first before it got cold. Priory Rise was more muesli-and-smoothie territory. The DC cast a few envious glances as he drove, reckoned his finances could just about stretch to a garage. Make that a kennel. Still, at least his imminently ex-missus had agreed to let the boys stay this weekend.

He glanced in the rear-view mirror, caught sight of a fit-looking lass coming out of one of the houses near Cross's place. He gave a low whistle. Even at this distance she was well tasty, legs up to her ear lobes. He drove on, taking in the sights. Summer was good for tottie: high temperatures, rising hemlines; great for bird-watching.

His face froze; the three-point turn was fluid and fast. The woman hadn't emerged from a house *near* Stephen

Cross's. It *was* his place. And unless Mac was very much mistaken, the bird he'd fancied a minute ago was one he'd spotted before.

"Laura *Foster*?" Bev's voice was so high-pitched it went off the register. Throat cleared, she tried again. "Laura Foster? You sure?" Another early bird, Bev had been busy catching worms of her own when Mac called. But it looked as if her DC had netted a big one.

"I was," he said. He'd given chase, but Ms Foster – if that's who it was – must've had wheels round the corner. He told Bev he'd tailed a Porsche for a couple of miles, thinking Laura was driving. At Fiveways roundabout, he'd clocked the face properly. Turned out to be some cocky bloke who gave Mac the finger for giving him the eye.

The DC was now on his mobile standing outside Cross's executive pile back in Priory Rise. Short of a battering ram, he wasn't going any further. No one had answered, let alone admitted him, despite repeated hammerings. Mac's activities were attracting more attention from a man across the road dragging an ancient spaniel and the woman at number eight who was a dead ringer for the Duchess of Cornwall.

"And now?" Bev sucked a biro, thoughts racing. What was Richard Page's right-hand woman doing with Stephen Cross? Cross hadn't given them much, but he was the only witness they had to what could have been Daniel's kidnap. "You still sure?"

Mac hesitated. Wished he'd focused more on the face. "Wouldn't swear to it."

"Shit."

"What does Cross do?" Mac asked.

"Architect. He's not a client of Page's, if that's what you're thinking." The ad agency list was on her desk; she'd already double-checked. She'd run Cross's details through criminal records days ago; they'd come out clean. "Even if he was on their books, why would she pay a home visit? And so early?"

"Working breakfast?"

She snorted, didn't buy it.

"Bit of how's your father?" Mac suggested.

"Shagging?" Her lip twitched. For an old lech, Mac didn't half mince his words.

"*Tres* eloquent."

Didn't matter how you put it, she doubted Cross put it anywhere near the female of the species. "I'm sure he's gay."

"Maybe he just hadn't come across the lovely Laura when you saw him."

"Fast fucking workers, then," Bev drawled. No, if Mac really had seen Laura leaving Stephen Cross's place there had to be another reason. She'd just not come up with it yet. Not when she was still trying to get her head round the worms she'd unearthed.

"What now, sarge?"

She sighed. No sense staking out the place. Couldn't afford to lose a body for one thing. "Best get to the agency. Hear what Ms Foster has to say." Phoning wasn't an option. If Laura had gone straight to the office, she'd be wearing the same gear. Might help Mac make the ID. And for anyone with something to hide, lying was a lot easier at the end of a line.

"Mac?" All she could hear was a dog barking and muffled voices in the background. She tapped the biro; at this rate she'd miss the brief. She assumed the heavy breather now offending her ears was Mac. "What was that all about?"

"Sorry, sarge. Some nosy twat over the road reckoned I was casing the joint and called the cops. I nearly got arrested."

At about the time Mac was evading arrest, there was no such get-out clause for Harry Maxwell. Control was on the phone to Byford: two uniformed officers acting on a tip-off to the hotline number had picked Maxwell up in a not-so-safe house in Handsworth. The crime boss was in the back of a police car on the way to Highgate, threatening to sue the arse off everyone from the Chief Constable down.

The steer must have come from someone in the know. Maybe there was honour among thieves and pimps. And porn chiefs? Byford allowed himself a raised fist and a silent *gotcha*. A slow smile spread across his strained face as he replaced the receiver.

Julia Tate had been hanging on for six minutes and fifteen seconds. The phone dug into her neck. She tapped nervous fingers on the kitchen table in time to a perfectly dreadful recording of Vivaldi. The old woman sighed, but supposed even a muzak version of the *Four Seasons* was preferable to the tinny singsong voice that kept telling her how important her call was to them.

"Vital, obviously," she drawled. She slammed the receiver on the rest, cradled her chin in her hands. Maybe it was God's way of telling her not to interfere? She sighed, reached for her cup, took a sip and grimaced. Even the Earl Grey was stewed now. She'd have coffee when she popped into Highgate.

Chores first. It was important to stick to a routine. She flicked surfaces with a duster, reflected on her frustration. It wasn't the first time she'd failed to get through. Fobbed off and cut off, she was now thoroughly browned off. Social services was a misnomer in Julia's book. The only real person she'd spoken to had been both condescending and incompetent. He couldn't help blah blah, she'd been transferred to the wrong department blah blah, she needed to contact blah blah. And then the call had been disconnected.

She swept the carpet with a glance; the hoover could stay in the cupboard. She wandered to the window: next door's drive was empty. Were they out? Should she knock again? Since the scream yesterday afternoon, she'd heard nothing. Was she seeing mountains where there were only mole-hills?

Julia folded her arms, stiffened her resolve. She would not be cowed. She knew what she'd heard and she'd rather make a fool of herself than do nothing. A few minutes later, she slipped through the front door wearing her new purple suit. It was important to maintain standards. She needed to pick up a few bits and pieces from the shops, told herself she had to pass the police station anyway.

The early brief had already kicked off when Bev crept into the kidnap room. Byford, pacing in front of the white-boards up at the front, registered her late arrival but didn't acknowledge it. She raised a hand in mute apology, sank into a hard chair at the back, glanced round at the troops. It was 8.22, day seven of Operation Sapphire and the squad looked dead on its feet. Missed sleep, skipped meals, lost chances. She knew the feeling. Her broken night and still dodgy insides were exacerbating the low-level but on-going exhaustion that went with every major inquiry. Ironic, really, she mused. As cases dragged on and they needed every cylinder operating, batteries were on the way out.

Nice metaphor, Bev.

"Get out there... question of time... do your best..."
The guv sounded dead chirpy, obviously trying to instil a
bit of positive energy.

She tugged at the hem of her favourite skirt, pencil-cut
steel-blue; it had cost a bomb and was hauled out of the
wardrobe when she needed a boost. She thought of it as
sartorial adrenalin. Thank God the hormonal variety
would kick in when the time came.

Couldn't be soon enough. They'd been at it seventy-odd
hours and had little to show but slumped postures and
dark shadows. Something pervaded the air, too, something
she sensed, could almost smell. Fear: fear of failure.

She waited until Byford threw it open, then chucked in
Mac's two penn'orth about Stephen Cross and Laura Foster.
It didn't set proceedings alight; mild interest was as far as
squad reaction went. "Mac's on his way. Should hear back
any time."

Byford was already gathering papers. "What's your
thinking, Bev?"

She still couldn't see a connection; hoped that in the
absence of anything else she wasn't making too much of it.
"Not sure, guv." She ticked points on her fingers. "Laura
Foster knows the Page family, works with Daniel's father.
Stephen Cross tells us he witnessed what could have been
the kidnap."

"Was he lying?" Byford asked.

"But why?"

"Ask him. Get uniform to bring him in."

She nodded. Made sense; it might involve hanging round
and she didn't have time.

Byford was in a hurry too. She caught up with him in the
corridor. "Guv?"

He didn't need to glance round. "I'm in a hurry, Bev."

"What's your definition of 'years ago'?"

Maybe it was something in her voice. He stopped, met her gaze. "What's your point?"

It was something Jenny Page had said during their first meeting. The words had returned to Bev during the early hours and were still bugging. "If someone told you something happened *years ago*, what's that in your book? Five? Ten? More? Less?"

Byford shrugged. "Strictly speaking, two. But people generally mean more."

She nodded. "Yeah. That's my take." So she'd run a few checks on Jenny's mother.

"Can you walk and talk at the same time?" Byford asked, nodding down the corridor.

"Chew gum and everything, guv." She fell into stride with the big man. "See, Jenny Page said she lost her mother *years ago*. But I checked: it was less than two."

Dorothy Hamilton had died in the same two-up-two-down end-of-terrace Bolton house where Jenny had been born. Broken neck was on the death certificate. The Bolton *Evening News* had been slightly more forthcoming: a few pars in the archives on the website reported that Dorothy had fallen downstairs. Body found by the milkman.

Byford halted outside his office. "Maybe they weren't close. Jenny could've left home when she finished school, not kept in touch. Sad. But these things happen."

Possible. But there was another discrepancy. "There's something else, guv." She wasn't even sure why she'd checked; it certainly hadn't shed any light. "I can't find a death certificate for the baby she lost."

His fingers were on the door handle. "Well, you know who to ask."

"I'm asking you, Maxwell." Byford and the crime boss were in Interview One. The e-fits of Doug Edensor's alleged attackers on the metal table between them. "Who are they?"

"You don't have to answer that question, Mr Maxwell."

Byford stifled already pent-up fury. According to Rumpole over there, Maxwell didn't have to answer a call of nature. The lawyer, Edward Cornwell, was smooth as Queen's silk. He could have tutored Houdini; show him a loophole, he'd jump right through. Elderly and prissy, Cornwell had been Maxwell's brief for fifteen years.

"What, exactly, are the charges, superintendent?"

"*Mr* Maxwell is helping police inquiries." Or not. Byford sat back, arms crossed, lethal stare fixed on the crime boss.

"So he's free to go whenever he chooses?" Silver hair, light grey suit, not an ounce of spare flesh on the lawyer's six-foot frame.

"Leave it, Ted," Maxwell drawled. "Let's get it over with. I want this bastard off my back." Byford suspected the casual sprawl was an act. Damp crescents darkened the armpits of Maxwell's blue shirt; beads of sweat showed on his sallow face, even through patchy stubble that peppered both chins.

"As long as you know, superintendent." Cornwell adjusted half-moon glasses, made a note on a legal pad.

"Take another look, Maxwell." The detective shoved the likenesses closer. "I'm told these goons are on your pay-roll." Byford was looking too – for every reaction, the slightest tic, the tiniest flicker.

"Says who?"

"A witness."

"Yeah, right." He lit a cigar, took his time, sneered through the smoke. "Never seen them before in my life."

"What about these, then?" Byford opened a file, pushed more paperwork across the desk: photocopies of the death threats sent to Robbie Crawford and Doug. The cigar halted fractionally on the way to Maxwell's fleshy lips. Cornwell leaned in, muttered a few words in the crime boss's ear.

"My client..." Cornwell began.

Byford flapped a hand. "Maxwell?"

"Yeah. I sent them. So what?" Cornwell tightened his grip on a classy fountain pen, but Maxwell's words were hardly an admission; his metaphorical fingerprints were all over the originals. Maxwell stared, defiant. "They needed a reminder... of what they done."

"Your boy's death was an accident." Byford's voice was level, quiet.

Lazy shrug. "Like Crawford's."

"How much did you pay the driver, Maxwell?"

"I don't have to listen to this crap."

"Where'd you get the insulin?"

"What?" The surprise might have been genuine. Or ingenuous.

"The insulin that killed Doug Edensor."

An eyebrow briefly arched. Byford couldn't interpret it. "I haven't got a clue." Maxwell tapped ash into a tin ashtray. "And neither have you, cop."

"Or proof, superintendent?" Cornwell fiddled with a cuff link.

"Tell me about the child porn, Maxwell."

As before in the pub, he didn't like that. Fat fingers bunched into fists; an unhealthy flush seeped from the neck up. "Dangerous talk, copper." Cornwell's liver-spotted hand reached out; Maxwell brushed it away, still glaring at Byford.

"Informants are grassing, Maxwell." Byford leaned across the divide. "I could turf Wembley with the spare." He read a hint of panic in Maxwell's eyes.

"I see now." Slow nod. Slitted eyes. "You fuckers are stitching me up. Bollocks to that." The crime boss lunged forward, grabbed the detective's shirt with both hands. "Go play with yourself," he snarled. "I'm outa here."

Byford smiled; his barbs had hit home. "No. You're not, Maxwell." If he walked, he'd probably leave the country this time.

"And the charge, superintendent?" the lawyer asked.

Byford made a show of smoothing his ruffled shirtfront. "Threatening a police officer will do as a start."

40

Phone tucked under chin, Bev hadn't even made a start. According to Richard Page, Jenny was asleep and not talking to anyone. She ended the call. Fuck it. She'd been fobbed off once too often. She grabbed keys and bag and was heading out of the office when the phone rang. Mac, on the move going by extraneous engine noises.

"Sarge. Laura Foster swears blind she was nowhere near Priory Rise this morning. Any morning, come to that. Says she's never heard of Stephen Cross."

Damn. "She would, wouldn't she?"

Mac wasn't brilliant at women's wardrobes but didn't think Laura was wearing the same clobber he'd spotted on Cross's house guest. Not that it meant much. She could keep any number of costume changes at the agency. Bev sighed. The Cross-Foster connection – or otherwise – would have to go on the back burner for the time being.

"OK, Mac. Meet you at the Page place, ten mins."

"I'm nearly back, sarge. Pick you up out front in two."

Kicking her heels in reception, waiting for Mac, Bev caught a bit of crossfire between Vince Hanlon and an old woman trussed up like a purple cracker.

"She give you a hard time, Vincie?" Bev smiled, as the old dear scurried through the swing door into the street.

"Nah, not really. Poor old thing. She's been getting the run-around from social services. Just needed to get it out of her system." He rubbed the back of his neck. "Broad shoulders, that's me, Bev."

Broad everything. She gave him the once-over, eyebrow arched.

"Don't even go there." The finger he wagged was like a sausage with a weight problem.

Bev helped herself to a humbug; Vince was addicted to the things. "Point her in the right direction, did you?" She glanced through the window. Where the hell was Mac?

"Pointed so often, she could've been a sodding compass – that was part of the problem. She went off feeling a bit perkier. I gave her the number she actually needs, for one thing."

"Saint, you are." Bev winked. "Vincent of the nick. Patron of old biddies." He'd even made a few notes to keep the woman happy. Bev peered at his scrawl. "You should've been a doctor, mate. What's that say?"

He lowered glasses from his shiny forehead. "Potatoes, carrots, mince, onions and milk." He grinned. "Not going the shops, are you?"

"Cheeky sod."

"Joke. Must be the old woman's."

Bev picked up the list. It was on the back of an old envelope. Julia Tate, 12 Marlborough Close. Just round the corner. "What was her gripe, Vince?"

A horn blared. She swivelled her head, frowning. Mac on a double yellow. She turned to the door as Vince said something about noisy neighbours, crying kids. "Usual stuff, Bev."

She saluted on the way out. "As I say, Vince. You're a bloody saint. Catch you later."

"I'm going nowhere till I've spoken to her."

Bev's size seven wasn't the only thing in the door. Her size twelve frame loomed foursquare as well. Arms crossed, fixed stare – it was gloves off, gauntlets down. The Morriss head of steam had built up in the motor on the way over to the Pages. Right now it could power the Rocket. Not that there wasn't a plan B. If the tough-guy strategy failed, Mac was going to plead a dodgy prostate and beg to use the loo.

Richard Page looked pleased to see them. Not. Pained was more accurate. "She's still sleep…" He stopped suddenly, stroked his forehead as if to relieve an ache. Maybe he saw the glint of steel in Bev's eyes. He stepped back. She opened her mouth to argue, closed it smartish when she realised he was letting them in. She threw Mac a puzzled glance, then stepped over the threshold before Page changed his mind.

Surly but resigned, he swung an arm in the direction of the sitting room. "Wait in there. I'll see if she's awake."

Colin Henfield popped his head round the door. "Any news?"

"'Fraid not, mate," she said.

Col looked crestfallen. Occupational hazard for family liaison: getting involved. He raised a hand, left them to it. Mac took the weight off his pins while Bev performed the usual prowl. Apart from another layer of dead skin cells, nothing appeared to have changed.

She perched on the settee, slipped a hand down the side. Mac raised an eyebrow.

"Force of habit, mate." She grinned. Never knew what you might come across. Nada in this instance.

"Taking his time, isn't he?" Mac asked.

She shrugged. "Maybe he was telling the truth and she's doing a Sleeping Beauty." She rose again, paced about. "Prince Charming's lost his sparkle, though," she murmured. There were footsteps overhead; a door closed, another opened. "Have to use that prostate scam another time.

Reckon it'd work?" *Stop wittering, Beverley.*

"You on edge, sarge?"

"No." She forced a smile, continued prowling. Mac was right, though. She felt wired and didn't know why. Except it had been too easy. Page's resistance had crumpled like a balloon with an air hole. She heard another door close overhead, more footsteps, quicker this time, then another door.

"What's going on up there?" Mac asked.

"Dunno." She scratched the side of her face, hoping to God the woman hadn't done anything stupid. There'd been enough pills in Jenny's handbag to make sleep a permanent state. But surely she'd only top herself if she thought Daniel wasn't coming back?

Mac's sharp intake of breath broke her thoughts. "What you got?" she asked.

"Force of habit, you said, sarge." Mac held a creased piece of paper. "It was stuffed down there." His side of the settee.

Her frown deepened as she saw what was written. It read like a little kid's wish list: Doctor Who duvet, a bunch of Harry Potter stuff, Dennis the Menace pyjamas, Spiderman slippers. "I don't get it…"

"I wrote it."

Richard Page defined haggard. How long had he been in the doorway? "They're Daniel's favourite things." Staring at the floor, he was distracted, not really there. The words were delivered carelessly as if they weren't important.

"And?" Bev asked.

"I realised last night. They're missing." Page leaned his head against the wood as if seeking support. "I noticed the mug wasn't there. Looked to see if anything else had gone."

Shit. Since when? And why? Bev glanced at Mac, whose

shrug echoed her own uncertainties. "When did you last see them?"

He raised a half-hearted hand. "I've no idea."

The absent tone, the posture, still suggested the list was the last thing on his mind. Bev's was screaming for answers. "Let's ask Jenny."

"We can't." Page's chest heaved. His words were barely audible. "She's gone too."

It looked as if the bed had been slept in. The duvet was rumpled, the pillow indented. Jenny Page – like Daniel's favourite things – was missing. Bev and Mac had searched every room in the house while Page attempted to pull himself together. Col was in the hall on the phone to Highgate. She knew the FLO blamed himself, though he couldn't have stopped Jenny if she'd been determined to leave the house.

"How long since you saw her, Mr Page?" Bev aimed for gentle concern. His son kidnapped, his wife missing, Page was close to the edge. He sat in a deep armchair, holding his head in his hands. "Yesterday evening. At about eight?" He seemed to be asking for confirmation.

"How did she seem?"

He snorted. "How do you think?" Contempt? Arrogance? Bev noted flashes of the original Page.

"Doesn't matter what I think." With effort she'd kept her voice level.

He closed his eyes. "Stressed. Exhausted. Desperate."

"So you stayed with her, tried to comfort her?" She'd seen the sleeping arrangements. Separate rooms, never mind single beds.

"I tried…" He held out empty palms.

"Was she asleep when you went to bed?" And are you

255

about to lie through your teeth?

"I don't know. We don't…"

"Sleep together?"

"Of course we do." His eyes flashed indignation. Bev's remained indifferent. "But…"

"What?" she prompted.

"Neither of us has been sleeping much at all. We thought it better…" He seemed incapable of finishing a sentence.

"Did you check on her during the night?"

He shook his head.

"Any idea where she could've gone? Friends? Relatives?"

Mac noted names, addresses, phone numbers; people the squad would check with as soon as the details were passed on.

"Mr Page?" She waited till he lifted his head. "Does your wife have access to your bank accounts?"

He frowned. "Of course. Why?" Could he really not see where she was coming from? She held his gaze but he hadn't made the connection.

"Is it possible she's in contact with the kidnappers?"

Page's face hadn't a lot of colour to begin with. It was grey now. "She wouldn't…" The panic in the voice and eyes said different. "She couldn't…"

Bev wished she could be so sure. She was picturing a Doctor Who duvet, the Harry Potter paraphernalia and a little boy's slippers and pyjamas. If Daniel already had his favourite things, when and how did he get them? And if not, was Jenny taking them to him now?

"We don't know, guv. Daniel's stuff could've been AWOL since day one."

Bev was on the phone, Mac doing a Schumacher as they raced round south Birmingham mopping up their share of

256

interviews with people Jenny might be staying with. Bev regarded it as an elimination exercise. She didn't see Jenny as a woman who confided in anyone. Certainly not Richard Page. "The husband's neither use nor ornament."

Byford was rubbing his chin, needed a shave; she could hear it. It was the only thing she could hear from the big man, whose head like hers was probably spinning with a zillion questions.

Bev shot an arm out. "Watch him, Mac." A drunken dosser was dithering on the kerb. The old guy looked like a down-market Dick Whittington with all his worldly possessions slung in a sleeping bag over his shoulder. She shuddered as Mac gave him a wide berth, had a sudden vision of Jenny Page roaming the streets clutching Daniel's things to her breast. It was just possible the poor bloody woman was having a breakdown. It was also possible she was following the kidnapper's instructions. And there was an outside chance she'd make straight for wherever Daniel was holed up.

"Stupid, stupid woman," Byford murmured. It had been the guv's worst fear. Bev knew that. Hers too: going it alone made fraught with danger look like a walk in the park. "What the hell is she playing at?" The guv could've been talking to himself.

"It's not a game," Bev said. "She wants her kid back. She'll do anything."

"Thank you, sergeant, for your valuable insights."

She pulled a face at the phone. Stating the bleeding obvious wasn't a road she normally went down, but if they'd recognised the strength of Jenny's feelings a bit earlier, maybe they could've headed her off before this. It wasn't for want of trying. The Pages had given her the bum's rush into a brick wall time and again.

"Bernie'll look after the press," Byford said. "He's called a news conference. Back here at midday."

"Dandy." At least they could bring the media in on this. Still no mention of Daniel's kidnap, of course; they'd sell it as a missing-woman story. In the meantime uniformed officers and as many of the squad as could be spared would soon be on the streets showing Jenny's picture to passers-by.

"Did you get anything on the missing death certificate?" Byford asked.

She frowned, couldn't think for a second what he meant. Given everything else that had gone on recently, it didn't figure large in her thoughts. But it was the reason they'd gone to the Pages in the first place: a stillborn baby whose death didn't appear to have been registered. She'd mentioned it in passing to Richard Page but he didn't have a clue. "Not yet, guv."

"By the way, Bev, Maxwell's in custody."

"Who? Oh, yeah. Right." One thing less to worry about was fine by her. "What's he saying?"

"Not a lot."

Maxwell could wait. Her focus was elsewhere. After days of going nowhere, the kidnap inquiry appeared to be heading for the home stretch against the clock. She had an image of a timer in her head. And the sands had started to run.

Maybe it was the heat. Maybe they were bored. The young PCs had been standing round in the sun for hours. There was no way they should have entered the premises. On the other hand, the window at the back was an open invitation to burglars. Really ought to be checked…

One of the uniforms waited on the drive while the other

slipped his considerably thinner frame through the gap. Had the two of them played it by the book, who knew how long it might have been before Stephen Cross's body was found?

41

"Stephen *Cross*?" Bev's sense of verbal *déjà vu* was surreal. Only six hours earlier she'd shrieked Laura Foster's name just as incredulously.

According to Daz, phoning from the crime scene, a uniform had discovered the architect's body at the bottom of his spiral staircase. In any other circumstances the fall might have been treated as accidental death. Except for the rank smell of metaphorical rats. A crime-scene team was sniffing around to see if more tangible evidence existed.

"What you doing there anyway, Daz?" She thought he'd been assigned to Kenny Flint, chasing Liam Fallon's mates.

He snorted. "Bloody moveable feast, sarge. Hacked off with it, tell you the truth." Daz's weren't the only mutterings she'd heard from the troops. Given the current workload, a lot of the guys felt like thinly spread jam – barely covering the surface and missing the corners.

Bev checked the time on the dash: just after two. They had a couple more house calls to make and Mac was moaning about missing lunch. "Be there in fifteen minutes, mate."

"We won't," Mac said. He took the phone from her, asked a few questions, made the right noises and ended the call. By which time, Bev had closed her gaping mouth. "Everyone's there," Mac said. "They don't need us. He was only keeping you in the loop. We've got our own stuff to clear and I'm starving."

"Fuck that…"

"Come on, sarge. You can't keep running round like a blue-arsed fly. No wonder you look rough. And it's counter-productive. Follow too many lines, they get crossed."

"They're *linked*, dumbo." Laura Foster-Stephen Cross-the Pages. She folded her arms before she bopped him. "Can't you see that?"

"And we're part of a team." He flung her a glance. "Can't you see *that*? Eighty officers at Highgate alone – what makes you think you're the only one who can save the world? Christ, you'll be wearing your underpants over your tights next."

"Not the sodding world I'm trying to save. It's a poor defenceless little…"

"Spare me, sarge." He lifted his palms. "We all want Daniel back. No need to go OTT."

Christ's sake. She didn't have to take this shit from a junior officer. "Fuck off."

"That's mature."

She turned her back, looked through the window. "Rough?" she snarled. Reluctantly and privately, she conceded he had a point. Several, in fact. She'd looked and felt ropey for the past few days. And the priority was tracing Jenny Page; and Daz had said not to bother putting in an appearance. But it was her way of working: being there, getting a feel for a crime scene. She sighed. Saw too many loose threads. She shivered despite the heat. Realised she was scared; scared the whole fucking shooting match was in danger of unravelling.

She was still miles away when he pulled over. Might've known: Ronald's golden arches. Good to see he'd got his priorities sorted. He took a tenner from his wallet and gave her a wink. "Fancy a Big Mac?"

"Daft sod." She smiled despite herself. He probably had her best interests at heart. The other sort she'd pursue when he wasn't around.

Daniel was very very hungry; he thought he might even eat the nasty woman's yucky scrambled eggs. Not that he'd been offered much food. She'd barely looked at him since she caught him knocking on the wall.

The lump on his head wasn't quite so swollen but it still hurt a lot. He'd examined the bump when she let him go to the toilet. He'd had several 'accidents' when he was tied up and she wasn't there. Tears pricked his eyes. Only babies wet themselves. He tightened his little fists.

The bump hurt. He itched to stroke it but his arms were tied fast round his body, and no matter how hard he tried he couldn't work the rope loose from his ankles. The skin was raw and bleeding. He wouldn't mind the pain if only his plan had worked; he was so sure someone had been knocking in reply.

His bottom lip quivered. No one cared. No one loved him any more. Where were Mummy and Daddy? Why hadn't they rescued him? Scalding tears ran down his cheeks. He hated the nasty woman. She told wicked, wicked lies. Mummy wasn't coming for him. The witch woman only told him things like that to hurt him more. He didn't believe a word she said. He wanted her to die. He wanted her to go to hell. He wanted to kill her.

"It arrived first thing." A worried Grant Young was on the phone to Byford. A wreath had been delivered to the media man's home in Kings Heath.

"Any message?" Not that it needed one.

"You could say that." The laugh sounded forced. "A card showing a coffin and my name on a headstone."

Byford's pen would snap if he didn't loosen his grip. Even behind bars, Maxwell pulled his puppets' strings.

"I've had calls warning me off, too."

"Why didn't you say?" Byford heard a rustle, pictured a shrug.

"I'm a big boy now. I can take care of myself." The attempt at levity didn't work. Young sounded uneasy.

"If it's any consolation, Maxwell's in custody." Not for much longer, though. He couldn't hold the crime boss indefinitely. And the army of goons was still out there.

"Maxwell doesn't worry me." The clipped delivery suggested the opposite. "Just thought you should know. In case I go missing or anything." Nervous laugh. "Do you want to see the wreath or the card?"

Byford checked the time. "I'll drop by this evening, pick it up. Get it off to the lab." He could send a uniform but it was on his way home, and he felt he owed Young a favour.

"Excellent! I can introduce you to a few of the crew."

"Crew?"

"The *Hard Time* team. I've asked a few people round. Drinks and nibbles. Nothing fancy. Just a bit of bonding, ice-breaking, whatever they call it these days."

"I can't prom..."

"One glass? Just say hello?" Young sounded his old self.

Byford gave a faint smile as he hung up.

"What do you mean, she's not here?" Bev loomed, hands on hips, over the young girl at Full Page Ads. Chelsea trembled in the swivel chair behind reception, ginger freckles swamped by a beetroot flush.

Mac leaned in, tapped Bev's arm. "Messenger, sarge. Don't shoot."

She took a deep breath, furious with herself more than the kid. Why hadn't they come to the agency the second they'd heard about Stephen Cross? Should've listened to her gut instinct, not fed Mac's fat face. It looked as if her

DC's earlier visit had acted as a wake-up call. The bird had flown. Or at least joined the missing list. Laura Foster wasn't expected back at work for two weeks and wasn't answering any of her phones.

"I don't think she's gone away," Chelsea said. "She cares for a sick relative."

"Who?"

"Laura."

Bev clenched her teeth. "Who's the *relative*?"

Blank look.

"What makes you say she's a carer?"

The girl hunched her shoulders. "Just a few things she's let slip. And…"

"What?"

Chelsea glanced round, lowered her voice. "She's hardly ever here, these days. Wish I could take…"

"Where's she live?"

The girl frowned. "How would I know?"

Bev tapped a foot. "Have a look in the files."

"I don't have access to personnel details." Poor girl had only been there a month. She looked as if she'd failed the probation, then suddenly had a bright idea. "You could ask Mr Page. He'd know."

She surely could. If she had the faintest idea where he was. Bev had been trying to reach him for a couple of hours. He wasn't answering his mobile, and according to Colin he'd left The White House shortly after lunch.

Four sachets of sugar and the canteen tea still tasted like piss. Bev could have murdered a pinot but needed all her wits about her. Listlessly she stirred the beige brew, gazed at the night sky from the top-floor window. Searching for what? Inspiration? Revelation? Perhaps she'd consult the stars. She had a galaxy of questions.

She looked again, really saw the sky this time: the beautiful, seemingly endless dark blue, a flawless backdrop for a perfect silver moon. The universe put things in perspective, didn't it? So vast, so deep, so unfathomable. Like this sodding case.

Where the hell was Jenny Page? They'd had a flood of sightings from viewers who'd watched the media appeals. A couple of reports had sounded promising, but didn't deliver. Teams were still monitoring calls, following up as and when.

At least Richard Page was back at the house in Moseley. Mac was there making sure it stayed that way. As for Laura Foster – she could be anywhere. She'd recently moved, and when Bev had asked Page, he said she hadn't given anyone her new address yet. Yeah, right.

What were the links? They had to be there. *Think it through, girl.* At least the canteen was empty this time of night. No distractions.

"Stir for Europe you could, BM." DI Powell nodded at the spoon in her hand, still doing the rounds.

BM? New one, that. "What you doing here?" She gave the tea a few more whirls, licked the spoon.

"The canteen?" He cocked an eyebrow. "Or at all?"

The resignation letter? Double shit. "Bit cryptic for me, that one."

"Thought you knew everything, BM. Before it happens, most of the time." Sweat beaded his hairline; she could count the droplets, he was that close. "Thieving from a senior officer? I could have you on a disciplinary."

She floundered for a fib. *PMT? HRT? PTSD?* "I didn't want you to go." The blurted admission shocked them both.

He backed off, frowning. "Say that again."

"I didn't want you to go." She peered at the cut on his forehead; it was healing nicely but would scar.

The DI flopped into the chair opposite. "You taking the piss?"

She'd nothing to lose. "Look, mate, you can be a right pain in the arse. There's times I'd like to give you a good slapping." She glanced away. "But I'd miss you if you weren't here."

"Fancy me, do you?"

"Pur-lease." She caught the smile tugging his lips. Best line he'd ever cracked.

It broke the ice floe between them. They chatted for a while: cases, cops, work in general. Being upfront had opened him up too; he was easy, relaxed. She'd have to suck up more often. She kept an eye on the time but Powell was off anyway. He scraped the chair back, delved in pockets for car keys. "Catch you tomorrow. And don't worry about the letter business. Next time though, keep it out, eh?" He tapped the side of his nose.

She was so busy lying through her teeth she didn't get the chance to ask what BM was short for. Had to be Bev Morriss. Didn't it?

When Bev left an hour later, the light was on in the guv's office. She frowned. What was he up to this time of night? Not far off ten. Maybe she'd nip in, mention where she was off to? Her inspiration was recent and she was keen to give it a whirl. Though SOCOs had already fine-tooth-combed Cross's place, had they looked for a link to Laura Foster? Only one way to find out. It was gut instinct again more than anything, and if she told the guv, he'd probably put the kibosh on it. No harm saying goodnight, though.

The door inched open when she gave it a gentle tap. "Guv…?"

He wasn't at his desk, she couldn't see his briefcase, the fedora was gone, the cactus looked to be on the way out. She shook her head with a smile: last time she'd buy him anything. She'd do him a good turn, though. He must've forgotten to switch off; the computer was booted as well. As she bent for the plug, her glance fell on a note.

Not that the guv had written a lot. Harry Maxwell's name underlined, plus Grant Young's circled. Maybe Young had come up with some goodies on the crime boss. The guv hadn't mentioned anything, though.

She shrugged. Please himself. End of the day, he was boss, she was lowly DS. That was the relationship. Having the hots for him didn't figure in the equation. It'd never work anyway. *How d'you know?* I just do. *Ask him out.* Get lost. *No way.* Back off.

The internal dialogue raged as she leafed through the diary. She almost talked herself into making him an offer involving Haagen Das and a lot of rubber. Until she saw where he was tonight: a party at Young's in Kings Heath for *Hard Time.* She sniffed. Good of him to share.

Not that she was exactly broadcasting her own imminent spot of moonlighting.

She hoisted her bag, ready to hit the road, then gasped, threw a hand to her mouth. "Holy Mary." There was a body hanging behind the door.

It took less than a second to realise her mistake. "Fuckwit," she snarled. It was the guv's black suit draped on a coat hanger over the lintel. Relief flooded Bev's system, already awash with adrenalin. She closed her eyes, took steadying breaths. Byford must have brought the suit in for the funeral tomorrow. She wasn't going, hadn't known Doug

267

Edensor well.

As she went past she caught a whiff of the guv's after-shave clinging to the dark material. She backed up, breathed it in. Then she remembered Jenny Page. Burying her face in her lost boy's t-shirt.

December 2005

Holly hadn't recognised the handwriting on the cheap white envelope. Why should she? Lots of mail had arrived after the programme, much of it badly written in green ink on lined notepaper, sick suggestions from pathetic perverts. The producer had warned about dodgy post. But she wasn't troubled by their fucked-up fantasies; she'd lived through worse. The letters went on the fire.

Appearing on television could succeed where everything else she'd tried had failed. The documentary was called Lost and Found? *– a showcase for reuniting loved ones. One of the other contributors met his birth mother for the first time within days of its transmission. But for Holly the question mark remained. Weeks went past and she began to believe her worst fear was founded.*

And then the letter had arrived.

It was not from her mother. But as Holly read, her heart raced, tears flowed even as she laughed in delight. She held the letter in both hands, danced round the room, already planning the visit.

Why had it never occurred to her before? Of course – she had a grandmother. *And granny, as she'd signed herself, was dying to meet Holly.*

Holly travelled to Bolton in blissful ignorance. She'd suppressed worrying niggles about the letter. It was snobbish to associate the cheap paper and untidy scrawl with common people. But her suspicions were more than founded. After watching Lost and Found? *her granny had seen Holly as a meal ticket.*

The old woman wanted cash for information, turned nasty

when requests were refused. At first Holly dismissed the vitriol as lies, clamped her hands over her ears. The witch said her mother was a slut who got pregnant at fifteen. That she had blackmailed the father – a married man – and had taken off with the hush money for a new life in London. That she'd never had any intention of keeping the baby.

Granny should have kept her mouth shut. Especially when she told Holly she'd chucked the filthy tramp out anyway.

After the 'accident' on the stairs, Holly searched the mean little house. The shock at seeing her mother's image for the first time was staggering. It was like looking at a photograph of herself. The picture was in a battered suitcase along with her mother's birth certificate and other documents. Enough to trace her.

Holly might have ended the search there. But she found the newspaper cuttings in a shoebox on top of the cheap wardrobe. That shock was even greater, the tears now scalding and bitter. Miracle baby, coldest night, lucky to be alive…

Her mother had left her to die.

Every hope and wish was destroyed in that instant. Everything changed: her past, present and future. Holly started planning her revenge.

Life wasn't the only thing the bitch would lose.

42

The key to Stephen Cross's pad was in Bev's pocket; she'd lifted it from an evidence bag in the exhibits room. The crime-scene guys had found nothing suspicious or incriminating, nada to suggest Cross's fall had been anything other than accidental. She'd studied their search report; it hadn't even mentioned Laura Foster. But maybe they were unaware of the possible link? Or maybe Bev thought she could do a better job. Either way, she'd not rest till she knew.

She parked the Midget a couple of streets away. Last thing she wanted was an audience and Priory Rise, as Mac had discovered, was full of nosy neighbours. She glanced round casually as she locked the motor. At least she could be sure it'd have a full set of wheels on her return. This was nob territory, not asbo turf.

An elderly man doffed his cap as he ambled past, so she must look respectable. She nodded, flashed him a smile. The evening was warm and still; Bev was hot and bothered. She took brisk steps, deep breaths. The air carried heady scents from immaculate gardens.

Hampton Place was peaceful, deserted; the gates of the school glinted in the moonlight. She recalled her first visit, the day Daniel was abducted. Her spine tingled; she hurried on, reminded of that stupid expression: someone walking over your grave. How the hell could you feel a pair of size sevens when you were six feet under?

The box for the burglar alarm was in the hall. The disabling code had appeared in the search report and was now scribbled on her wrist. The job would be easier with house lights on but she didn't want to alert the neighbours. The pencil torch and moonbeams would have to do.

Start at the top. Cross wasn't big on clutter. The rooms were sparse: bare walls, polished floorboards, sleek lines, sharp designs. All class – little character. What seemed hours later, she stood in the hall. Here and there she'd caught a whiff of perfume. She'd smelt it before, couldn't pin it down. Apart from that, the place was clean, far as she could tell. The kitchen was the only room left to search. Was it worth it?

Wished she hadn't bothered. Cross was as stainless as his steel and gleaming pots. Might've known he was too cute to leave clues lying around. Talk about anti-climax: pissed off wasn't even close. Her reflection in the huge mirror said it all.

She stiffened. Another face stared back – but not human. The clock. Breath bated, she backed and turned. Arms raised, she ran her fingers along the ledge under the dial.

A slip of paper. Don't get your hopes up, girl. It could be a bill, a receipt, a…

A handwritten address. She'd see it before but was pretty sure it hadn't been in Cross's contacts book. She took it through to the hall, checked it against every entry. No match. Not there, then. Where?

Come on, girl. Come on. She studied the writing again. The squiggle in the bottom corner of the paper put her in mind of Frankie's flamboyant curlicues. She smiled briefly then frowned. What if…? She squinted, looked closer. The writer had done a Frankie – run his or her initials together in an almost indecipherable scrawl. Almost. Interpreting the squiggle differently, this time Bev traced the letters with a finger: an L and an F.

She gave a low whistle. Laura Foster – the no-longer-missing link. As for the address, she'd definitely seen it before and recently. Suddenly it clicked. Bev grabbed her bag, ran out of the house. The grave walker was on her case again.

"What did she say, Vince? The exact words?" The phone was tucked under Bev's chin. She was either way off-beam or knew where Daniel was being held. And who was holding him. Either way, she'd be there in ten minutes. The driver in front sat on a red for a second; Bev hit the horn, flashed the lights.

"Just trying to think," Vince muttered. The TV blared in the background. She'd caught the desk sergeant at home, hoping he could supply a brushstroke or two to the nascent picture in her head.

"Come on, come on." It emerged louder than she'd intended.

"Hold your horses."

She tapped the wheel, only vaguely aware of her surroundings. People were having fun. The streets were buzzing, life was going on as normal. But the bright lights were a blur, her focus elsewhere. She was seeing an old lady in a purple suit complaining to Vince about noisy neighbours.

The old woman's address had been on the back of the shopping list dropped at Highgate: 12 Marlborough Close. It'd rung a bell as soon as Bev stumbled across the scrap of paper in Stephen Cross's kitchen. Apart from being one house number out, she'd been spot on.

"It was mostly about a kid crying."

"Yeah, Vince, but you said something else." As Bev had been leaving. God, don't let her regret that. "Dig deep, mate." She counted to ten.

"Nothing out of the ordinary. Most complaints are a damn sight worse. It hadn't even been going on that long."

She tightened her grip. "How long?"

"'Bout a week."

And how long had Daniel Page been missing?

Byford sat in the Rover outside Grant Young's place, debating whether to stay for a drink or just pick up the wreath and the card and get off home. He wondered what Young's media cronies made of George Road. Back-street Birmingham would be way out of their comfort zone.

He looked in the mirror, straightened his hair with his fingers. Must be getting vain in his old age. He gave a wry smile. If he went ahead with the programme, when he hit his dotage he could play it to his grandkids. Bore them to death about the good old days.

Silly ass. The big man rubbed both hands over his face, knackered. What he really needed was an early night. But it had been a gruelling few days; maybe a break from the grind was what he needed. And he owed Young a favour. Bit of *quid pro quo* wouldn't hurt.

Curry and cabbage odours lingered in the evening air. Black bin liners spilled rank contents on to the pavement. Byford sidestepped a chicken carcass and cracked eggshells. Early shout for the bin men tomorrow as well as the squad.

Tomorrow. He halted briefly. Doug Edensor was being buried in the morning, a week to the day since Robbie Crawford's funeral.

Night had fallen; the air was still. As Bev drove past the nick, she gave a grim smile; Marlborough Close was just round the corner. How ironic would that be? Nah.

She shook her head, almost convinced by now she was chasing phantoms, figments of her wishful thinking. Crying is what kids do.

But enough to persuade a concerned neighbour to contact the police after less than a week? So why ignore the voice in her head urging her to call for backup? She told herself it was about protecting Daniel. But was it? Breaking the case would restore her shaky self-confidence and credibility at a stroke. She sniffed, dismissed the notion; more pressing concerns to get on with.

She pulled over two doors down from number 14, switched the engine off. The houses were redbrick Edwardian: solid, reassuring, sitcom land. Easy to forget that the main drag was so close. Except for road-rage sound effects. And the police sirens. She frowned. They were going off like there was no tomorrow.

She dropped the window an inch, lit a cigarette. Number 12 was in darkness. She glanced at the clock on the dash: half-ten. The old woman was probably in bed. In an ideal world she'd have a word with Julia Tate first, but this was Highgate.

She inhaled deeply, savoured the nicotine hit, flicked the butt out of the car. Now or never. Momentary hesitation. Should she think it through a tad more? Sod that. She'd be here all night. She snapped the seat belt, grabbed her bag. As she locked the car, her gaze homed in on number 14. Even if she'd got it totally wrong, worst-case scenario was egg on her face.

Snatches of Mozart, a buzz of conversation from within. Byford arranged his features into a sociable smile, rang the bell. Better late than never. The party volume increased when Young opened the door.

"Bill! Come in – good to see you." He took the big man's

fedora, hung it from a hook in the hall. The wreath was against the wall. "Drinks are in there." He pointed to the end door. "Go through. I'll do the intros."

It sounded as if the party was in full swing. Byford took two steps into the room; froze. It didn't make sense. Only two people were in there. Instant silence as the party sound-track was switched off. Agonising pain as something crashed into the back of his head.

In the split second before he hit the floor, he realised he'd seen the two faces before. But then, though no one touched the lights, everything went black.

As Bev approached the house, a light came on at an upstairs window. They'd probably close the curtains in a min, see her if they looked out. She hung back; the element of surprise was about the only advantage she had.

Thank God she'd waited. Her phone started up like a burglar alarm. Talk about early warning. Best switch the sodding thing off. She delved in her bag, peered at the screen. Brighton number. Paula Ryland. The DI wouldn't phone for a friendly chat this time of night. She sighed, hit return call. It'd take a minute, max.

"What took you so long?" Not friendly: brisk and businesslike. The man charged with Andy Quinn's murder, Ronnie Stone, had offered a deal, she said. If they dropped charges, he'd drop his paymaster in the shit.

"We talked a reduced sentence, maybe, and he finally went along."

"And?"

"Andy Quinn was number three on a hit list. His boss is going after cops."

"Robert Crawford and Doug Edensor?" Bev closed her eyes.

"One and two. There's one more to go."

She didn't need to ask. She was surprised she could talk, let alone sound reasonably calm. "What's happening now?"

Highgate was handling it, Ryland said. The superintendent wasn't answering any of his phones, but as far as she knew an armed response unit was ready to go.

"Go where?"

"Kings Heath."

"Why there?" Bev frowned. "Anyway, Harry Maxwell's in custody."

A pause, two heartbeats. "Who's Harry Maxwell?"

Then she saw it. The guv's diary. The Kings Heath address. There was a roar in her ears; she clung to the wall for support.

"Jesus Christ. Paula, get on the radio. Warn Highgate." Her voice broke. "Byford's in there."

Bev dropped to her haunches, stomach heaving. She had to get there, make sure the guv was OK. First had to wait out the shallow breaths, shaking limbs. As she reached the Midget, she glanced back at the house.

And knew she had to stay. A little boy was standing at the window. A little boy with a shorn head, green eyes and tears sliding down his cheeks.

The pain was blinding, breathtaking. Arms pinned back, body strapped to a hard chair, Byford couldn't move. Eyes slowly opening, he gasped as he saw his distorted reflection in a lens. Two cameras on tripods were trained on him – and a gun. He tried not to flinch as Young stroked the barrel down his cheek.

Byford sensed they were alone. No sign of the two men he'd recognised before blacking out. The witness's e-fits had been accurate. They were the goons who'd murdered

Doug Edensor. Sent by Young. Not Maxwell.

Byford winced as his head was yanked savagely to the side. The cameras recorded every tic, every bead of sweat. Young jabbed the gun at a monitor. "Private screening. Watch."

He squinted. The hand-held jerky shots were difficult to make out. But Byford knew, felt his blood run cold. Three crime scenes, three dead cops. The bastard had filmed the murders.

"No long lens for you, though, big man." He recoiled as Young's saliva slithered down his face. "Up close and personal."

"You won't get away with it." It was a line from a crap film.

"I know." Young's eyes were already dead. "But I'll take you with me."

43

The armed response unit was at Young's place; Bev had elicited that much from control. Officers on the ground were keeping comms to a minimum. She slipped the police radio in her bag anyway. Right now all she wanted was to grab Daniel, get this thing over, get to the guv. Fired up, distracted, she hammered on the door.

Not Laura Foster. Jenny Page. Jenny was the last person Bev expected to see. But a closer look showed that it wasn't Daniel's mother. A younger version – the blonde hair a shade darker, the green eyes more vibrant. Same gene bank, though. No time for twenty questions. No time for any.

"Police. I know Daniel's here." She flashed her warrant card. "I'm taking him home and I'm taking you in."

"Don't be ridic…"

She raised a finger. "The bedroom. I've seen him."

"Shouldn't have untied him, should I?" The woman gave a resigned shrug. "You'd better come in."

Wrong-footed, Bev followed warily, darting uneasy glances. The sitting room was minimalist, neutral shades, nothing fancy; french doors leading out back, sliding door into the rest of the place. Bev stood with her back to the wall. "Fetch Daniel, please."

The eyes held a warning. "Not yet." In the silence, more sirens.

Bev took a step closer. Getting the boy out was priority. If it came to a fight, the woman was on a loser. "Have you hurt him?"

"All relative, isn't it?" She sneered. "You may as well sit. He's going nowhere till I've seen his mother."

"You'll be lucky," Bev mocked. "She's legged it."

"Wrong again, *detective*. She'll be here any minute." An eyebrow arched in contempt as she took great delight in putting Bev right. Jenny Page was simply following instructions, lying low in a back-street hotel until the handover.

"Why the f...?"

Haughty. Defiant. "Because I wanted her to."

Bev shook her head. It was a power thing, the act of a control freak. A zillion thoughts swirling, she watched as the blonde lowered herself on to a leather sofa, languidly crossed her legs, raised a wine glass to her lips. And then it dawned. The mannerisms, the voice, the pose: the picture in Bev's head was turning into a family portrait.

"You're the daughter," she breathed.

The blonde put down the glass, started a slow handclap. "Give the dog a bone." Malevolence in the green eyes. "Not very good at this detecting lark, are you, Bev?"

She blinked. The ID had only been flashed.

"You really don't know, do you?" She laughed, too loud, throwing her head back.

Bev itched to knock it off her shoulders. Her own head was spinning. The young woman had to be Jenny's supposedly stillborn daughter. That explained the lack of a death certificate. But not how she knew Bev's name...

She froze. The woman was reaching into her bag. Knife? Gun?

Glasses. Fashionable dark frames. Bev recalled trying them on, posing for Mac. Fucking shame they hadn't improved her eyesight.

"They're clear glass. Amazed you didn't pick up on that." The woman laughed again. "I use contact lenses, myself. Blue ones."

To go with the Laura Foster ebony bob. Bev closed her eyes. Poor vision? Blind, more like. But what had Jenny Page done to deserve revenge as savage as this? There was only one answer. And it suddenly slotted into place.

"She gave you away, didn't she, Laura?" Bev's phone beeped; she ignored it.

"Gave?" The laugh chilled Bev's bones. "The bitch *dumped* me, the day I was born. Just before Christmas, in a public toilet. On the coldest night of the year. A miracle baby, they called me." She raised her glass. "And my name is Holly."

Bev shook her head. Why hadn't she seen it? From day one the kidnap had been intensely personal, an attack aimed at the mother. She aimed for damage limitation. "Maybe she thought…"

"The bitch didn't think." Holly poured a refill from an almost empty bottle. "It was out of the frying pan into the furnace for me." Impassive, she described a grotesque childhood that turned Bev's stomach. Abducting Daniel was payback time.

Bev bit her lip. Though never excusable, taking Jenny's son was maybe understandable. But what could she say? Sorry your life's been shit. Now I'm taking you in.

"Your phone." It was beeping again. "Turn it off."

Reluctantly Bev reached into her bag; somewhere the balance of power had shifted. She cast a quick glance at the screen: missed calls and messages. Dear God, let the guv be OK.

"What's she like?" Holly asked casually, elegant ankle swinging.

"Your mother? You've never…?"

"Not in the flesh. Twenty-two years old and I've never actually seen her. Liam met his birth mother days after doing the telly."

She must've misheard. "Sorry?"

"Liam Fallon. He was on the programme with me – *Lost and Found?* I'll miss Liam."

Bev knew nada about any TV show. Far as she was aware, Liam was the Selly Oak misper who might or might not have perished in the Monks Court fire. She was getting a bad vibe. "Why will you miss him, Holly?"

"He's dead, of course. He couldn't get out." She bit the skin round her thumbnail, winced when it drew blood. Bev wiped clammy hands on her skirt. What the hell had she got herself into? "We kept in touch after the programme." Holly smiled. "We even had a bit of thing going for a while. I told him about the abuse, what I'd been through growing up. He was more than happy when I asked him to help me set the blaze."

It took a superhuman effort not to react. "Monks Court? Why did you do that, Holly?"

The blonde stared at her hands. "My adoptive father used to bring his sick friends along sometimes for a little extra fun. Satan's cronies, I called them. I may not know all the names but I never forget a face. I bumped into one of them in the street. He didn't even recognise me, but I followed him back to that pervs' hostel. It's sad about Liam, but men like that…"

Bev swallowed; pictured a young police officer with a sunny smile. Itched to beat the shit out of the woman. Then a thought occurred. "Stephen Cross…? Was he another crony?"

"His was a name I did remember," she spat. "I tracked him down. Amazing how helpful he was, to protect his precious reputation. Until the spineless bastard got too scared, threatened to go to the police."

Bev tried to keep a lid on her rising panic. The woman was barking. The abuse hadn't just damaged her childhood. "Holly, don't worry about…Satan. Give us his details. We'll bring him in."

"You'll be lucky." More brittle laughter.

"Dead, is he?"

"And his bitch of a wife. It was a shame Amy died too."

No question, Bev thought; she was in striking distance of a psycho serial killer. She jumped when Holly leaped to her feet, walked to the window, gazed out. "Where the fuck is she?"

A knock on the door answered the question. Bev had one too. "What are you going to do?"

"What do you think?" The knife must've been on the sill. Smiling, Holly slashed it through the air. Bev blinked as light glinted on the blade.

"Life for a life, eh, old man?"

Byford screamed as a bone cracked in his face. A second later Young smashed the gun into the other cheek. Blood already gushed from the superintendent's nose, dripped from his chin. Two teeth were on the carpet, others loose in the gums, lips split.

"Didn't hear you, cop," Young sneered, whipped back the gun. Byford braced himself, eyes tight. There was a rush of cool air as Young took a swing, stopped a hair's breadth from impact. "Not time yet, old man. Don't want you passing out on me again."

Byford could barely speak; if he could, he wouldn't give the bastard the satisfaction. Anyway, Young was revelling in the sound of his own voice. He'd told the detective every gory detail. Bragged about how he'd planned the deaths, how hit men had carried out the killings, how he'd bankrolled it all with his compensation money. And how he'd pointed Byford in Maxwell's direction, every false step of the way. The big man groaned. Every confessional word was a nail in his coffin.

Young's white suit was already splattered with Byford's blood. "Remember what you got me sent down for, cop? Do you *know* what happens to child killers inside?" The ex-con wanted eye contact, smacked the detective's face till he got it. "They get a hard time like you wouldn't believe." Cold steel bit into raw flesh. "You believed, though, didn't you? *Hard Time*?" He sniggered. "There's no programme, you arrogant twat." Another spit in the face. "Fucking flatter yourself, cop."

Fixated on Maxwell, the superintendent hadn't even checked Young's information. Even though it had always been his mantra to Bev: check, check, check again. Her picture flickered in his head: heart-shaped face, teasing smile, wide mouth. The image was still there when he closed his eyes.

"Wake up, cop." Young slammed a boot into Byford's shin. "Don't worry. You'll get your moment of glory." A wild wave of the gun took in the cameras. "Time to shoot your famous final scene."

A Bob Seger track. Byford heard the music in his head as Young breathed curry fumes in his face. The detective prayed silently to a god he'd spurned since childhood. The gun was hard against his temple; Young's voice hissing in his ear.

"Twenty years, I've waited for this." Slow pressure on the trigger. "Time to die, cop."

44

Seconds to decide. Seconds to save – or lose – a life. Holly wouldn't give a fuck about her own. It had been crap from the word go. She'd killed before; she'd murder her mother in a heartbeat. Bev's pounded her ribs. Jenny would take a blade if she didn't act.

"Don't even think about it." A man's voice from behind. It couldn't be...

Startled, confused, Bev whipped her head round.

Holly laughed. "Quite the family reunion, isn't it?"

Richard Page, unsmiling, stood in the sliding door, Daniel limp in his arms. Holly strolled over, kissed Page full on the lips. "Couldn't have done it on my own, could I, darling?"

Bev closed her eyes: the great fucking detective. Page had traded Jenny in for a younger model: fuck mother, fuck daughter. Grim-faced, Holly beckoned to Bev. With the knife. "Let the bitch in."

Mind racing, she walked slowly to the door, playing for time that was fast running out. Her plan: grab Jenny, leg it, alert control. Page wouldn't hurt his son.

A calming breath. Plan wasn't perfect... The blade pressed into her spine. Plan wasn't possible.

"One false move," Holly hissed, "you'll never walk again."

Slumped shoulders, sunken cheeks – in the long black coatdress Jenny looked as if she was in mourning. The moonlight cast dark shadows on a complexion the colour of ash. Barely a glance at Bev; the wary green eyes were focused to the side. The face showed emotions Bev could never imagine. Jenny knew she was staring at the daughter she'd left to die.

"Seeing a ghost?" Mocking, contemptuous. The expression had been meaningless to Bev before. But Holly was right. Jenny looked haunted by a past she'd tried to bury.

"Bring her in," Holly ordered.

Bev glanced over Jenny's shoulder. The street was deserted. Where the fuck was Mac? He was supposed to be tailing Richard Page. In the seconds since the smarmy bastard had shown up, it had been her chink of light at the end of a long flooded tunnel.

The room was getting crowded. Jenny registered nothing but her son. She dashed to the settee where Daniel lay on his side. "If you've hurt him, I'll..."

Bev glanced round, desperately seeking a weapon. If she could reach the lamp, the bottle...

"You'll what?" Holly mocked. "Give me a smack? Send me to bed without any supper?" Her voice grew ragged. "There was a time I'd have given my right arm for you to do that. But you weren't there." She ran a finger along the blade. "Were you, *Mummy*?"

On her knees, Jenny stroked Daniel's brow, didn't even look round. "Take the money. Please. Just go."

"We will. And Dan-Dan's coming with us."

Jenny's hand stilled; her eyes followed her daughter's gaze. God knows what was going through her mind; one word issued from her lips. "Richard?" He couldn't look at her; watched his feet shuffling the carpet.

Bev flung him a contemptuous glance, then froze. Willed herself not to react. Trick of the light? Or had she caught a fleeting shadow outside?

Daniel mumbled in his sleep, threw an arm over his shorn head.

"I'd love to stay and chat, catch up on old times." Holly laughed. "But places to go, planes to catch, you know how it is."

"Fat chance." Bev sniffed. She needed to draw metaphorical fire. Mac's fat frame had just flashed across the french window again.

"Lippy cow, aren't you?" If looks could kill. At least she had Holly's attention.

"You're kidding yourself, sunshine." Bev's stare was flat, unafraid. "Only one place you're going. One-way ticket. Do not pass go, do not collect two hundred pounds."

"We're wasting time." Richard's voice trembled. "Let's get it over with."

Holly's gaze was still fixed on Bev. Even set in a sneer, her face was stunning, breathtaking.

"Take after your mum, don't you, love?"

The barb hit home, but recovery was quick. "And from." She turned to Jenny. "Kiss the boys goodbye, *Mummy*."

Tears welled; Jenny's face was wet from those already shed. She rose, her expression unreadable as she looked into her daughter's eyes. "Can I kiss you first?"

Holly's mouth gaped in stunned silence. Jenny's voice faltered, her stare stayed rock steady. "I never ever stopped loving you. I dreamt of holding you in my arms. I knew you'd been found. I keep the cutting in my purse." An unwitting smile, faded. "Every single day of your life, I've lived with guilt."

"Bullshit." Holly tapped a foot, knife held at her side. "You were a money-grabbing tramp. The only way you could have ditched me faster was with an abortion. Don't look so shocked, Jen." She gave a sly smile. "I heard it from your witch of a mother before her –" She made a shoving motion with her hands – "accident."

"But I didn't, did I?"

A flicker of uncertainty. "What?"

"Abort you. It never crossed my mind for a second."

Holly mimed a violin playing.

"You have every right to hate me…"

"I do." Holly's eyes shone. "With a passion."

"You'll never know how much I ached to hold you." Tears flowed down Jenny's cheeks.

"Then why?" She took a step closer, eyes searching her mother's face. "Why did you dump me?"

"I was little more than a child myself. I couldn't give you the life you deserved."

"You left me to die."

"I never meant to hurt you, Holly. I know it's too late." Jenny held out her arms. "But one kiss, one hug, then I'll go."

Holly wavered further, then stepped forward.

Jenny wrapped her in a warm embrace.

And knifed her in the back.

45

Bursts of static, barked orders. A voice cut through the babble: *officer down, officer down.* Hammer blow. Bev hunched, retched, willed herself to keep driving, to get there. Kings Heath seemed a lifetime away. Live commentary played on the speaker as terrifying pictures ran unbidden in her head.

"Dear God. Dear God." *Don't let me be too late.* White knuckles showed through Holly's dried blood on her hands. She dashed angrily at scalding tears, left warpaint smears on her face. "If the guv dies…" The warning was hissed through clenched teeth. "I'll kill you!" God? Grant Young? Page? Holly? Jenny?

She fumbled for a baccy, lit it with trembling fingers. Bad for the health? Yeah. Like psychos. Deep drag, then another, then another, red glow in the dark. Whatever gets you through. "Don't die on me, guv." Sod the age gap, the rank divide; if the big man made it, first chance she got she'd hit on him like there was no tomorrow. *What if there isn't?*

While she was playing Happy Families, the guv had been in the hands of a cop killer. Another throat-burning drag. Should've left the Pages to their pathetic devices. She'd legged it the second she could. Left Mac and the team mopping up.

He'd tailed Page's motor but it was the Midget parked in the close that rang Mac's alarm. Unlike Bev, he'd not played superhero. He'd radioed control, requested assistance. At Marlborough Close, officers had entered at the front as Mac smashed his way through a back window.

Richard Page put up no resistance; last she'd seen of him

was in the back of a police motor; Holly in the back of an ambulance. Her wound wasn't fatal. The entry angle missed vital organs. A wonder the stiletto went in at all, given how Jenny had attached it inside her sleeve. Holly would live, then get life. Extenuating circs would probably lead to a suspended sentence for Jenny. Right now, Bev didn't give a fuck. Even the tearful mother-son reunion left her cold. Kids. Who'd have them?

She leaned on the horn, ran a red. More radio static. Shouts. Silence. Had they gone in? What was going on? She slammed a palm on the wheel.

George Road was cordoned off. Tough. She mowed down the police tape, narrowly missed a police officer. Flashing a card, Bev ignored shouts, returned hand signals. There'd be a disciplinary to face for the Page fuck-up: if you're going to hang, sod a sheep, make it a flock. Adrenalin, nicotine, incandescence? Whatever. She was more wired than she could remember.

Two wheels straddled the kerb, door gaped; she glanced around, took in events. Four armed officers on the street. How many located out of sight? An AR vehicle was up at the top. She jogged towards it. Heightened senses; shortened breaths. Something was wrong. Three flak-jacketed men stood in a group, talking. Too casual. There were too many people around, too much idle noise. Bev was clammy-palmed, light-headed, nauseous – a classic panic attack. Sod that. She started to run, tripped, almost fell. A horn blasted behind her. Flashing blue lights. An ambulance. And a meat wagon. It was all over.

Byford had no doubt he was about to die. The gun was cold against his temple; Young's hot breath in his face. The superintendent closed his eyes, not ready but resigned.

A shot rang out, deafening in the small room. His body's desperate heave toppled the chair sideways. Overwhelming pain as his head hit the floor.

Unconscious, he was unaware that the shot, from a police marksman, had taken out the light. And totally unaware of the second shot that took out Grant Young.

They brought Young's body out first. Paramedics were working on Byford. They'd been in there twenty minutes, feeling like another lifetime to Bev. The senior officer, a burly thickset woman she barely knew, wouldn't let her in. Crime scene; fair enough.

"Will he make it? All I need to know..." She'd asked just about everyone else. No one would look her in the eye. Not even Mike Powell, who was about somewhere.

"I'm no expert," the woman said. "He's drifting in and out. Head injuries causing concern."

Disciplinary? Suspension? Sod it.

"Hey! Where are you going?"

Bev didn't look back. The guv was on a stretcher, unrecognisable. Face a bloody open wound, a black hole where his teeth had been, chips of bone showing white through the battered flesh. The paramedics were talking to him, trying to keep him awake. *Keep him alive?* Fractured skull, pressure on the brain, touch and go. Drips were in place, the medicos making leaving noises. One of them turned at the sound of her footsteps. He opened his mouth, said nothing. Maybe her face said everything.

She knelt at Byford's side, gently stroked the blood-matted hair, voice soft and low. "Looking good, boss." His eyelids fluttered. He couldn't smile: needed a working mouth for that.

Hers was tight as she fought tears. "Not George Clooney

good…but, hey, you can't have everything." She bit her knuckles, tasted blood. "Loads to tell you, guv." Gently she ran a finger along his jaw. "Best let you go for now. Get a few running repairs, eh?" His eyelids fluttered.

She bent close. "Ever do this to me again…" She pressed her lips against his forehead. "I'll bloody kill you."

Six weeks later

He'd missed *her* birthday; she was taking *him* presents. How did that work?

Bev was walking to the house, trying to get fitter, keep down the kilos. No hardship on a day like this. The long avenue of trees formed a cool green canopy backlit by the sun. The sky was the colour of her eyes; the new dress a close match. Her fringe was a pain; she'd not had a chance to get a trim, but maybe she'd keep it longer anyway.

The goodies in her bag weren't Bev's only gift to the guv. She'd given him her time too, visited him every day in hospital, brought vineyards of grapes. Not that there'd been a bunch else to do. Her suspension still had two weeks to run: insubordination (two counts); contaminating a crime scene (one); failure to communicate (countless). The disciplinary board hadn't ruled out busting her down a rank.

Yeah, right. Excommunicating Jack Pope had been a major boob, and the board didn't even know about that. The reporter had twice tried to speak to her, to tell her about the likeness between Jenny Page and a young woman on a TV programme, *Lost and Found*? By ignoring him, she'd not even looked.

A stone took the brunt of her frustration. It wasn't as though the guv could put in a good word; he'd not be back at work for months, if at all. The teeth weren't the only things he'd lost: his memory and balance had taken a bashing. He'd come out of intensive care after a week, took three more coming out of the coma. Talk to him, they'd said. So she had. She gave a wry smile. Very nearly talked him to death.

Only one thing she hadn't told him. Hadn't told anyone. Not even her mum.

She sat on a bench, lifted her face to the sun; didn't want to arrive early. She'd mostly avoided mentioning work to the big man, just passed on the odd snippet from Mac. Daniel was back with Jenny, pending her court appearance on the wounding. Richard Page was on remand, looking at a lengthy custodial. He was denying collusion but had clearly been involved for months. Page was in it up to the neck he was now desperately trying to save.

Holly was unlikely ever to be released. Criminally insane and cunning as a box of foxes, her game plan had had a long smouldering fuse. Landing a job at Page's ad agency was the first carefully calculated step; seducing a besotted Page the next; kidnapping Daniel the final move.

The kidnap had played right into Grant Young's hands, not to mention Operations Hawk and Phoenix. The police had been running round like headless poultry anyway; by fingering Maxwell, Young had not only kept himself out of the frame but had muddied already murky waters. The child-porn rumours stemmed from only one source: Grant Young.

The media man had served time with Maxwell years back; knew about his hatred of cops, heard his boasts about the wreaths and the death threats. Who better to point the police at? Throw in a few anonymous tip-offs and pay serious money to one of Maxwell's heavies to film a funeral and the signposts were all there. Garden path, big time.

Holly had inadvertently helped Young's anti-Maxwell campaign when she hired Dunston as post-boy. Dunston was just a loser who'd get sent down on the menacing charge. The crime boss – at least in this instance – was innocent. Probably why he was still kicking up a stink about unlawful arrest.

Bev scowled: nasty taste in the mouth. Seeing what it had done to the guv, the job had seemed futile for a while: a load of fuckwits fouling up their lives, cops having to take the fall-out, clear up the shit. Simon Wells's funeral had added to her grief. Later, a chat with a five-year-old *Doctor Who* fan had gone a small way to a change of heart, if not mind. Helping people, especially kids like Daniel, was why she'd become a cop in the first place.

Had to admire Powell in that respect. He was convinced gang masters had killed the Eastern European couple's son as a warning to other illegals who wanted a life as opposed to slavery. The DI was angling for a trip to Albania, hoping to cast a net with the authorities there. Powell saw it as his personal mission to track down the bastards. He'd also ditched the BM business. She gave a wry smile. Mind, she did have a big mouth.

Couple more minutes. Delving for a ciggie, she was reminded she'd given up. Didn't taste the same, anyway, without a pinot in the other hand. She hadn't had a drink since her birthday, the big three-O. Sick as a dog for days after. Oz's guest appearance with a female DI on his arm might've had something to do with that. She sniffed. Frankie's surprise party had certainly lived up to its name. Yeah, well, get over it. Today was worth celebrating.

Two o'clock, he'd said. She rose, hoisted her bag. First day back from hospital, the guv had wanted a few hours to acclimatise. Her stomach was a butterfly farm as she rang the bell. First time she'd seen him in a suit since the attack.

"Looking good, boss." The smile lit her eyes.

"George Clooney good?" That was another thing she'd mentioned.

"Can't have everything." She winked.

They sat in the garden, drank tea, laughed a lot. She sensed his gaze on her; studied him when he wasn't looking. The bruising and swelling had gone, the stitches were out, teeth were temporary but they'd get fixed. That reminded her. She dug in her bag, brought out the pressies. The Laphroaig went down well. The box of straws was probably a tad tactless. Took it in good spirit, though.

Everything was warm, relaxed, felt good. She didn't want to leave, knew she couldn't make a move. Not now. Not till she'd decided.

Byford sat forward, elbows on knees, suddenly serious. "So, Bev, what you going to do?"

She scrutinised his face again. The guy was a medicine man, not a detective. He couldn't possibly know. "'Bout what, guv?" Dead casual.

"I can read the signs, Bev."

She felt the blush rise. Oz's last stand. Talk about a fucking mistake. Stupid, careless, life-changing, career-threatening, and yet…

"Dunno what you mean." Hated lying to him. At the time she'd put the nausea and feeling rough down to a crap life-style. And she'd been right. But a month later the sickness had returned – and hadn't gone away.

Byford pointed at her bag. It wasn't closed properly, and the pregnancy kit she'd bought, to double-check the positive result of the first test, was well visible. "If you are, will you keep it?"

Oz Junior? Morriss minor? Would she? She hadn't got a clue.

Author's note:

At the end of *Baby Love* – the previous title in the series – I likened Bev to a cactus with tiny pink flowers. I wrote that passage four days before Christmas, and later that afternoon, I happened to see a cactus, complete with tiny pink buds, languishing outside a florist's near my home. I had to buy it, didn't I? It flowered brilliantly then nothing but leaves for twelve months. As I was writing the final chapters of *Hard Time*, I noticed pink shoots emerging. By the time I delivered the first draft, the cactus was in full glorious bloom. No journalistic licence here: I captured it on camera.

The script went through several revisions and as time passed, not surprisingly, the flowers faded and fell. I thought that was it florally for at least a year. Several weeks later as I started work on the final draft, I noticed two more tiny buds. As I finished the novel, they were in flower.

As Bev might say… Sentimental? Moi?

Maureen Carter
February 2007

More witty, gritty Bev Morriss mysteries from Maureen Carter:

Working Girls

Fifteen years old, brutalised and dumped, schoolgirl prostitute Michelle Lucas died in agony and terror. The sight breaks the heart of Detective Sergeant Bev Morriss of West Midlands Police, and she struggles to infiltrate the deadly jungle of hookers, pimps and johns who inhabit Birmingham's vice-land. When a second victim dies, she has to take the most dangerous gamble of her life - out on the streets.

ISBN: 978-0-9547634-1-1 £7.99

Dead Old

Elderly women are being attacked by a gang of thugs. When retired doctor Sophia Carrington is murdered, it's assumed she is the gang's latest victim. But Detective Sergeant Bev Morriss is sure the victim's past holds the key to her violent death.

Her new boss won't listen, but when the killer moves uncomfortably close, it's time for Bev to rebel.

ISBN: 978-0-9547634-6-6 £7.99

Baby Love

Rape, baby-snatching, murder: all in a day's work for Birmingham's finest. But she's just moved house, her lover's attention is elsewhere and her last case left her unpopular in the squad room; it's sure to end in tears. Bev Morriss meets trouble when she takes her eye off the ball.

ISBN: 978-0-9551589-0-2 £7.99

Bev's dry, sometimes caustic sense of humour remains firmly in place... her passion for what she does shines throughout...
- Shots Magazine

New for 2007:

CRÈME DE LA CRIME PERIOD PIECES

GRIPPING DEBUT CRIME FICTION
FROM DAYS GONE BY

**A new strand from the UK's
most innovative crime publisher.**

BROKEN HARMONY

Roz Southey

Charles Patterson, impoverished musician in 1730s Newcastle-upon-Tyne is accused of stealing a valuable book and a cherished violin. Then the apprentice he inherited from his flamboyant professional rival is found gruesomely murdered.

As the death toll mounts Patterson starts to fear for his health and sanity – and it becomes clear to characters and readers alike that things are not quite as they seem…

Published April 2007
ISBN: 978-0-9551589-3-3   £7.99

TRUTH DARE KILL

Gordon Ferris

The war's over – but no medals
for Danny McRae. Just amnesia and
blackouts: twin handicaps for a private
investigator with an upper-class client
on the hook for murder.

Newspaper headlines about a Soho
psychopath stir grisly memories in
Danny's fractured mind. As the two
bloody sagas collide and interweave,
Danny finds himself running for his
life across the bomb-ravaged city.

Will his past catch up with him
before his enemies? And which would
be worse?

Fast-paced post-war noir, with a
grimly accurate London setting.

Published May 2007
ISBN: 978-0-9551589-4-0   £7.99

THE CRIMSON CAVALIER

Mary Andrea Clarke

Regency London: a dangerous place for an independent, outspoken young woman – especially one with an unusual taste in hobbies.

A prominent unpopular citizen is murdered, apparently by an infamous highwayman known as the Crimson Cavalier. To the chagrin of her self-righteous brother, Georgiana Grey sets out to track down the real culprit.

But her quest for the truth is obstructed on all sides, and soon her own life is at stake.

A CRÈME DE LA CRIME PERIOD PIECE

The Crimson Cavalier

Mary Andrea Clarke

Published August 2007
ISBN: 978-0-9551589-5-7   £7.99

NEW TITLES FOR 2007 FROM OUR BESTSELLING AUTHORS

From ADRIAN MAGSON: a fourth rollercoaster adventure for Riley Gavin and Frank Palmer.

NO TEARS FOR THE LOST

A society wedding…
A crumbling mansion…
A severed finger…
For once, Riley Gavin and Frank Palmer are singing from different hymn books. As bodyguard to former diplomat Sir Kenneth Myburghe, it's Frank's job to keep journos like Riley at bay.

But Sir Kenneth's dubious South American past is catching up with him. When he receives a grisly death threat involving his estranged son, the partners-in-crimebusting stop pulling against each other.

Helped by former intelligence officer Jacob Worth, they discover Sir Kenneth has more secrets than the Borgias, and his crumbling country house is shored up by a powder which doesn't come in Blue Circle Cement bags.

Published July 2007
ISBN: 978-0-9551589-7-1   £7.99

From **LINDA REGAN**: **a sparkling follow-up to**
BEHIND YOU! (ISBN 978-0-95515892-2-6), the sell-out
debut from a popular actress turned crime writer.

**DI Banham and DS Grainger take a walk
on the seedy side of Soho in**

PASSION KILLERS

A convicted murderer has recently come out of prison, to the horror of six women who were involved in his crime.

Twenty years ago they were all strippers in a seedy nightclub.

Now some of them have a lot to lose.

Two of the women are found dead – murdered, and each with a red g-string stuffed in her mouth.

Enter D I Paul Banham, ace detective but not so hot when it comes to women. He focuses his enquiries on the surviving women, and finds that no one has a cast-iron alibi.

Everyone is a suspect and everyone is a potential victim.

And Banham is falling in love…

Published September 2007
ISBN: 978-0-9551589-8-8   £7.99

MORE TOP TITLES FROM
CRÈME DE LA CRIME -
AVAILABLE FROM A BOOKSHOP NEAR YOU

From Adrian Magson:

No Peace for the Wicked

Old gangsters never die – they simply get rubbed out. But who is ordering the hits? And why?

Hard-nosed female investigative reporter Riley Gavin is tasked to find out. Her assignment follows a bloody trail from the south coast to the Costa Del Crime as she and ex-military cop Frank Palmer uncover a web of vendettas and double-crosses in an underworld at war with itself.

Suddenly facing a deadline takes on a whole new meaning…

ISBN: 978-0-9547634-2-8   £7.99

No Help for the Dying

Runaway kids are dying on the streets of London. Investigative reporter Riley Gavin and ex military cop Frank Palmer want to know why. They uncover a sub-culture involving a shadowy church, a grieving father and a brutal framework for blackmail, reaching not only into the highest echelons of society, but also into Riley's own past.

ISBN: 978-0-9547634-7-3   £7.99

No Sleep for the Dead

Riley has problems. Her occasional partner-in-crimebusting Frank Palmer has disappeared after a disturbing chance encounter, and she's being followed by a mysterious dreadlocked man.

Frank's determination to pursue justice for an old friend puts him and Riley in deadly danger from art thieves, black gangstas, British Intelligence – and a bitter old woman out for revenge.

ISBN: 978-0-9551589-1-9   £7.99

Gritty and fast-paced detecting of the traditional kind, with a welcome injection of realism.

- Maxim Jakubowski, The Guardian

From Penny Deacon: two dark, stunningly original futurecrime chillers

A Kind of Puritan

Would anyone care if a killer was murdering people with no status, no worth to society? Boat-dweller Humility – a low-tech person in a mid-21st century hi-tech world – cares a lot. When she finds a body in the harbour, she is determined to track down the killer. But it puts her in the gravest peril. Soon enmeshed in a deadly maze of sabotage, arson and missing identities, she's struggling to stay alive.

ISBN: 978-0-9547634-1-1   £7.99

A subtle, clever thriller…
- Daily Mail

A Thankless Child

Life gets more dangerous for loner Humility. Her boat is damaged, her niece has run away from the commune, and the man who blames her for his brother's death wants her to investigate a suicide. She's faced with corporate intrigue and girl gangs, and most terrifying of all, she's expected to enjoy the festivities to celebrate the opening of the upmarket new Midway marina complex. Things can only get worse.

ISBN: 978-0-9547634-8-0   £7.99

…moves at a fast, slick pace… a lot of colourful, oddball characters…
a page-turner…
   - **new**booksMag

MORE EXCITING DEBUT
CRIME FICTION

IF IT BLEEDS   **BERNIE CROSTHWAITE**

Chilling murder mystery with authentic newspaper background.

Pacy, eventful… an excellent debut. - Mystery Women

ISBN: 978-0-9547634-3-5   £7.99

A CERTAIN MALICE   **FELICITY YOUNG**

Taut and creepy crime novel with authentic Australian setting.

a beautifully written book… draws you into the life in Australia… you may not want to leave.

- Natasha Boyce, bookseller

ISBN: 978-0-9547634-4-2   £7.99

PERSONAL PROTECTION   **TRACEY SHELLITO**

Erotic lesbian thriller set in the charged atmosphere of a lapdancing club.

a powerful, edgy story… I didn't want to put down…

- Reviewing the Evidence

ISBN: 978-0-9547634-5-9   £7.99

SINS OF THE FATHER   **DAVID HARRISON**

Blackmail, revenge, murder and a major insurance scam on the south coast.

… replete with a rich cast of characters and edge-of-the-seat situations where no one is safe…

- Mike Howard, Brighton Argus

ISBN: 978-0-9547634-9-7   7.99

4